Herring on the Nile

L. C. TYLER

Allison & Busby Limited
12 Fitzroy Mews
London W1T 6DW
allisonandbusby.com

First published in 2011.
This paperback edition published by Allison & Busby in 2016.

A CIP catalogue record for this book is available from
the British Library.

10 9 8 7 6 5 4 3 2 1

ISBN 978-0-7490-1948-8

Typeset in 10.5/15.5 pt Sabon by
Allison & Busby Ltd.

The paper used for this Allison & Busby publication
has been produced from trees that have been legally sourced
from well-managed and credibly certified forests.

Printed and bound by
CPI Group (UK) Ltd, Croydon, CR0 4YY

To Will and to the MNWers, past, present and future

'The Truth is rarely pure and never simple'

Oscar Wilde

CHAPTER ONE

Q: What's the worst possible way to begin a detective novel?

A: Tedious scene-setting stuff. Explaining basic things for people who haven't read the earlier books in the series.

Q: You write under several names, don't you?

A: Yes, I write crime as Peter Fielding and J. R. Elliot. I also write romantic fiction as Amanda Collins. None of those is my real name.

Q: What would you see as the main influences on your writing style?

A: I've always admired the crime writers of the Golden Age – Christie and Sayers in particular. For some reason I never have got to grips with dear old Margery Allingham. She's useful if you want to know how the English upper class in the 1950s thought the English working classes spoke – I mean, cawdblimeah, guv! – and she does quite a nice line in endearing cockneys, but I couldn't recommend her otherwise.

Q: *Our readers are always interested in how writers work. Describe the room you are writing in now.*
A: I'm at work on the dining table of my flat. The table bears the remains of this morning's breakfast. From where I'm sitting, I can just see out through the bow window and down to the village square below. The winter's first flakes of snow have started to settle; but, here inside, my ancient radiator is pumping out heat. The room is not large, but it's enough for me and for my books, which are pretty much everywhere. Occasionally books get mixed up with slices of toast, but that's fine.

Q: *What do you like most about Sunderland?*
A: I'm sure it's a very fine city, but I've never visited it.

Q: *What is your favourite restaurant in Sunderland?*
A: Sadly, I've never had the pleasure of dining in Sunderland.

Q: *Where would you go for a great day out in Sunderland?*
A:

'The Elsie Thirkettle Literary Agency. How can I help you?'

'Elsie,' I said, clutching the phone in one hand and scrolling down the screen with the other. 'Those interview questions you emailed me. Why are they asking me about Sunderland?'

'Which interview is that, Ethelred?'

'The *Sunderland Herald*, strangely. They seem to think I'm some sort of expert on eating out on Wearside. They want to know my favourite restaurant.'

'Could be a trick question. Hold on while I Google it . . . no, there really are restaurants in Sunderland.'

'Yes. What I meant was: Why are they asking *me*?'

'I don't know.'

'Yes, you do.'

'Fair enough,' said Elsie, who only lied properly to people she respected. 'I thought they'd be more likely to run the interview if I told them you were a local lad. It's only bending the truth a tiny bit, Ethelred. You *are* a local lad, just not local to Sunderland. What have you said so far?'

I read out my answers while Elsie made the disapproving noises that she has spent much of her life perfecting.

'You can't say that about Margery Allingham,' said Elsie. 'Unlike you, she has a lot of admirers out there. Your professed contempt for Allingham implies that anyone who enjoys her books won't enjoy yours. So that's a few thousand sales you've just thrown away quite unnecessarily. It's much better, Ethelred, if people get to decide they don't like you *after* they've paid for the book. Conversely, when you think about it, each writer you mention favourably is money in the bank. You can't claim too many influences – drop in all the names you can. And don't forget to plug the other writers at this agency and mention their books, because one day—'

11

'Yes, yes, I do get the picture,' I sighed. 'So I like Margery Allingham, do I?'

'You've adored Margery Allingham ever since you read *The Tiger in the Smoke* with a torch, under the bedclothes in the dorm.'

'In which part of your imagination did I go to a boarding school? Was it in Sunderland, by the way?'

Elsie's appreciation of irony is strictly limited to her own.

'As a writer of crime fiction,' she said, enunciating her words with more than usual care, 'you should be able to manage the odd fib or two if it will boost sales. Saying-the-thing-that-is-not is your job. I'm only a literary agent. Do you hear me complaining about having to lie? I described you as a "much-respected author" the other day. I may have even called you a "bestselling author". There are whole weeks, Ethelred, when I scarcely get to tell the truth from the moment I wake up to the moment I go to bed.'

'Is that true?'

'Don't try to get clever with me, Ethelred.'

'And the question about which football team I support?' I asked, looking further down the list.

'Wait, I'll Google that one for you too.' There was a pause and the sound of a biscuit being munched in far-away Hampstead. 'OK . . . it looks as though Sunderland is up near Newcastle, so I'd tell them you support Newcastle United if I were you. That should go down well. How are the other interviews that I emailed to you? I promised we'd turn them round in a few days.'

'We?'

'You.'

'I'll try to finish them all in Egypt and email the answers back to you.'

'Egypt? Who said you had permission to go to Egypt?'

'I'm doing some research. I did tell you.'

'Did you? Well, if you really must put pleasure before duty, at least take your laptop along to the pyramids.'

'I shall most certainly have my computer with me. I said, "it's research;" it's not a holiday. I shall be working hard the whole time.'

'I see – "research" is it?' said Elsie.

'Yes,' I said. 'It's research. But without the inverted commas you just put it into.'

'Yeah, right.'

'And not the pyramids either, as it happens. I'm going on a cruise down the Nile – or possibly up the Nile. I wasn't paying much attention when I booked it. It's the boat that is the great attraction.'

'You're travelling alone, I hope?'

'I'm going with Annabelle,' was treated to another outward and audible sign of Elsie's disapproval.

'She's keeping a close eye on you, now you're engaged.'

'We're not engaged,' I said.

The resulting snort of derision was intended to convey a number of things to me:

1. I was, though perhaps not formally engaged, nevertheless subject in all respects to Annabelle's whims.

2. Whether Annabelle and I became engaged would be a decision made solely by Annabelle, who would inform me when she considered the time was right.

3. I, uniquely amongst the male population of West Sussex, was incautious enough to have allowed such a situation to develop.

4. Annabelle was, contrary to anything I might have been told, not a natural blonde.

'I wish you would *try* to like Annabelle,' I said.
'I like her as much as I need to.'
'She says she likes you.'
'She'll be able to coach you in telling fibs then.'
'I really wish—'
'My boredom threshold is pretty low this morning, Ethelred. I'm putting the phone down before you mention that woman again. Have a nice day, now.'
'—you'd try to get on with Annabelle.'
'Piss off, Ethelred. It's almost lunchtime and, if I'm going to sell your Latvian rights to Nordik, I'll need to take this afternoon's mendacity to previously unexplored levels.'

'The Elsie Thirkettle Literary Agency. *Ka es varu jums palidzet?*'
'It's me, Elsie, not Nordik.'
'Ethelred, I've been practising that for the past half hour. You've just made me waste my best attempt to ask a Latvian if I can help them. You are a total plonker. Go away.'

'Sorry. Elsie, just a thought. You don't fancy coming to Egypt, do you?'

'No, Ethelred. My first rule in life is not to share a rusty old boat with gold-diggers sporting fake tits. I've stuck to it since I was a girl and it's made me what I am today. You'd do well to try it yourself sometime. In the meantime, you and Annabelle have fun.'

'Annabelle may not be coming.'

'May not, in what sense?'

'Isn't.'

'So – let's pause for a moment and get this absolutely right – Annabelle isn't coming and therefore, as a poor second choice, you're now inviting me at a week's notice? Thanks a bunch.'

'Eight days' notice.'

'Eight days? Why didn't you say so? That really does make all the difference.'

'Does it?'

'That was irony, Ethelred. Look it up in *Fowler's Modern English Usage*. Now, as I may have observed before: Piss off.'

'Sorry.'

'Don't keep saying "sorry".'

'Sor – I was offering to pay for the whole trip, of course . . .'

'I'm busy,' said Elsie. 'I can scarcely drop the entire work of an important literary agency, like this one for example, and clear off up the Nile on some three-legged paddle steamer you've booked yourself on. You'll have picked the oldest, slowest and most uncomfortable boat in Egypt as a matter of principle. I'm sure you'll enjoy it.'

'The *Khedive* is actually quite well appointed,' I said, 'though it is a paddle steamer, of course.'

There was a pause in the conversation during which a literary agent in Hampstead wrestled with a minor problem that had nothing to do with her.

'Why exactly *has* Annabelle dropped out?' Elsie asked, shelving for one moment the work of an important literary agency.

'She changed her mind.'

'Why?'

'She just did. Maybe she'd just had enough of my company for a while,' I added, jokingly.

'Fair enough. I can see that,' said Elsie. 'Even so, I don't change my mind. And I never play second fiddle to women who don't realise they are too old to wear short skirts. Check your contract – it's in para 23.2.'

'Sor—' I said again.

'Nothing would induce me to go on that boat, whatever it's called.'

'The *Khedive*,' I sighed. 'It's called the *Khedive*.'

'Ethelred Tressider speaking.'

'Elsie here. I've just Googled this brilliant boat we're going on. Have I explained Google, by the way? Somebody like you might think of it as this magic librarian that can tell you—'

'Elsie, I use Google all the time. As far as Egypt is concerned, don't worry. I'm not going now. I'm about to phone up and cancel the trip. I'll set the next book in Pembrokeshire or somewhere instead. Pembrokeshire is quite interesting in late November.'

'I don't think so, Ethelred. Sadly, there's no market for books about Pembrokeshire these days. More to the point, you didn't tell me that the word "luxury" featured twenty-seven times in the description of the *Khedive*. There seem to be staff whose sole duty is to top up the ice in your drink. The general picture I'm getting here is the Ritz with a paddle attached to the back. This trip must cost a fortune.'

'Possibly.'

'You haven't checked the cost down to the last penny? Does that mean you've finally sold the Big House?'

'I've found a buyer for it and I think we're about to exchange contracts. It has all happened a bit suddenly, but I really have to take any serious offer that comes along. Houses that size don't sell easily at the moment and the running costs are hideous. The gardens alone require somebody full-time.'

I paused, aware that a simple 'yes' would have been a better answer if I wanted the whole thing to sound routine and uncontroversial. Mentioning the gardens was almost certainly a step too far. But I was perfectly entitled to sell the house if I chose, whatever Annabelle had said.

'So, you're back in your old flat?' asked Elsie, pleased, it would seem, by all aspects of my answer. 'On your own? No unnatural blondes?'

'Wasn't that clear from my interview answers?'

'I thought that was just building up a background, creating a nice picture for the sort of readers you have – lonely, bored, a bit insecure, semi-literate.'

'No, Elsie, it was the truth. I never really moved out of

the old flat. Technically, the house has been mine only since probate was granted. Annabelle had every right to remain there in the meantime.'

I was doing it again. I had to stop sounding defensive all the time.

'And now?' asked Elsie.

'We'll have to work something out,' I said, summarising in six words a discussion with Annabelle that had occupied most of the previous evening plus a short and abruptly terminated phone call this morning. 'But, to answer your question, yes, the house is as good as sold and money isn't so much of an issue now.'

'Even so, I wouldn't want you to lose your deposit on the trip.'

'That's kind of you, but it's not your problem.'

'Ethelred – my authors' problems are my problems, you know that. Do I get a really enormous cabin? On the top deck?'

'The boat was pretty empty. I'm sure that could have been arranged – but you don't want to go.'

There was a crunching noise in Hampstead as somebody ate another restorative chocolate digestive. In the background I thought I heard an empty packet hit the wastepaper bin.

'You deserve a holiday, Ethelred. I should hate to see you cancel just because I wasn't there for you. I like to support my authors every way possible. Are we flying first class?'

'The quickest way of getting there is a charter flight straight to Luxor from Gatwick. And it's research, not a holiday.'

This time, I noticed, she didn't say 'yeah, right'. Elsie did not take unnecessary risks.

'I'll put up with a charter flight if I have to,' she said. I couldn't see her at the other end of the phone line, of course; but I knew that, just as soon as she had finished her biscuit, her expression would be one of noble self-sacrifice, probably modelled on the statue of Nurse Edith Cavell outside the National Portrait Gallery.

Five minutes later I was ringing the travel agent to say that I would now be accompanied by Ms Elsie Thirkettle rather than by Lady (Annabelle) Muntham, and that a cabin on the top deck would most certainly be required. As I paid the additional charges I felt a momentary pang of guilt that I was, in a sense, spending Annabelle's money.

But it had – I reminded myself – been Annabelle's decision not to come. Even she, surely, would have conceded that much? And, had I been able to see into the future as I read out the three numbers printed on the back of my card, I might have felt that she had made a very wise decision indeed. But of course, you never do see into the future. If I'd noticed any references in the tour brochure to a dead body floating in the Nile or to the cold barrel of a gun pointing at a spot precisely midway between my eyes, I might have decided South Wales in a blizzard was in fact the much better option. But perhaps they'd hidden that sort of stuff in the small print, along with the fuel surcharges. They often do, I find.

CHAPTER TWO

Q: *Our readers are always interested in how authors work. Describe the room you are writing in now.*
A: Actually I am on a plane. It's quite crowded, and I think only one toilet is still working. Otherwise it's fine. My computer is balanced on top of an unopened meal that I didn't ask for. It has 'CHK' written on the lid. It's chicken I think.

Q: *Which crime writers do you most admire?*
A: I've always admired the crime writers of the Golden Age – Christie and Sayers, of course, but especially the inimitable Margery Allingham, whose work I first read by the light of a torch under the bedclothes at my boarding school in Sunderland. She had an ear for the speech of the ordinary working man. Of the present-day writers, I enjoy Colin Dexter, Ian Rankin, Val McDermid, Donald Westlake, Martin Edwards, Sue Grafton, Simon Brett, M. C. Beaton, C. J. Sansom, Chris Ewan, Henning Mankell, Hakan Nesser, P. D. James,

Kate Atkinson, Brian McGilloway, Colin Bateman, Peter James, James McCreet, Colin Cotterill, N. J. Cooper, Louise Penny, Mike Ripley, Laura Wilson, R. J. Ellory and Malcolm Pryce. My work is strongly influenced by all of them in approximately equal measure.

Q: What is your writing schedule like?
A: I tend to be very organised. I like to write at least a thousand words a day – including when I am travelling. I always take my laptop with me, even on holiday (though this trip is research, obviously).

Q: Where would you go to boogie in Dunstable?
A:

'Elsie,' I said. 'Though I fear I may already know the answer to this question, why do they think I know anything about partying in Dunstable?'

The plump, slumbering figure in the seat beside mine stirred and opened one eye.

'Are we there yet?' It is a common misconception amongst those who doze off in a public place that nobody else has noticed. Elsie was now trying unsuccessfully to sell me the idea that she had been alert since take-off and, for all I knew, that it was normal to snore when wide awake. She was also, when she noticed it, going to have big problems explaining the dribble.

'We're somewhere over Italy, I think. I'm working on the next interview. A paper in Dunstable this time. I don't know what you told them, but I can't have grown up there and in Sunderland.'

'I may have said that you had an elderly aunt living there or something.'

'Who boogies on a regular basis?'

Elsie's expression quickly squashed any idea I might have had that I was qualified to mock other people's boogying. 'Maybe the aunt was in Salford,' she said dismissively. She leant back and closed her eyes again. 'Just say something vague about the exciting buzz there is in Dunstable these days.'

'Nobody's going to believe that.'

'They will in Dunstable. They don't get out much.'

'Maybe I'll just skip that question,' I said.

Elsie yawned and stretched. The lack of legroom on the charter flight was not a problem for anyone her size. My own joints, conversely, were beginning to ache from being forced into unnatural positions. I checked my watch again.

'Remind me – why exactly did Annabelle decide not to come?' asked Elsie, suddenly opening her eyes.

'She just changed her mind,' I said. I thought we'd dealt with that question already and my answer was true – well, after a fashion. And, if I had missed one or two small details, why should I be completely candid with Elsie, who regarded honesty much as she would an expensive pair of shoes: something to be cherished, admired even, but to be used only occasionally and not without some discomfort.

'Isn't she going to get jealous if you go off with some other woman?'

'But I'm going with *you*,' I said, laughing. 'Yes, fair enough, you *are* a woman, but Annabelle's hardly going to get jealous . . . I obviously don't mean that you are unattractive in any way, only that you and I . . . Of course, I wouldn't wish to imply that . . .'

'Shall I stop you there?' asked Elsie. 'Or do you think you can dig yourself in any deeper?'

'You're my agent,' I pointed out. 'It's a purely professional relationship.'

'With a one-month notice period.'

'Your joining me in Egypt does not affect my relationship with Annabelle in any way at all.'

'You are choosing your words very carefully, Ethelred. What does affect your relationship with Annabelle? The sale of Muntham Court? You can tell me. If she's given you the push because you've sold the ancestral home that she was hoping to live in for the rest of her days, then I may be forced to order champagne at your expense, but there is no other downside that I can see to your admitting you've been dumped.'

'She just didn't want to come to Egypt,' I said. 'And it's not an ancestral home – hers or mine.' Was that another point I'd made to Annabelle? It sounded familiar.

'Fine – just so long as she doesn't book herself a cabin at the last minute and join us on the *Khedive*,' said Elsie.

'That's very unlikely, though there are plenty of spare cabins apparently. It's a quiet time of year.'

'Suits me if it is a bit quiet. I too have work to be getting on with once we are back in touch with the world.'

Elsie produced a flashy mobile phone and would, no doubt, have explained in some detail how it worked, had I not produced the identical model from my jacket.

'Snap,' I said. 'I've got the same one.'

She took my phone dubiously, and then held hers and mine side by side, trying to identify any minute differences in functionality that would make hers cooler. There were clearly fewer than she had hoped.

'I bet I've got more apps,' she concluded lamely.

'We're just passing over Naples,' I said, unscrewing the top of the small bottle of wine that had accompanied the unrequested CHK.

'Don't change the subject,' said Elsie. 'My phone is cool. Your phone sucks.'

She took a paperback out of the seat pocket in front of her – Agatha Christie's *Death on the Nile*.

'I didn't know you were a Christie fan,' I said.

'It's rubbish basically,' said Elsie, though this was her default position on any work of literature that was not actually under contract to her.

'It's generally reckoned to be one of her best,' I said.

'So, how likely is it that you'll get a bunch of murderers, spies, writers and other disreputable people on board one small boat? And, if you did, why would you choose to shoot somebody in a place you couldn't make a decent getaway from? The problem with a small boat is that almost every move you make is observed by somebody else.'

'But the killer's movements *are* observed – that's why they have to kill again.'

'Precisely – it's a crap way to carry out a murder. The whole plot is too complicated. You shouldn't mix detectives and spies – they're different genres. And the incident with the boulder seems a complete red herring, which is just brushed away at the end.'

'Well, that's what you get in detective stories. Lots of red herrings – even on the Nile.' I smiled to show that I knew that herrings are limited to the temperate waters of the North Atlantic and North Pacific.

'You get crocodiles in the Nile,' said Elsie.

'Not below the Aswan Dam,' I said. 'Not any more.'

'Just get on with the interview questions, Tressider. You're starting to get pedantic and irritating. And lay off the duty-free wine – it just makes you maudlin and pessimistic, which is even worse.'

'No, it doesn't. And I'm not pedantic.'

'Yes, it does. And being pedantic is like snoring – the person who is doing it can't tell. Right now I need you upbeat and positive for those interviews. Screw that top back on. You can wake me when we're in Luxor, so I can look at the nice crocodiles. And not a moment before.'

Elsie's snores recommenced, proving at least one of her points was true. As a preliminary to disproving her other points, I poured my wine and watched it splash, warm and red, into the cheap plastic cup. I took a sip or two and reflected on Life. It seemed OK. Not fantastic, but as good as it was ever likely to get. I took another few sips, then swallowed the rest of the wine in a single gulp. I reached decisively for my computer and began to type again.

CHAPTER THREE

Q: *Many of the readers of our magazine are budding authors. There are so many genres to explore. What started you writing crime novels?*
A: I wish I could remember. There must have been a point at which I thought it would be fun.

Q: *You write under several names. Why is this?*
A: See above. Like so many things, it just seemed a good idea at the time. As Peter Fielding I write the Sergeant Fairfax books. I also write historical crime as J. R. Elliot and romantic fiction under yet another name. Occasionally people confuse me with Paul Fielder – the former secret service man who writes thrillers – but he's obviously a lot better known than I am.

Q: *What books are currently on your bedside table?*
A: It's funny you should ask that. I did take a glance at my bedside table before I left home. There's quite a stack of them. Some are books that I feel I ought to

read because everyone else is reading them, though deep down I despise both the books and the people who read them. There are also the books I've started reading but never got round to finishing – *A l'ombre des jeunes filles en fleurs* to name just one, though technically it is currently *under* rather than *on* the bedside table. And there are a number of copies of *History Today* in which I have vainly sought inspiration. My bedside table is, when you think about it, an allegory of blighted hope. Sometimes I simply want to weep.

Q: Great! Have you started writing another book? Is it a sequel to the one being published now?
A: I'm doing research for a new historical series – set in Egypt. Crime writers have to produce series. There's no escape. Do you know – all I wanted was to write one great work of literary fiction. Just one. Was that really too much to ask?

Q: Which contemporary writer do you think people will still be reading in a hundred years' time?
A: Dan Brown. I bought *The Da Vinci Code* last year and I'm still only on page seven.

Q: And finally, what advice would you have for anyone wanting to write fiction themselves?
A: Write it by all means, but do not expect it will make you rich or especially happy – and above all, do not expect that it will make you more attractive

to the opposite sex or you will be very disappointed indeed. On the plus side, you don't need to buy many ties.

Q: I'm sure all budding authors will find that tremendously encouraging. Thank you, Paul Fielder!

'Are we there yet?'

'We are flying down, or possibly up, the Nile. Up, I guess, since it flows from south to north and we are flying almost exactly due south.'

'Have you finished those interview questions?' asked Elsie, looking suspiciously at the two empty wine bottles.

'Three sets so far.'

'I hope you're being cheerful and upbeat?'

'Of course.'

'You're not being cynical and tedious?'

'No.'

'You're not going on and on about wanting to write great literary fiction?'

'I just ask one very short question about it.'

'And you are being very complimentary about other writers?'

'Yes. I even gave a plug to Dan Brown.'

'There's a good boy.'

'I thought we had the boat to ourselves,' said Elsie, as we joined a small queue to be allocated our cabins. 'I hope I am not going to be made to share my ice waiter with somebody else?'

'Evidently there were some last-minute bookings,' I said.

Ahead of us a middle-aged lady, who had clearly arrived a short while before, was returning a key to the desk. She was wearing the practical, loose, dust-coloured dress of the habitual traveller, and a hat with a large floppy brim covered much of her greying hair. Her wrist carried several substantial silver bracelets, bought quite possibly in the suq in Luxor that morning. They clinked happily as she handed over the key.

'Thank you,' she said in the clear precise way the English speak to foreigners, as an alternative to learning their language. 'I thought an upper cabin would be better, but on reflection I am very pleased with the one originally allocated to me. The other cabin is too close to the dining room. Tell the porter that my cases may remain where they are. I have locked the cabin door.'

It was not unlike listening to a passage from a phrase book in which a number of eventualities for booking a cabin are envisaged and set down for the traveller to use as necessary. For a moment I thought she might go on to ask for a telegram to be sent to her head office in Oldham about a shipment of cotton samples, or whatever scenario the book's author had next seen fit to cover. But she simply nodded once and smiled. The purser returned her smile weakly and dropped the key into a wooden box beside him without a further glance at it. The lady however showed no sign of being in a hurry to return to her original cabin. She was on holiday and had plenty of time to display old-world good manners, no matter how much inconvenience and irritation it might cause.

'It was however very kind of you. I appreciate your allowing me to inspect it,' she continued, as though she had just remembered a further optional piece of dialogue, illustrative of the gerund.

The phrase book should, undoubtedly, have had the purser reply that he was honoured and delighted to have been of service, but he seemed not to have read that section. The lady, therefore, received another weak smile in return. The queue of passengers, including one literary agent who had hoped to have the boat largely to herself, was growing impatient.

'Thank you for locking the cabin and returning the key,' said the purser. 'Perhaps, madam, you would now permit me to check in the other guests?'

'But of course,' she said, turning to the rest of us in the most leisurely manner I could recall ever having seen. 'I do apologise for having delayed you all. It is very rude of me. I shall not hold you up for another second.'

For a moment I could have sworn she was about to drop a curtsey, but then she turned sharply and swept away towards the lower deck.

'Next,' said the purser, raising his eyebrows in rather unprofessional mock despair.

'Professor Campion,' snapped a tall, bald man who had managed to position himself at the front of the queue by means of a rapid exit from the coach and an agile pair of elbows. He slapped his ticket on the desk. He clearly resented having been made to wait and resented it even more when, in spite of being a professor, he was asked for his passport, the search for which encompassed his jacket, his rucksack and finally (with much greater success) the back pocket of his trousers. He fiddled with a pair of reading glasses while his documents were being checked and his key located, though in the end he found nothing to read with them and finally made great play of folding the glasses away again into a small tubular case. He did this slowly and precisely. It was as if delaying the rest of us somehow evened up the score with the lady with the floppy hat. He too disappeared, but towards the upper deck, following a porter who had swooped lightly onto his small suitcase.

'I'm Sky Benson. I think you'll find I have a lower-deck cabin.' The next passenger was a young woman whom, had I been looking for a quiet, efficient secretary, I might have shortlisted on the spot. She was quite pretty, but her lack of make-up was so conspicuous as to amount to a statement of intent. She had on a fairly simple necklace of blue stones and what seemed to be a matching bangle. Propped coquettishly on her small nose was a pair of surprisingly heavy and old-fashioned glasses – surprising because the lenses did not appear to be very strong, and she might have disposed of them completely had she been at all concerned about her appearance. The spectacles too seemed a statement of some kind – a suitable accompaniment to the plain skirt, high-necked blouse and the absence of make-up. It struck me that sometimes the ultimate vanity is a desire not to appear vain.

She retrieved her ticket and passport from a well-organised plastic folder, then chatted inconsequentially to the purser as he ticked her name off the list. She appeared slightly tense and awkward, and kept looking over her shoulder as if she feared additional passengers might join the queue and delay us further. Once or twice she gave a short nervous laugh in response to her own jokes. Perhaps it was being in a strange country or perhaps she was always like that. Doubtless I would find out in due course, as all of the passengers would in due course find out about each other. For the moment we were still a collection of strangers, eyeing each other with varying degrees of trepidation and disdain.

Eventually a porter was summoned and Miss Benson too was dispatched on her way.

Another young woman travelling alone was quickly dealt with. She gave her name as Lizzi Hull, tipping her peaked cap back on her head as she said it. While her booking was checked, she rolled up her sleeves, revealing a fashionable selection of tattoos. She must have noticed me looking at them, because she gave me a quick wink before turning back to the purser.

'*Shukran*,' she said, as she pocketed the key. She declined any assistance with her rucksack, which she hoisted onto a shoulder before striding off towards her cabin.

Two Americans in their mid-twenties were now all that separated us from our own keys.

'I wonder why they were pretending not to know each other,' said Elsie.

'Who?'

'Professor Campion and Miss Benson. They were sitting together on the plane, but pointedly took seats at opposite ends of the coach for the drive from the airport. They didn't exchange a single word here on the boat – not even to say what a pain the floppy-hat bitch was being in the queue.'

'Maybe they'd said everything they had to say to each other on the plane,' I suggested. 'They didn't look as if they had much in common.'

'I'm surprised she could afford a trip like this, if her cheap jewellery is anything to go by.'

'Was it cheap?'

'Oh yes. New but very disposable. I wouldn't go to her hairdresser either.'

'No?'

'You might, but I wouldn't.'

'Maybe she inherited some money recently. It happens.'

'Yes, but the first thing you do if you inherit money is go out and have your hair done and buy the most expensive shoes you can find.'

'Not a rich heiress then?'

'She doesn't really fit in at all. Think about it – Campion and the floppy-hat lady, both spending their early-retirement lump sums by the look of them. And then the two American boys . . .' They had fortunately also moved on, though their presence would probably not have prevented Elsie from continuing as she did. 'East coast old money. Ivy League. Probably both taking a year out between graduate school and joining Goldman Sachs.' It seemed quite possible – or, at least, no more unlikely than any other scenario. They had the perfect teeth and untroubled countenances that only the very best sort of money buys.

'And the young lady with the tattoos?'

'Bristol or Durham history of art graduate on a gap year. Decorating her arms in a way that she hopes will gladden the hearts of her parents on her return to Guildford.'

What Elsie's snap judgements lacked in accuracy, they invariably made up in detail.

'So there are eight passengers on the boat?' I said to the purser, as much to make conversation as anything.

'There are thirteen,' he said, checking the list. 'No, twelve. We had thirteen bookings but the final number is confirmed as twelve. In addition to Miss Watson and the seven of you who have just arrived, there are also two gentlemen sharing a cabin on the lower deck and two gentlemen in single cabins. They are already here. So, once we have everyone accommodated to their *entire* satisfaction, I shall inform Captain Bashir that he may set sail for Esna.'

I was handed my key and Elsie hers. The box with the remaining keys in it was shut with a flourish and the box itself was then locked away. I too might have swung my small bag over my shoulder and set off unaided, but the purser had no intention of allowing such a breach in etiquette to occur twice on his watch. I accordingly followed my uniformed porter to the upper deck, where my cabin had been eagerly awaiting me for some hours.

My luggage took only a short time to unpack, unlike Elsie's large suitcase, the contents of which seemed designed to cater not only for all social occasions but also for extreme and as yet unpredicted climate change. I was therefore alone on the sun deck of the boat, watching the deceptively clear waters of the Nile oozing by, when I spotted a familiar face on the far side of the boat. Even at a distance the crookedness of his teeth was all too apparent as he broke into an insincere smile. In return I nodded as briefly as politeness allowed, but that was not enough to discourage him from ambling slowly in my direction. It was rather as if the Nile had just spewed up a surplus crocodile onto the deck – a rather scrawny crocodile in bright pink Bermudas, but authentically scaly. I suppose I knew deep down that I would run into Herbie Proctor again one of these days – I'd just hoped it would be later rather than sooner. I know very few private detectives – too few certainly to be able to say whether duplicity, parsimony and an ingratiating manner are essential qualities for a good private eye. Not that Proctor had ever, to my knowledge, been a good private eye.

'Ethelred! I thought I'd probably find you here – out in the midday sun.'

'Indeed,' I said, ignoring his outstretched hand.

'As in "mad dogs and Englishmen",' he added. His grin served only as an unfortunate reminder of some cheap dental work.

'Yes,' I said. 'I did get the allusion.'

'One of Flanders and Swann's,' said Proctor, with more confidence than accuracy. 'Well, we're two mad dogs out here together, eh, Ethelred? What were the chances of our turning up in the same joint again?'

'Greater than I had hoped, clearly. What exactly brings you here, Mr Proctor?' I asked. 'Isn't this a little expensive for your tastes?'

'Not quite my usual holiday destination,' he said. Herbie Proctor had the ability to make most things sound disparaging, though he rarely had the chance to dismiss an entire civilisation in six words. He scanned the far bank of the river and was not impressed. 'Load of smashed-up old stones in the desert. Great blocks of useless masonry.'

I wondered whether to quote 'Ozymandias' to him, but decided not to waste my time. Proctor had in any case now taken out a very old mobile phone and was playing around with it unhappily.

'Can't seem to get a connection,' he said.

'The older ones don't always work overseas,' I said, surprised to be ahead, for once, of anyone on technical matters. 'Or not outside Europe at least.'

'Don't they?' asked Proctor, looking rather mournfully at the unresponsive device in his hand.

'Are you expecting somebody to contact you?'

'It's not important,' said Proctor, replacing the phone in his pocket, where it made an impressive bulge.

'I take it that this is a working visit?' I asked.

He gave me a conspiratorial wink, then looked around theatrically before whispering: 'Very perspicacious as ever, Ethelred. I do have a little job on, as it happens. Maybe you can help me. Can I talk to you in confidence?'

'That depends entirely on what you have to say.'

'I'm here to prevent a murder, Ethelred.'

'That's very decent of you.'

'Yes, isn't it? My client has been kindly alerted to the fact that somebody wants to kill him. He thinks that the person threatening him may be on board this boat.'

'Then he would do well to move to another boat entirely. That would leave you free to do the same.'

Proctor eyed me, an irritating smile on his lips.

'My client doesn't frighten easy, Ethelred. A bit like me, you might say. And he's not the sort of man you'd want to cross. He can take care of himself when he needs to, if you get my drift. My job, since he is travelling alone, is to be his eyes and ears. He just wants a fair fight with no surprises.'

'Which of the passengers is he?' I asked.

'I'd like to be able to tell you,' Proctor smirked, 'but that will not be possible.'

I made a quick tally of the male passengers – the problem of identification did not seem to be quite as impenetrable as Proctor implied. If the client in question was indeed travelling alone, that ruled out the two Americans, and also the two gentlemen sharing a cabin who had arrived shortly before we had. If he was male, then that ruled out most of the rest. Put bluntly it left me, Professor Campion and one other. It wasn't me. I had just seen Campion and he didn't quite fit the description of a man you would not wish to cross; in fact I'd have said he would have been safer to cross than most people, provided you were prepared to put up with a little scholarly petulance. I hadn't met the second gentleman, but had noticed from the purser's list that he was called Purbright. He might well be seven feet tall and built like a gorilla for all I knew. Time would tell.

'Presumably your client is Purbright,' I said.

'He might be travelling under that name,' said Proctor. His tone implied that I had used underhand means to obtain confidential information.

'Why does he think his life is in danger, though?' I asked. I was reluctant to continue the conversation longer than I had to, but professional curiosity made me ask. As I say, I don't know many real-life detectives. And this was, after all, a research trip. Not a holiday.

'He received a letter a week or two before he was due to leave England. A tip-off from somebody well inclined towards him. It said that a couple of people who did not wish him quite so well were on his tail and were planning to follow him here. That's when Mr Raffles wisely contacted me.'

'Raffles being the real name of your client?'

'Precisely. Clever of you to spot that, Ethelred. I can see why you're a successful crime writer.'

I turned and looked at Proctor. It was not always easy to tell when he was being sarcastic and when he was merely being stupid – something that may well have helped him in his chosen vocation as a low-rent private investigator.

'And why are you telling me all this?'

'A further pair of eyes, Ethelred – that would be six eyes in all, including Mr Raffles' own. Also six ears. Three noses. I'm good, but even I can't be everywhere at once.'

'The name Raffles is vaguely familiar,' I said. 'What has he done that might upset anyone?'

'Successful businessmen make enemies, Ethelred. Pure envy, most of it. It is indeed a sad reflection on the society in which we live that honest citizens go in fear for their own safety.'

Though that was possibly true as a generalisation, it did not prove that Raffles was an honest citizen himself or that he had received a death threat on account of his integrity and charitable nature.

'So, are we working together again?' Proctor enquired.

The invitation was like having my skin rubbed with slimy sandpaper.

'Working with you before was not a happy experience,' I said. 'The only good thing I can say about our previous collaboration is that it was brief.'

'Always joking, eh? I could make it worth your while, though, Ethelred. A couple of crisp tenners has to be useful to a mid-list author like you.'

'If you'll excuse me,' I said, 'I have some work to do.'

'Writing a literary masterpiece?' The irony in his voice was unmistakable.

'Stranger things have happened, Mr Proctor,' I said.

CHAPTER FOUR

Q: Our readers are always interested in how writers work. Describe the room you are writing in now.
A: It's pretty plush actually. There is a large bed in the middle of the cabin and a couple of armchairs upholstered in blood-red velvet. There is also a rather ornate, brass-bound, mahogany bureau, on which my computer is currently resting. Good taste seems to be slightly different in Egypt. A door leads to a small private veranda, with a rather fine iron railing, from which I shall, in due course, be able to watch the world go by.

Q: What books are currently on your bedside table?
A: There's an enormous bowl of fruit taking up most of it – complimentary I think. I also have my copy of *Egyptology Made Easy*. It looks pretty authoritative and has some nice pictures, though one pharaoh tends to look much like another – possibly because of centuries of inbreeding.

Q: I always think crime writers must be very clever to think up all of those plots. How do you do it?

A: Thank you. Most crime writers would agree with your general premise. In terms of plotting, I tend to do one of three things. Sometimes, like Agatha Christie, I offer up a whole crowd of potential murderers before revealing that the killer was the least likely of the bunch. Sometimes, conversely, I like to give lots of clues pointing to the real murderer early on. This tricks experienced crime readers into rejecting the genuine murderer as being far too obvious – the simple double bluff. Most of all, however, I like to present the reader with half a dozen dead certs, only to reveal at the end that it wasn't murder at all. The only problem is when your readers don't spot all of the twists they are supposed to. Readers who can't keep up with you are a nuisance – though readers who are cleverer than you are a nuisance too. Actually, clever readers are a real pain in the neck.

Q: And finally, tell us one thing about yourself that nobody will know!

A: My bath towel has been arranged on my bed in the shape of a camel.

That's fascinating. Thank you very much, Peter Fielding!

I had been looking forward to the boat's departure – its first nosing out into the stream, with the water churning aft and the whole journey still ahead of us. An asthmatic coughing and rumbling from the distant engine room, and the oily plash of a giant paddle wheel alerted me to the fact that, with my own nose pressed against the computer screen, I had just missed that moment. Through the cabin window I could now see clouds of steam rising and swirling around the boat. As the river rolled majestically northwards, we were now battling south against the current, towards Esna. I opened the glass door onto my veranda, and stood for a while watching the flat landscape with its groves of ragged palm trees and low, square houses begin to drift slowly by. It was a romantic moment that I had once envisaged sharing with Annabelle. Well, I could at least share it with my agent.

My knock on Elsie's door went unanswered. I reasoned that she was most likely to be in the air-conditioned bar, demanding that yet more ice should be added to her drink. The bar was however deserted except for the floppy-hat lady. She was drinking a purple-coloured liquid that looked much like Ribena. Though the purser had mentioned her name, I had already forgotten it. We introduced ourselves. She proved to be called Jane Watson.

'Did you see that ridiculous little man in pink shorts?' she demanded. Even though I was not a foreigner, she chose to address me in a loud voice that would have been audible some way off. She clearly either shared Elsie's minimalist approach to tact or believed that most of the other passengers were deaf.

'Herbie Proctor, you mean?'

'Oh, so you know him? Sorry – is he a friend?'

'No, not a friend. I met him once in France. We were staying at the same hotel.' There had been rather more than that to it, but that was as much detail as I now cared to remember. 'He's a private detective,' I added.

'Well, I suppose even private eyes must go on holiday from time to time.'

'He says he's here on business.'

'Really?'

'Really,' I said. An early Christian martyr of the better sort might, perhaps, have forgiven Proctor his offer of a couple of ten-pound notes and decided not to blow his rather flimsy cover. I was not, however, at that moment, feeling remotely charitable. 'He is here to prevent a crime, so he tells me.' I raised my eyebrows and gave her a lopsided smile.

I had naturally expected Jane Watson to share the joke, and to join me in mocking Proctor's pretensions, perhaps returning to the subject of his ridiculous shorts, which certainly merited further discussion. But the colour drained instantly from her face. I realised that, farcical though I found everything that Proctor did, others might take him seriously.

'Sorry – I really didn't mean to alarm you,' I said. 'I can't imagine there will be any trouble on a boat like this – still less that Mr Proctor would be of any value to his client if there were.'

Jane Watson was far from reassured. 'His client . . . who exactly is that?'

'I'm not sure,' I said lamely. I felt a bit like a comedian whose sure-fire gag has just died. Blowing Proctor's cover had seemed fair game. But causing panic amongst my fellow passengers hadn't been my plan at all. Moreover, informing the world at large that Mr Purbright was the intended target, when I had no evidence for that other than Proctor's hints, now seemed unwise in all sorts of ways. 'Look – forget I even mentioned it.'

Jane Watson's look was severe. 'I have to say that you have greatly worried me, Mr Tressider. You might at least tell me all of what Mr Proctor said or I shall not sleep a wink tonight. That much you owe me, don't you think?'

'I'm sorry – I've obviously already said too much . . . what he said was in confidence and—'

'In confidence? I would have said Mr Proctor had already been very free in divulging his client's affairs. If he can tell you, I would have thought you could tell me. Or was he telling you as a very close friend?'

'Absolutely not. He's no sort of friend of mine.' I wished to clear that one up. 'Mr Proctor's client – the person he is protecting – is apparently a businessman travelling alone. I don't think I should say more than that.'

I smiled apologetically, but Jane Watson took no longer than I had done to solve that particular puzzle.

'Travelling alone? The client then is either Professor Campion or Mr Purbright?'

'Honestly, I don't know,' I said. 'Campion doesn't strike me as a businessman. But—'

'So, in that case, he is here to protect Mr Purbright?'

'Proctor didn't actually say so.'

'I can't think who else it can be, can you?'

'No,' I said.

'This Proctor person – you are certain that he is just a private detective? Not, say, a policeman or MI6?'

'MI6? Good grief, no. He's just a cheap private investigator, operating more or less on the right side of the law. Most of his work is probably spying on cheating husbands and process serving.'

'And you think Mr Purbright has actually employed him as some sort of bodyguard?'

'I really don't know – but if Herbie Proctor is right, then Purbright is merely an alias.'

'An alias?'

'Yes.'

'So, let's get this straight – Mr Proctor is convinced Purbright is a businessman travelling under an alias, and that he can in some way be of service to him?'

'Yes,' I said. 'But . . .'

'How extraordinary,' said Jane Watson. For some reason I had cheered her up enormously. She had finally seen the joke and was now positively beaming.

'Look,' I said, wishing both to reassure her and prevent her from jumping to any more conclusions than she already had, 'the most likely thing, it seems to me, is that Herbie Proctor is simply on the wrong paddle steamer and that Purbright is nothing to do with him. Please therefore don't mention this to anyone else. Though I am reasonably sure Mr Purbright is in no danger, I have no wish to alarm the whole boat.'

'I see. That's what you'd like, is it? Yes, on reflection, I agree that it would be unwise to worry the others as you have me. That was thoughtless of you, though it has afforded me a certain amount of innocent amusement. And there is *certainly* no cause to trouble Mr Purbright, who I am sure wishes only to enjoy himself. We shall therefore both keep this to ourselves. How well do you know this Proctor person?'

'Reasonably well. We spent a few unpleasant days together in a hotel in the Loire.'

'Is he armed?'

'I've really no idea, though I hope not. I should think it would be difficult to import a gun into Egypt.'

'Yes, that's right,' she said, frowning. 'Well, at least we don't have to worry about a shoot-out on board the boat. And does he have any idea who might be threatening his client?'

'If he does, he didn't tell me,' I said.

'Male or female?'

'He implied there was more than one.'

'*More than one?* This gets more and more interesting.'

'Does it?'

'Oh yes. There aren't many of us on the boat. If Mr Proctor is right, then it would seem to me that about half of us must either be trying to kill poor Mr Purbright or to protect him. You alarmed me at first, Ethelred – I may call you Ethelred, mayn't I? – but I am beginning to feel that your ridiculous Mr Proctor could liven up the cruise considerably.'

'He's not *my* Mr Proctor.'

'I'm pleased to hear it. Ethelred, let me give you some advice. If your life is ever in any danger, do not pin your hopes on a man in bright pink shorts.'

I nodded. I'd never planned my life any other way.

* * *

46

'We've done Italy, we've done Greece, so we just *had* to do Egypt. It was the complete set of ancient civilisations or nothing. No half measures. That's how it is with us.'

The young American flashed me a smile. His friend punched him on the arm and then turned and pointed a finger at me.

'Just don't tell Tom about Mesopotamia. Or Assyria. You know, I'm beginning to think we'll *never* get back to Kansas.'

'John is *dying* to get back to Kansas,' said Tom.

'You both come from Kansas then?' I asked.

'No, New York,' said Tom.

The two young men burst out laughing, as if I had missed something obvious.

'It's just that Tom keeps telling people he has the feeling we're not in Kansas any more,' explained John. 'It wasn't funny, even the first twenty times.'

'Ah,' I said.

'Don't believe anything Tom tells you anyway. His father is a prominent and well-respected New York mobster. That's how we can afford this trip.'

'Don't believe anything John tells you. His father worked for Nixon. John didn't hear anyone speak the truth until he was seven. It's a foreign language to him. Even now he speaks it with an accent.'

This conversation had now been going on for five minutes. Its great advantage was that I was not called upon to say a lot, but I wasn't sure that I knew much more about the pair of them than I had before I met them. I was reasonably sure they came from New York and that they were both lawyers. One of them had possibly been educated at Brown, the other almost certainly at Princeton. One of their fathers might well have been a Nixon aide way back. They had been to Paris and London in addition to the other places they had mentioned. But most of the conversation so far had been one long private joke, the key to which was always slightly beyond my grasp. They reminded me of two large puppies bouncing around, their play constantly verging on, but never quite becoming, a genuine scrap.

'Have you met many of the other passengers yet?' I asked.

'We've only spoken to you so far,' said Tom. 'We're very particular who we speak to.'

'No, we ran into that lady with the hat in Cairo, didn't we?' said John. 'We spoke to her there.'

'Oh yes, in the museum. She was with that guy with a moustache. He didn't like us much. Small world, eh?'

'She didn't seem too pleased to see us on the boat.'

'Only because you kept on and on about Kansas last time. She thinks you're mad.'

We turned and watched the bank flow past us for a bit, secure in our floating air-conditioned world. The land stretched away, flat as only a flood plain can be, under a vast, hot sky. The fuzzy horizon was in a constant state of gentle agitation. On the near bank, travelling north in a cloud of dust, was a pick-up truck with a camel sitting sedately in the back, slowly chewing the cud, a ragged scarf tied over its ears. Tom winked at John.

'Toto, I have the feeling we're not in Kansas any more.'

* * *

Elsie's cabin was larger and plusher than mine. Whatever I had, she seemed to have at least two of. Her towels were arranged on the bed in the shape of a swan. It was more like a swan than my camel was like a camel.

'Where have you been?' she asked.

'Meeting and chatting with people,' I said.

'Me too.'

'I'm beginning to think there's something odd going on here,' I said. 'You'll never guess who I ran into – Herbie Proctor, of all people. He claims to have a client on board the boat who is about to be murdered or something. But, and this won't come as a surprise, I'm not sure he knows which passenger has employed him. It's the most ridiculous story I ever heard. I'm not planning to alert the police that we have a killer on board.'

'You won't need to alert them,' said Elsie. 'The police are already onto it.'

CHAPTER FIVE

Elsie

In one of my previous lives I was almost certainly the Queen of Sheba. Unless of course there was somebody else who used to recline on cushions in an even classier manner, while really fit slave boys fed her peeled grapes. I'd be a natural at that sort of stuff, though getting really fit slave boys in Hampstead these days is almost as difficult as getting a plumber. Still, if I was ever going to get properly pampered while I waited for my fresh orange juice to be squeezed, the *Khedive* looked as likely a place as any. I was pleased that I had let Ethelred persuade me to come.

I went to his cabin to share this thought with him and to check if he knew the Arabic for 'Peel me a grape', but he'd gone walkabout. So I took a stroll up to the covered deck and had a look at Egypt. It was a bit flat and the trees looked all the same. There weren't any pyramids.

'Your first trip on the Nile?'

I turned. The speaker had one of those leathery faces that you acquire by spending a great deal of your time in places like the one we were in. The way the leather was ingrained –

50

and the permanent bags under his eyes – suggested much of that time might have been spent partying. There was a small scar on his cheek. If it wasn't the face he deserved, then he'd been dead unlucky. Overall, I'd have said he was a bit old for me and probably divorced once too often for comfort. Still, there was no sign yet of any tendency to middle-aged flab and only a few grey hairs. I wasn't necessarily going to chuck him off the boat.

'I've always loved paddle steamers,' I said, thinking mainly, I have to admit, of the old *Medway Queen*, plying its trade between Southend and Margate.

'This one is a bit special, though,' he said. There was a huskiness to his voice that indicated nobody had told him yet that it was dangerous to smoke more than forty a day. Beneath that huskiness, though, lay a sort of relaxed confidence. 'It was built for the King of Egypt. British shipyard, of course – one of the many shipyards that have vanished over the years. It's probably been converted into a yachting marina or a lesbian sushi bar or something. The *Khedive* would have been the last word in luxury, though it wouldn't have had air-conditioning in those days.'

'You've done this trip before?' I asked.

'No, not really.'

'But you live out here?' I asked.

'Sort of. What is it that you do?'

'I'm an agent,' I said.

He looked puzzled.

'A literary agent,' I said. 'Ethelred is one of my authors – you might know him as Peter Fielding.'

Purbright frowned for a moment, as if in recognition of the name, then said: 'You're not a secret agent then.'

'No,' I said. 'It wouldn't really work being a secret literary agent. And I'm not with MI5. And you?'

'Not MI5 either,' he said. 'I wonder how long we'll be going at this speed.'

'What's wrong with our speed?'

'It's only half what it should be. I've just had a word with the captain. They're going to need to do some work on the engines at Aswan. Until then, this is as fast as we can go. We'll be travelling through the night.'

'Suits me,' I said. 'I wasn't intending to go anywhere else.'

'Yes. As long as there are no other problems.'

'Are there likely to be?'

'Looking at the programme they left in my cabin, all they envisage is cocktails and dinner. I may as well get changed,' he said.

I'm not sure when, during that conversation, the two Arab-looking passengers had shown up. I noticed them only after the suntanned guy had gone. They were looking at me from the other side of the boat. I saw one of them nod at the other and both moved casually but purposefully in my direction. They introduced themselves as Mahmoud and Majid.

'Who was that bloke?' asked Majid, in the sort of Estuary English I'd learnt at my mother's knee.

'I don't think he said.' I'm reasonably good with names, unlike Ethelred, who is quite capable of forgetting his own if he's not carrying his laminated Crime Writers' Association membership card. No, I was pretty sure he hadn't mentioned a name.

'He didn't say he was called Purbright?' asked Majid.

I shook my head.

'You are travelling with your husband?' asked Mahmoud.

'You mean Ethelred? Are you kidding? He's a crime writer. Nobody in their right mind marries a crime writer. I'm his agent.'

'So, Ethelred is a famous crime writer?'

I took a deep breath. No opportunity for PR should ever be overlooked. 'Yes, he's highly respected,' I said, wondering if my nose was growing visibly as I said it. 'A bestselling author, in fact. You'll see his books everywhere. Great reviews for all of them. He writes crime novels as Peter Fielding and J. R. Elliot.' Well, the last sentence was true anyway.

'A most valuable client for you to have.'

Hmm, if they really thought that, I wondered what else I could get them to believe. I'd probably already pushed Ethelred's luck as far as it would go, though the truth is quite stretchy and you never can tell what you can do with it until you try.

'He's pretty big in Latvia,' I added.

Mahmoud nodded. He raised one eyebrow at Majid, but I didn't see Majid's response.

'Can we speak to you in confidence?' asked Mahmoud after a pause.

I looked round the deck. It was empty. I told them therefore that they probably could. I always encourage confidences. In my experience, stuff people tell you in confidence is usually more interesting than the other stuff.

'OK. Let me say at once that there's no need to be alarmed,' said Mahmoud.

'About what?' I asked.

'We're policemen,' said Majid, producing an identity card from his pocket. 'Inspector Hafiz Majid and Inspector Hamid Mahmoud. Cairo police.'

'Your English is pretty good,' I said.

'We both studied in the UK. We're working in cooperation with the British police, tracking a couple of criminals who we think are on this boat.'

'I thought you said you weren't going to alarm me?' I said. 'Change of plan?'

'There is no need to be alarmed. But we may need your help.'

'Does it involve any danger to me?'

'No,' said Majid.

'To other people?'

'Possibly.'

'But not to me?'

'No.'

'That sounds OK. What had you in mind?'

'We can't say as yet. At a certain point we may need to make an arrest. We have to ensure that the passengers that we know we can trust are aware who we are – we don't want any confusion at a crucial point.'

'You mean I try to trip you up, thinking you are a terrorist or something?'

'That is the sort of misunderstanding we would prefer to avoid, if at all possible.'

I thought of Ethelred and made a note to give him a heads-up on that one. Tripping up a policeman in pursuit of a criminal was one of the few things I was sure he'd be good at.

'So, which of the passengers are the villains?' I asked.

'That's the one thing we can't tell you,' said Inspector Mahmoud. 'I can only say that our information is that there are two of them.'

'Are they posing as passengers or crew?'

'Again, that's not something we can tell you.'

'I can't say any of the passengers looks particularly likely.'

'Don't be fooled. Criminals look very much like anyone else. It could be any of them. Mr Purbright, for example.'

'Purbright? You mentioned him before. Is that who you are after?'

'I merely gave him as an example. Still, his behaviour is very odd, don't you think?'

'Were you listening to what we were saying to each other just then?'

'Yes. That's our job.'

'Cool. Now you mention it, I suppose he was a bit vague about where he was from and what he did,' I conceded. 'And he looks as though he has been partying non-stop since the early seventies. So, is he your man – or one of them anyway?'

'He is certainly somebody that we are watching closely.'

'And I should therefore stay away from him?'

They looked at each other.

'No,' said Mahmoud. 'In fact, it might be better if you could gain his confidence and report back to us anything that he says.'

'OK,' I said. It sounded like harmless fun – better than visiting temples anyway.

'And don't let him or anyone else know we are policemen. Don't mention this conversation to anyone.'

'These lips are so sealed,' I said.

'They're policemen, then?' said Ethelred.

'Yes,' I said, spitting a few bits of grape accidentally onto the cabin floor. 'But it's a *secret*. Could you peel those a bit faster, please?'

'Can't you peel your own?'

'Ethelred, if you have to peel them yourself, it completely misses the point. The whole *raison d'être* of the peeled grape is that somebody else does it for you. Don't you understand decadence?'

'Yes, I do. What I don't understand is why Mahmoud and Majid would tell you all this,' said Ethelred, handing me the meagre results of some three minutes of wrestling with some rather straightforward grape skin.

'Are you saying I can't be trusted with a confidence?' I deeply resented this slur.

'I mean,' said Ethelred, 'they can hardly be expecting you to help if it comes to a tussle with armed villains. They can't possibly have suggested that.'

'The point is,' I said, 'that Purbright isn't Raffles, as Proctor suggested to you. According to my policemen, he's actually the guy *who is going to kill Raffles*.'

'You don't know that,' said Ethelred cautiously.

'I might.'

'But, actually, you don't.'

'Have I ever told you how boring you are?'

'I'm merely pointing out that you can get into a lot of trouble by jumping to conclusions too quickly.'

'Yeah, right,' I said. As if I'd do that. 'Still, it's exciting, isn't it? I get to follow Purbright round the boat, then cleverly trick him into giving himself away.'

Ethelred looked doubtful.

'Everything they said sounds pretty odd to me,' he said, with his usual capacity for getting things totally arse about face. 'They must have been pulling your leg.'

'They had Egyptian warrant cards,' I said.

'And you know what an Egyptian warrant card is supposed to look like, do you?'

'Yes,' I said. There are times when it is pointless *not* to lie. 'Anyway, you have to admit that it's odd that both Proctor and my nice policemen think that a murder is about to be committed. And it's also odd that they are both talking about two murderers.'

'Did your policemen mention the word murder?'

'More or less.' I wasn't having a perfectly good theory wrecked by minor points of detail.

Ethelred sniffed. 'Well, I suppose that is a bit more convincing if they really did say that. But if Purbright is the hired assassin, or whatever, then who is Raffles? It can't be Professor Campion, surely. There's simply nobody left on the boat fitting Proctor's description of his client. In which case, as far as Proctor is concerned, the most likely thing in my view remains that he has simply boarded the wrong boat, and his client is being quietly done away with on another part of the river entirely.'

'Ethelred,' I sighed. 'If you don't mind me saying so, you have a very vivid imagination.'

CHAPTER SIX

The sun was setting to starboard. The dancing horizon that had threatened all afternoon to dissolve into a mirage was taking a break, and the broad western sky glowed red and orange. The Nile's green fringe was turning black, a strange twilight world in which things moved obscurely here and there amongst the palms. I leant against the varnished rail and watched it all go by. It was an ancient landscape, through which we moved noisily, the engines throbbing and the giant paddles swishing at the stern.

The sound of footsteps behind me made me turn. It was one of the passengers I had not yet met. Even without Elsie's somewhat sketchy description of him, it seemed almost certain that this had to be Purbright. At first sight he did not appear to be either a gorilla or a gangster. 'Dissolute' was the closest I could get to a single-word description.

'Mr Purbright, I presume?'

'And you must be Ethelred Tressider. I see that we have both studied the passenger list. You obviously notice things. Is that because you are a writer?'

'Possibly. You've read my books then?'

'Yes, I love them.'

I basked briefly in a rare moment of recognition. 'Which ones have you read?' I asked.

Purbright named three books by Paul Fielder. Somewhere on the far bank a waterbird cried out, ushering in the last of her chicks or trying to pull a passing male. The silence that followed it, to the extent that I could appreciate it with the *Khedive*'s paddles going, seemed empty and desolate.

'It's a beautiful evening,' I said, suppressing a sigh of resignation.

'Cooler anyway,' said Purbright. 'Your first time in Egypt?'

'Yes,' I said.

'It's a good time of year to come. Not too hot, but before the crowds arrive. The boat seems half empty.'

'An interesting mixture of people,' I said.

'Yes. You could say that. Is that strange man in pink shorts called Proctor?'

'That's right.'

'Any idea why he keeps winking at me?'

'Perhaps he thinks he knows you.'

'A lot of people know me. I can't think of any who wink at me like that.'

'Probably not,' I said.

'Must be something else then, wouldn't you think?'

I didn't feel able to say, though it did strengthen the case for concluding that this was certainly not Raffles and that Herbie Proctor needed to be on another boat entirely.

'I'm told there's good shooting round here,' said Purbright. He too was now leaning against the rail, his shoulder inches from mine. It all felt quite confidential. 'Waterfowl and so on,' he added.

'Really?' I said. It seemed possible, but it wasn't really my type of thing. It might have been Purbright's type of thing – out on the grouse moors at the crack of dawn after a night's heavy drinking – but I couldn't imagine that it was an activity that would be on offer on this trip. An afternoon of bird photography was as much as the *Khedive*'s programme envisaged.

'You must have had a lot of experience of guns,' Purbright continued. 'Your main characters tend to favour the Walther PPK – James Bond's gun, of course.'

As a former secret service agent, Paul Fielder probably did know quite a lot about guns. Before becoming a writer I, conversely, had worked in a tax office. Of the characters I wrote about, my Sergeant Fairfax never carried a firearm and the villains he pursued tended not to get much beyond a vaguely described sawn-off shotgun.

'I know a bit,' I hedged. Crime writers get to know a bit about a lot of things – much of it by using Google. I had also, after all, fired airguns at the local fair, occasionally denting a tin duck. Purbright nodded as if this confirmed what he had thought. The chance seemed to have passed, at least for the moment, for me to tell him that I wrote crime as Peter Fielding (and slushy romance as Amanda Collins). I'd bring the subject up tomorrow, if necessary, over breakfast. 'Is that a temple over there on the far bank?' I asked.

'I guess you could still handle a pistol if you had to?' He wasn't that interested in temples.

I smiled and shrugged. For some reason this also

appeared to have been a good answer on my part.

'I was planning to travel with a colleague of mine – a very good shot,' said Purbright, standing back from the rail again.

'But he couldn't make it?' I said cautiously. It explained the missing passenger on the purser's list anyway.

'Apparently not.' Purbright glanced behind him.

On second thoughts perhaps he *was* Herbie's client, but had originally planned to bring along somebody reasonably capable of protecting him. If Proctor had been called up at the last minute to replace this gun-toting colleague, Purbright would have been naturally dismayed when he came to view the detective actually on offer.

'Were you planning to do some shooting together?' I asked, still trying to feel my way through a rather obscure conversation.

'Something like that,' he said. 'Yes, you're right. I think that is a temple over there. The valley's full of them. There's nothing really worth looking at until we get to Edfu, of course.'

'You seem to know this stretch of river well,' I said.

'Look, Paul . . . or Ethelred if you prefer,' he said suddenly. 'I realise it's some years since you worked for Her Majesty – you must have left the service round about the time I joined. But you are probably the one person on board the boat I can trust at the moment.'

Only for a brief instant did I entertain the possibility that he might have worked for the Inland Revenue back in the eighties. I decided that it would be better not to delay explanations until breakfast, but to tell him now that I was not Paul Fielder, and only fired guns when there was a good chance of winning a goldfish.

'I'm not sure I can help in the way you think I can,' I began. 'You see—'

'I'm not expecting you to do anything too risky – however much you'd like to. It's just that there are a couple of gentlemen that I need to keep an eye on. If things get tricky, it may all look a little confusing to the average bystander – if you know what I mean. Even if the passengers can't help much, it's important they don't get in the way.'

'You mean I might think you were a terrorist or something?'

'That type of thing.'

'You're not connected even tangentially with Mr Proctor?' I asked. 'You didn't invite him onto the boat? Perhaps to stand in for your colleague?'

It was Purbright's turn to look puzzled.

'Connected? Not at all,' he said. 'And why on earth should he be able to stand in for my colleague?'

The theory that Purbright might be Raffles was fading in my mind almost as soon as it had been resurrected. On the other hand, that I was being briefed on something because Purbright thought I was a well-known author of spy stories, who had formerly worked for MI6, was as close to certainty as you got in this world.

'Anyway,' Purbright was saying, 'the fact that you can handle all sorts of firearms could prove very useful indeed.'

Only if the main threat was tin ducks.

'Maybe I should clear something up—' I said.

'Don't worry,' he said reassuringly. 'The chances are

that you won't be called upon to do anything at all. In the meantime, it would be helpful if you could keep your eyes on the two Arab gentlemen.'

'I'd be happy to do that – it's just that I think you are making a mistake,' I said.

He paused. 'No, our information is pretty good. Watch them. Talk to them if you can. Let me know what they say. We'd better resume this conversation later – there's somebody coming.'

He winked and slipped away, down the stairs to the deck below. Oh well, hopefully there would still be time to explain things to Purbright at breakfast tomorrow. I should have tried harder to correct him, but (on reflection) I had rather enjoyed being mistaken for a man of action. Or even for a bestselling author. What harm could there possibly be in that?

'Who were you talking to just then?' No sooner had Mr Purbright slipped away than Sky Benson suddenly materialised beside me. She was dressed as before: prim skirt and blouse, no make-up, just a hint of perfume. It reminded me for some reason of Annabelle's perfume – probably, as Elsie would inform me in due course, just a cheap imitation of it. But a pretty good imitation for all that. Though Miss Benson wore no earrings, I noticed that her ears were pierced. Perhaps then she was just reserving her finery for some later date. 'He's called Purbright,' I said.

'Ah,' she said. The contrast to Purbright could not have been greater. He had seemed totally self-assured. She on the other hand still looked ready to start at the first shadow.

The sun was setting. There were a lot of shadows around.

'So, we're all here? The missing passenger did not show up?' she asked.

'No,' I said. 'We left without him – or her.'

Relief briefly fluttered across her face, but only briefly.

'Whoever it is might still join us at Esna or Edfu, I suppose?' she asked.

'Yes,' I said. 'I suppose they might.' Our progress was slow enough that we could have been easily overtaken by somebody driving a car – a train would have flashed past in seconds. I was, as I say, now assuming that the absent traveller was Purbright's colleague – the man who was good with a gun – though that was not of course necessarily the case. 'Is the missing person a friend of yours?'

'No,' she said, as if that should have been obvious to me.

Having raised the matter of the missing passenger, Miss Benson seemed disinclined to discuss him further. She briefly observed that the weather was hot but not as hot as she had expected.

'Your first time in this part of the world?' I asked.

'Majorca,' she said distantly. I must have looked puzzled because she added: 'With Brenda and Susan. That was hot too.'

'Of course,' I said. That, I thought, placed her. For those not used to travel, a very different culture, like Egypt's, could be overwhelming. 'Egypt's a bit different from Majorca. But here on the boat, you won't have any hassles.'

'Hassles? What hassles?' she asked.

'Well, people trying to sell you things, for example . . .'

'No,' she said. 'I wouldn't imagine that they could sell

you things here on the boat.' But she glanced nervously over her shoulder as she did so. Her knuckles gleamed white against the mahogany rail. If my game plan had been to put everyone on the boat on edge I was doing well. Two down, nine to go.

After five minutes of a very one-sided conversation about the Nile and the sites we were due to visit the following day, she made a short apology and walked unsteadily back down the stairs, in the direction that Purbright had taken a few minutes earlier.

'Sorry, I made you jump.'

'Not at all,' I said quickly. 'Well, not very much. You sort of crept up behind me. You're Professor Campion, aren't you?'

'How do you know that?' He looked at me with deep suspicion.

'I was just behind you in the queue for keys,' I said.

He tilted his head at an angle that might have been intended to show sagacity but in practice revealed a great deal of nose hair. 'Ah,' he said.

'Your first time in Egypt?' I asked.

'No, I've been here quite a few times. I teach Egyptology.' Again, I was made to feel this was something I should have known.

'Good to have an expert on board,' I said. 'I'm sure we'll learn a lot from you.'

Campion's expression changed to that of a man who, out on a pleasant stroll through the countryside, notices for the first time the bull that is sizing him up from a shady corner of the field. 'I've no plans to run courses . . .'

'No, of course not. Still, it helps to have somebody on board who knows their way around.'

'Does it?' He still seemed worried I might know of a way to make him teach us Egyptology.

'I think so. It's a completely different culture here, isn't it? Sky Benson seemed a little nervous.'

'Miss Benson?' This was a new problem for him. He tipped his head to one side, as if miming 'Thought', and frowned. 'Who exactly is she . . . ?'

'Oh, sorry, I thought you knew each other. You were sitting next to her on the plane?'

'Ah, yes, the plane.' He seemed on the verge of asking which plane, then thought better of it. '*Benson* – was that it? And what was her first name again?'

I repeated it. He repeated it, though with a pathetic note of uncertainty in his voice. I sympathised. I am not that good at remembering names either, as I may have said. At his third attempt he seemed reasonably satisfied that he now knew about whom he was talking.

'Or perhaps she was nervous about something else,' I said, picking up the conversation from where we had left off.

'She seemed fine on the plane,' he said. 'To the extent we conversed, anyway.'

'I think she hasn't travelled much,' I said.

'No,' he said, but the way he said it suggested her concern was not only avoidable but also reflected, in some obscure way, badly on himself. Maybe he too had tried to reassure her earlier and failed.

'Well,' I added, 'it's not your problem anyway.'

'*Exactly*,' he said, but I had, somehow, just placed an unreasonably heavy burden on his already stooped shoulders. My score was now three.

Another very one-sided conversation followed, this time about dinner and how we might or might not dress for it. Here too I was not a success. I said that I thought that, on the first night at least, dinner jackets would not be required. He said that he had not packed such a thing. I replied that I doubted very much that it mattered what we wore on any night, but he shook his head sadly. He clearly blamed me, and me alone, for the fact that he would be wrongly attired – perhaps not tonight, but almost certainly on some future occasion. He too took his leave after an awkward silence. Bearing in mind we were all on holiday, a high proportion of the passengers seemed nervy and tense. Purbright alone had seemed relaxed, in spite of the absence of his colleague, equally fearless of being murdered in his bed or caught in the wrong sort of dinner attire.

The bell sounded for our first meal on the boat, and we all made our way, in ones and twos, to the dining room.

Though dress was indeed informal, no effort had been spared to continue the illusion of old-world luxury. The mahogany panelling shone sumptuously and the gold palm fronds, carved onto the top of each pillar, gleamed as if freshly painted. Burgundy velvet curtains, of a kind positively designed to capture the desert dust in every rich fold, formed graceful arcs around the windows. The chairs were vast and antique, though perhaps a little too soft and yielding to be described as truly comfortable. The table linen, by contrast, was rigid with starch and the massed ranks of bright cutlery arranged on it promised more courses than I felt entirely comfortable with. It was a room from which the twenty-first century had been banned.

I found myself at a table with Elsie, Purbright (the probable MI6 man), Professor Campion, Lizzi Hull and Jane Watson, the pleasant if excitable lady in the floppy hat. At another table sat two Arab passengers (who seemed nice enough, but did not look much like policemen), the two Americans, Sky Benson (who I could only conclude did not know Campion) and Herbie Proctor, who was already boring the other guests to sleep.

CHAPTER SEVEN

Elsie

I found myself at a table with Ethelred, Purbright (the cunning master criminal), Professor Campion, Lizzi Hull and Jane Watson, the annoying cow with a floppy hat. At another table sat the two policemen – the only ones I really trusted on the boat – together with the two young Americans, Sky Benson (who clearly *did* know Campion – do me a favour) and Herbie Proctor, who was already boring the other guests to sleep.

I watched with mild curiosity as Sky Benson, with her back to me at the far corner of the other table, gave a sudden nervous laugh and knocked her water glass and knife to the floor at a single stroke. A waiter, in his black uniform trimmed with white braid, swooped immediately to clear them away. Further down my own table, I heard Professor Campion give a despairing sigh, but when I turned to him he was examining a fish fork with great care, as though they were rarely encountered in academic circles.

'What a cosy little table we are,' said Miss Watson, in a way that suggested she rather enjoyed the role of jollying people along, particularly those who did not much want

to be jollied. 'I'm quite pleased the boat is half empty –
we'll all get to know each other so much quicker.' She shot
a glance to her right, but I didn't see whose eye she was
trying to catch – Purbright, Campion, Ethelred? It was, in
any event, Campion who spoke next. Her jollying had, in
his case, been a complete lost cause from the start. He was
the only passenger, male or female, to be wearing a suit
and he looked hot and annoyed. He scowled at Purbright
and Ethelred, both dressed in open-necked shirts, as though
they had tricked him in some way that he could not yet
quite put his finger on.

'We still appear to be one passenger short,' said
Campion. This seemed to piss him off even more, though
what business it was of his was a mystery.

'Apparently,' I said.

'Perhaps, if he or she has missed the boat, whoever it is
may still join us at Edfu?' asked Campion. 'Does anyone
happen to know?' I noticed Ethelred give Purbright an
enquiring glance at this point, as if he might.

'It's possible,' said Purbright. He implied that, if it was
a problem of any sort, it wasn't his problem. Ethelred
shrugged apologetically, but Purbright was in any case
now looking across at the other table, behind my back.
His eyes were narrowed at somebody – Proctor? The two
policemen? Sky Benson?

We were served clear soup with bits in it. I declined
a roll, feeling that if we were in for the full six courses I
should show a little restraint. It's the only way, I find, to
stay girlishly slim.

'Have you all just flown in?' Purbright asked

71

inconsequentially, giving his soup an experimental swirl with his spoon.

'Most of us were on the same flight,' said Ethelred.

'Though not I.' Miss Watson addressed Purbright diagonally across the table. 'I had things to do in Cairo en route. Things to do and people to see. Always busy. And how about you, Mr Purbright? Have you been long in this very pleasant part of the world? Do you work here or do you live entirely for pleasure?'

Purbright's reply was curt. Another one who could take jollying or leave it, apparently. 'Yes, I've been here a while,' he said.

'And you are happy here?'

'Shouldn't I be?'

'I've no idea,' said Miss Watson. 'Some people get what they deserve – some of us don't.'

Purbright opened his mouth as if to reply, then shook his head and turned to ask Lizzi Hull what she did when she was not on a Nile paddle steamer. She proved to be a train driver.

'Surely not?' asked Miss Watson, overhearing her.

'Goods,' said Lizzi Hull.

'Your first visit to this part of the world?' asked Purbright.

'I worked in Khartoum for a while,' she replied. 'And I've been to Palestine.'

'Not obvious tourist destinations,' said Purbright.

'I'm not an obvious tourist,' she replied. 'You have to go and see things for yourself. The papers always lie, don't they – especially the Tory ones?'

Since I suspected that the other two men at our table

read much the same papers as Ethelred, this may not have been the most tactful response. I admired that.

'Indeed,' said Ethelred, implying his reading matter was entirely left of centre. He did occasionally buy *The Guardian* to check whether they had reviewed him – I've no idea why. 'First-hand research is vital,' he added, as if making some point for my benefit. Whatever.

'So, we begin our *research* tomorrow at the temple at Edfu?' I said, to show that I had read the itinerary on my bedside table.

'Ptolemaic,' said Professor Campion, looking up from his soup. He dabbed his thin lips delicately with an over-starched napkin before continuing. 'Dedicated to the falcon god Horus and completed in 57 BC by Ptolemy II. It has a massive 36-metre-high pylon and reliefs of Horus and Hathor. Also carvings of the great battle between Horus and Seth. Seth is shown as a tiny hippopotamus, being skewered on a lance. It's all about a zillion years old and blahdy, blahdy, blah, blah.'

Or something like that – I confess I may have paraphrased the last bit. If you're not bothered whether Hathor is the cat or the canary, and you can't work out why they needed a pylon if they didn't have mains electricity, then it's all somewhat theoretical. Campion seemed very keen to give us a brief lecture – but really just that and no more. Ethelred asked some questions about Edfu and Campion answered them, though with an increasing reluctance that I couldn't quite account for.

Since it didn't take much sensitivity to realise that Campion had had enough of the conversation, it was no surprise when Ethelred persisted doggedly with his questions.

Once or twice Campion looked perplexed, but mainly he just looked bored and hacked off – a common reaction to Ethelred in my experience. Purbright occasionally chipped in some obscure fact, though (thinking about it) nobody came up with any facts that I would have been prepared to describe as riveting. So fascinating did Ethelred and Campion make it all sound, in fact, that I wondered if I could just plead conscientious objections when they tried to round us up and make us go to the temple. A freshly squeezed orange juice by the pool – followed by some dedicated sleuthing on my part – sounded a better option. Anyway, I was almost asleep by the time the waiters brought us some reviving coffee.

As we left the dining room, I could see that something was troubling Ethelred. His dear little brow was furrowed. I hoped he wouldn't feel the need to tell me why.

'I'm sure Professor Campion was wrong about Ptolemy II,' he whispered to me, as if it could matter. 'It couldn't be that Ptolemy.'

'Not that Ptolemy? Wow! And you think somebody might actually give a shit?' I said.

Ethelred nodded. He clearly thought they might. 'I'll check in my guidebook.'

'Let me know straight away if you're right,' I said. 'I shan't sleep, worrying that it might have been Ptolemy III.'

'Ethelred,' I said, opening my cabin door an inch or so. 'I was being ironic. Nobody on the planet gives a monkey's about who built the temple except you, Ptolemy and Professor Campion. At this precise moment in time,

74

Professor Campion is asleep and Ptolemy is mummified, so save it for tomorrow.'

'You don't understand,' he said. 'Can I come in? Wow! Did somebody peel all those grapes free of charge or are they being put on my bill?'

'Tell me what it is I don't understand,' I said, diminishing the grape pile by one, 'then let me get back to sleep.'

'The point,' said Ethelred, with a touching belief that I shared more than a microgram of his enthusiasm, 'is that I was certain it wasn't Ptolemy II who built the temple.'

'Yeah, whatever,' I observed, wishing to show interest in his little ideas, as you must occasionally with your authors.

'So, I checked it in my guidebook – and what do you think?'

'It was Ptolemy III?'

'No.'

'IV?'

'No.'

'V?'

'No.'

'VI?'

'No.'

'Well, which sodding pharaoh was it then?'

'Ptolemy II.'

'II?'

'Yes. By the way – you don't pronounce it "Eye-Eye."'

'So, just like Campion said?'

'Yes.'

'You woke me up to tell me that?'

'You weren't asleep.'

'That is a pure technicality, and you know it. You have disturbed what might have been my beauty sleep to tell me that Professor Campion was right and you were wrong. Why not phone the BBC and let them know too? That's also irony, in case you are actually tempted to do it.'

'No, the point is that both the book *and* Campion are wrong. Think about it – there were fourteen Ptolemies, so Ptolemy II couldn't possibly have been around in 57 BC. It's just a misprint. As you know, Ptolemy I blah, blah, blah, bloop, bloop, blippy, blip, blap, blappy, blap.'

Again, I have had to paraphrase some of what he said to make it more intelligible for you.

I waved my hand to indicate I was now as big an expert on pharaohs, up to and including Ptolemy Ex-Ivy, as I wished to be.

'Or, alternatively,' I said, 'just accept you could be wrong and everybody else could be right.'

Ethelred frowned thoughtfully at this novel suggestion, unaware that the conversation had already finished. Then in the silence we heard, from not that far off, an entirely different and more interesting tête-à-tête. The door leading to my balcony was open and somebody on the deck immediately above was having a very urgent discussion with somebody else. Sadly we had already missed part of it because Ethelred was shit scared I might be confusing two different, though equally mummified, pharaohs.

'. . .at Edfu,' said Professor Campion. He was cross but we had (and you are quite right in blaming Ethelred for this) missed the reason why.

'I should never have agreed to do this,' said Sky Benson.

'But you did. Indeed, I seem to remember you were quite insistent that you should be part of it.'

'I don't know that I can go through with it. But maybe we won't have to?' There was an almost plaintive note in her voice. Campion's response was brief but mean.

'We've got to go through with it now. If the opportunity arises, we have no choice. We can scarcely go back and say that we simply changed our minds.'

'No,' said Sky Benson.

One or other of them sighed. Possibly both of them. Neither had sounded exactly content with their lot.

'Just try to relax and at least act normally,' Campion said. 'If you constantly look as though you're about to commit a murder, people will start to get suspicious.'

'I'll do my best,' she said.

'Now, go back to your cabin before anyone overhears us.' A bit late for that, obviously. Sky Benson muttered something we could not quite make out and quick footsteps tapped across our ceiling (their floor). After a carefully judged but, as it happened, completely redundant delay, a heavier tread above us and some carefree but tuneless whistling announced the professor's own departure.

'So, I was right then,' I said, without the slightest trace of smugness. 'They know each other. And Campion is forcing her to do something she doesn't want to do.'

'Do you know how smug you look?' asked Ethelred.

But this conversation too was quickly superseded by another. The spot above my cabin was clearly a sheltered corner in which people imagined they could have confidential chats. A second couple had taken up their stations.

'This is an unexpected surprise,' said Purbright. His tone of voice gave little away, but it was fairly clear that he did not mean it was a birthday cake or a free chocolate bar. 'Are you about to tell me your presence here is a complete coincidence?'

If there was a reply, the other person present was very softly spoken. Perhaps Purbright's words had simply been greeted with a shrug or smile because he continued: 'I can't easily throw you off the boat, but I'm warning you not to get in my way . . . is that a light down there?' The last words were spoken in a hoarse whisper. Whatever conclusions the two of them reached about the light, we heard no more – just footsteps crossing the deck, one briskly, the other with deliberate, almost irritating, slowness. Then there was just the rumble of the engines and the swishing of the paddles to break the stillness of the night.

'That's your fault, that is,' I said.

'Mine?'

'If you hadn't disturbed me, my light would have been off and they would have stayed and talked a bit more.'

'If I hadn't disturbed you, you would apparently have been asleep and missed both conversations.'

There is no reasoning with Ethelred sometimes. I therefore ushered him, still protesting, out of my cabin and got back into bed. Though I stayed awake for some time, there were no further discussions, secret or otherwise, on the deck above me.

I was just drifting off to sleep when it struck me that I had not checked my new phone for the many important messages that would have arrived for me from both friends and business contacts. I duly switched it on and accepted the Egyptian network on offer. Disappointingly there were no missed calls and only one new message, from an unidentified caller. I opened it. It proved to be from Ethelred. I read it three times before it sank in, but the message was really admirably clear.

It said:

I am going to kill you,
Ethelred

If this was because I dissed his Ptolemy theory, he really needed to chill out a bit.

I got up and checked that my door was locked. Then I went to sleep.

CHAPTER EIGHT

My father must have spent a great deal of my childhood thinking up words of advice that would benefit me in later life. One of the few aphorisms that I still follow – or indeed can now recall – is that, on holiday, you should always opt for an early breakfast. In my father's opinion, the fruit juice and boiled eggs were that much fresher. The stocks of cereal and jam would still be complete. The staff would be that much more attentive. The view from the window would be softer, still in the glow of the newly risen sun. It is true that he based this policy on the shortcomings of certain cheap hotels in the Peak District or North Wales in which he, and therefore my mother and I, endured our summer holidays thirty or more years ago. Nevertheless, it was one of his better dicta. There really is something about an early breakfast that puts a spring in one's step and makes one's spirits rise.

'What are you playing at, you pillock?'

My thoughts were interrupted by a short, plump literary agent thrusting a mobile phone in my face.

'That's my phone,' I said, eyeing it from roughly three inches away.

'No,' said Elsie. 'This is *my* phone. Unless you are sending text messages to yourself. Why are you threatening to kill me?'

'What are you talking about?' I tried to focus on the screen in front of me. By moving my head back slightly I managed to get the words to take shape: *I am going to kill you, Ethelred.*

'I'm talking about that!' said Elsie, whipping the phone away again. 'You are not allowed to send me death threats, Ethelred. It's in your contract. Para 65.2 b.'

'Are you sure it's in the contract?'

'It's a standard clause. Ask any agent.'

'But I didn't send you that message,' I said.

'Then how come it's on my phone?' asked Elsie. She clicked once or twice to reveal the number of the sender. 'Are you saying that isn't your phone number?'

I sighed. 'No, that isn't my number. But that is my phone.'

Elsie looked blank.

'When you compared phones on the plane, you must have taken the wrong one. I've clearly got your phone and you have mine there in your hand. That's *my* phone.'

'But . . .'

'Read it again. That message doesn't mean: *I am going to kill you, kind regards, Ethelred.* It means: *My dearest Ethelred, I am going to kill you.*'

Elsie looked at the message again, then at me, then at the message again.

'Your phone?'

'Yes,' I said.

'A message to you?'

'Yes.'

'Not a message to me?'

'No,' I said.

'So who is the message *from?*' she demanded.

'Nobody you know,' I said.

'Ethelred, you are a crap liar. Your face gives you away every time.'

'It's just a joke,' I said. 'From a friend.'

'You have weird friends,' said Elsie.

'Better than weird enemies,' I said. Though obviously it wasn't much better.

Elsie might have taken this conversation further, but there were other more pressing matters on her mind. She had switched to tapping her fingers on the table and looking round the dining room impatiently.

'So, where are the sensible people?' she asked, in what would probably prove to be a rhetorical question. 'Ah, yes – they are all asleep in their beds. That's why there are only morons here at present.'

'As far as I can see, it is just the two of us,' I pointed out, having briefly checked the room. 'I am sure that the others will all be here in a few minutes, regretting their tardiness. In the meantime, I am going to get myself a fresh omelette.'

'Ethelred, the normal people won't be here for another couple of hours. You have time for at least a dozen omelettes, some using eggs from hens as yet unborn, before the first of the other passengers shows.'

'Since we are to visit the temple at eight, it would be

most unwise of them to delay so long.' I gave a little chuckle at this excellent riposte.

Elsie showed her contempt by buttering a croissant with slow, sarcastic strokes of her knife.

'In any case,' I added, 'I am curious to see what happens next.'

Elsie nodded, her mouth now full of butter mingled with small quantities of croissant. On this point at least we were in agreement. The conversations that we had overheard established that Professor Campion and Miss Benson not only knew each other but had some plan of action that they wished to keep quiet for the moment. So would they again opt for different tables? Purbright too was already acquainted with one of the other passengers, and he had not been pleased to see him – or her. Would a glance or remark give away who it was?

'So, who *was* Purbright talking to?' asked Elsie.

'Proctor?' I suggested. 'We know that Proctor thinks he is here to guard Purbright. Maybe that was Purbright telling Proctor his services were not needed. He couldn't throw him off the boat, but—'

'But Purbright isn't Raffles,' said Elsie. 'The policemen have him down as the man who is planning to *kill* Raffles. So, he can't be Proctor's employer.'

'They're not policemen,' I said.

'Whatever,' said Elsie. 'I still say Purbright is acting suspiciously. That conversation up there on deck last night was very odd.'

'Purbright is . . .' I began. Then I stopped. If Purbright really was MI6, then the last person I should tell was Elsie.

'Purbright is?' she asked. 'Ethelred, any sentence from you lacking a complement always makes me suspicious. You have deliberately terminated what you were about to say, your brain having belatedly caught up with your tongue and given it a good slapping. So, what have you just decided not to tell me about Purbright?'

'I think somebody has been pulling your leg,' I said, providing both subject and predicate in full this time. 'Policemen don't just blow their cover in the way you say these two have. They're simply a couple of passengers who decided to have a joke at your expense. If you want to believe any of the stories we've been told, collectively or individually, then we can at least be sure that Herbie Proctor *is* a detective – of sorts. And he'd hardly be on this boat unless somebody was paying his expenses in full.'

'So you are dismissing my two nice policemen and relying on the word of the worst private detective known to man?'

'Your rather touching assumption that they are policemen is based on a couple of pieces of paper purporting to be warrants and waved briefly in front of you,' I said.

'And you think I can't spot a real Egyptian warrant?' she demanded.

'I do indeed. If the warrants were in Arabic,' I pointed out patiently, 'you wouldn't have been able to read them. If conversely they had been in English, then they would most certainly be forgeries made entirely for your benefit. Or perhaps they were in Latvian?'

'God, you're pompous,' said Elsie, as she usually does when I am right.

'They are not police,' I said. 'Take my word for it.'

'Well, if we have two fake policemen on board, then we really have problems. Either they are with the Cairo police or they are up to something very funny indeed.'

Here Elsie had a point. 'Perhaps,' I said, 'we should alert Captain Bashir . . .'

'They said to tell nobody,' said Elsie.

'But the captain—'

'Obviously they feel they can trust no one on board – except me.'

Which of course was final and absolute proof that they could not possibly be policemen. Elsie was about to reply when she noticed we had company. I was not, after all, alone in believing that an early breakfast was best.

'Mind if we join you?' The two young Americans were both wearing sleeveless cashmere jerseys against the early morning chill – Tom's was beige, John's rose-coloured. They seemed to be enclosed in an aura of soap, toothpaste and aftershave.

'Do we just collect stuff from the buffet?' asked John, as he sat down.

'Yes,' I said. 'You go and choose but you'll find the waiters then bring it over for you. That's as close to self-service as this boat gets.'

'Interesting learning the local customs. Interesting place generally. Folk back home think we're nuts coming here, what with all the terrorists. Of course, we try not to look too much like Americans,' said John.

'You look totally like an American,' said Tom.

'And you don't?'

'Observe,' said Tom. 'Beige cashmere. Not pink. I blend with the desert. At fifty yards, the upper half of my body is completely invisible.'

'And the cream slacks?'

'You reckon the terrorists are going to hang around when they see a pair of disembodied cream slacks heading for them? I don't think so somehow.'

'Ignore him. He's mad,' said John.

'Ignore him. He's from Kansas,' said Tom. 'Never trust anyone from Kansas, even if they have a cute dog with them. Sooner or later they'll dump a house right on top of you and steal your ruby slippers.'

'If you don't mind my saying so, that sounds rather unlikely. Is this seat taken?' Miss Watson sat down without waiting for a reply. The black-uniformed waiter, who had been following a few paces behind her, whisked the bowl of fruit he had been carrying onto the table and unfolded her napkin for her with a well-practised flourish.

'*Shukran*,' she said. Then to the two Americans she added: 'I think we met in Cairo.'

'So we did,' said Tom. 'You were with an Egyptian gentleman.'

'Unsurprisingly since it was Cairo.' She seemed in no hurry to explain who it was. She took a grape out of her bowl and held it for a moment between finger and thumb before popping it into her mouth, unpeeled.

'Weren't those mummies scary?' said Tom. 'Didn't you think they were about to burst out of their glass cases and grab you?'

'No,' said Miss Watson. 'That's not what they do. Except possibly in American films. I think yoghurt might go well with this, don't you? In a moment, I'll get one of the waiters to carry over a pot from the buffet. They seem to enjoy carrying things.'

Our watching the various parties from last night's conversations proved inconclusive. Campion eventually entered clutching a book neatly covered in brown paper but of a similar size and shape to my own *Egyptology Made Easy*. He nodded at us all briefly and went to the other table with his bowl of cereal, where his reading was interrupted by Purbright a few moments later. Purbright seemed chirpy but Campion was keen to read his book, whatever it was, so the conversation at that table was intermittent at best. Sky Benson glanced briefly at our table and then at Campion and Purbright, both silently munching cornflakes, before electing to join us.

Eventually all were present and accounted for except Elsie's 'policemen'. I still needed to correct Purbright on the Fielder/Fielding business but it seemed unlikely that I would now be able to mention it casually over an omelette, he being at one table and I at the other. Perhaps there would be a chance at the temple this morning. There was no urgency. I could experience being a famous author for a little longer.

It was as Elsie and I were finishing our breakfasts that the purser appeared. He glanced from one table to the other and then coughed. Everyone turned and looked at him, including the small queue that had built up (*precisely* as I had predicted) in front of the omelette chef.

'Ladies and gentlemen. You will be aware that your

trip is to be accompanied by a guide. Unfortunately he failed to join us at Luxor. I had hoped that he might still travel down by train overnight, but regrettably that will not be possible. I now hope that our usual guide will be able to join us tomorrow. We are trying to contact him. In the meantime, you will of course be issued with tickets for each of the temples, and a member of the crew will accompany you, but your visits will be without an expert.'

'That is really too bad,' said Miss Watson, looking up from her yoghurt. 'We have paid for a proper guide.'

'I am sure there will be a refund . . .'

'That is scarcely the point.'

I wasn't sure that the purser appreciated being addressed like a naughty third-former. I felt sorry for him, though it has to be said that Miss Watson was speaking for most of us. We had all paid for a guide, even if one of us was hoping to recharge everything to their elusive client.

'We shall manage,' I said, with what I hoped was good grace. 'We do have Professor Campion with us. You won't mind giving us the benefit of your knowledge, Professor?'

It was clear that some of the party had not known we had an Egyptologist amongst the passengers, and several heads turned curiously in Campion's direction.

For a moment he said nothing, then he exclaimed indignantly: 'I am supposed to be on *holiday*, you know!'

'We wouldn't expect very much,' I said quickly, remembering his reaction when he thought I was suggesting he should run a course. 'You need only to point us all in the right direction and tell us what to look out for.'

'The problem . . .' he said, uncertainly. He was not happy.

Sky Benson conversely seemed quite perky and on the ball. 'Professor Campion,' she said, 'as an internationally renowned expert in Egyptology, it would be only natural for you to offer to help us, surely?'

'Would it?' he asked.

'I think so.'

Miss Benson, perhaps because of the previous evening's conversation, rather seemed to be enjoying putting Campion on the spot – at least, from the safety of our table.

'That would appear to be settled, then,' said Miss Watson, mainly I think because that was so far from being the case. 'I am so much looking forward to being guided by Professor Campion.'

'Then if I must . . .' Campion was both on the spot and backed into a corner and didn't seem to like being either.

'Excellent,' said the purser. He had wisely remained silent during this conversation, but now decided it was time to close the deal. 'Ali will accompany you to the temple and purchase tickets. The *very* distinguished Professor Campion will most kindly guide you round. For sure, I wish you all a very fine day.'

Campion rose, sighed and dropped his napkin tetchily on the table. 'So be it. I shall see you all in half an hour, when it will be my pleasure, *for sure,* to escort you round the temple of Edfu,' he said. 'In the meantime, please do enjoy your breakfasts, while I prepare for the visit.'

As he left the room, clutching his book, he flashed a look at me that was malevolent in the extreme, though all I had done was to try to help the other passengers. He clearly would have also liked to put the evil eye on Sky Benson, but she was already in conversation with the two Americans and so missed Campion's petulant exit and his final blameful gaze in her direction.

'Odd,' said Miss Watson, as she folded her napkin.

'Odd?' I asked. 'You mean Professor Campion's evident reluctance to guide us round the temple?'

'No – if Egyptology is his job, I can see why he might object to having his services commandeered in this way. It's a bit like getting a professional opera singer to entertain us with a bit of karaoke or getting a brain surgeon to check out your piles over coffee. If your day job is teaching hieroglyphics to people who are beginning to wonder why they didn't apply to read media studies or sociology, then you'd probably resent having to do the same to a group of people who are thinking mainly about what to have for lunch. I meant it's odd that they have sent for the *usual* guide as a replacement. Because the question is: Why didn't we have the usual guide in the first place rather than this thoroughly unreliable person who has failed to appear?'

'The boat is half empty,' said Purbright, turning to us from his seat at the next table. 'They've probably given their usual guide the week off and employed some first-year archaeology student from Ain Shams, who has now had a better offer at the last minute.'

'That is a remarkably confident assertion coming from somebody who clearly knows nothing about it,' said Miss Watson in the sweetest possible tones.

'I am only speculating,' said Purbright, with practised patience.

'I'll ask the purser,' said Miss Watson with a sniff. 'He's more likely to know than you are.'

Since Miss Watson had made her views of the purser known only minutes before, this was not a comparison intended to flatter.

'Do, by all means,' said Purbright. He stood up and made his exit, thus ensuring that he had at least had the last word.

Miss Watson watched him leave. 'I shall,' she said, as the door closed behind him. 'I most certainly shall.'

I'm not sure – returning to Miss Watson's analogy – how I would have felt if I had been asked to read from my novels to amuse the passengers. I suppose I would have done it. There was a time – I have to say a much better time in my view – when writers were simply required to write. Now your publisher, and indeed your agent, expects you to keep up your website, to blog and to appear regularly in order to read, sign and generally be pleasant. Elsie constantly reminded me that my natural modesty was quite charming but unfortunately sold no books. I did not doubt that, had she thought it would shift even a single copy, Elsie would have had me reading to the passengers every evening, pointing out (no doubt) that this was after all supposed to be a working visit.

As, of course, it was.

Campion's annoyance was, in that context, perhaps quite understandable. Miss Watson's comment to him, by extension, seemed tactless – but perhaps no more so than her remarks to Purbright, who had done nothing to offend her. Like Elsie, she apparently felt that people were entitled to know her views in full. Hopefully, like Elsie, she also had a finely tuned sense of what she could get away with – I was completely with Agatha Christie on the issue of whether you could murder somebody on a Nile paddle steamer. You can murder somebody anywhere. It's getting away with it that is always the tricky bit.

In the end, Campion's lecture to us on the main features of an Egyptian temple was informative, but our questions to him were almost invariably dismissed with every sign of wearied irritation.

'It's just a list of the pharaoh's titles, one after the other,' he said curtly, in reply to a question from Jane Watson about the meaning of the hieroglyphs on the face of the vast pylon in front of us. Even first-year students, he implied, would have known that.

'Such as?' asked Herbie Proctor. At breakfast Proctor had dismissed any idea of joining our excursion, but had eventually trailed along – mainly to be unkind to Campion, as far as I could tell. He had displayed no real interest in anything he had been shown, but had occasionally tried fiddling with his phone to see whether he could get a signal.

'Well,' said Professor Campion, peering at the carved characters, 'this one says, "He of the Sedge and Bee".'

'And that one?' asked Proctor, pointing randomly.

'That says "King of Upper and Lower Egypt".'

'And the one up there?'

'That's the Golden Horus.'

'Fascinating,' said Proctor. 'That's *really* interesting.'

Proctor's little world was, it seemed to me, a curious one. He shared Elsie's view that the majority of his fellow men were idiots, placed on earth primarily for his own personal annoyance. While Elsie's fellow men were never left in any doubt about how she felt about them, Proctor limited himself to snide ambiguities, which might later be disowned if they proved inconvenient. Scratch Elsie, however deeply, and you would just find more of the same. Proctor's bravado was no more than a thin veneer, easily damaged but perhaps too cheap to cause him concern if it was.

Campion looked uncertainly at Proctor. Somebody who was sufficiently vain might have taken Proctor's words as a compliment. Somebody who was sufficiently thin-skinned would almost certainly have bridled at Proctor's tone. Campion was possibly both, and therefore unable to decide what the appropriate response might be. In the end, he shook his head as if he had never come across anything quite like Proctor before, and then led us through the door in the pylon and into the peristyle courtyard, where the impromptu lecture continued.

'The prof seems to know his stuff,' said Purbright later, as we stood in the shade just outside the hypostyle hall, its towering columns and stone ceiling creating a welcoming gloom for those inside and a narrow line of shadow for us outside. Purbright wiped his neck with an old-fashioned spotted handkerchief and stuffed it back in his pocket. The sun was now higher in the sky, and Egypt was starting to feel a whole lot warmer. Our little group had dispersed after viewing the sanctuary, and was now wandering round the temple in ones and twos, each at his or her own pace and in the shade as much as possible. The boat was not due to sail for another hour. Elsie and I had re-examined the great pylon – a solid, almost modernist slab with its vast figures striding stiffly across its face to some never-fulfilled meeting in the middle. We had plunged into the twilight of the temple to view the sacred barque in the narrow inner sanctum. We had glanced briefly up a steep staircase that apparently led to the roof. Had I been tempted to venture up there I would have been quickly dissuaded by a sign that read: 'CLOSED – REPAIR WORK IN PROGRESS'. Nothing prevented us physically from ascending, other than an old piece of rope tied crookedly across the passage. My natural inclination to follow official instructions might still have been countermanded by Elsie, who has a theory that you are only ever banned from doing good stuff. Before she could drag me over the rope and up the stairs, however, she had spotted somebody with an ice cream and decided that locating the shop that sold them was a higher priority than subverting petty bureaucracy.

Thus I found myself talking to Purbright in the growing mid-morning heat. I was beginning to wish that I had joined Elsie, but told myself that there would be plenty of time for keeping cool once we returned to the *Khedive*.

'Yes,' I said to Purbright. 'Professor Campion was very informative. I think he blames me for landing him in it, though.'

'I got that impression too,' said Purbright. 'I don't think you've made a friend there somehow. Still, it has been very useful for the rest of us.'

I nodded. Though the Ptolemy business still worried me, I could not fault Campion's role as a guide. At the back of my mind both now and earlier that morning, however, had been the strange overheard conversation between Campion and Miss Benson. It was true that, when Campion had been leading the group, Miss Benson had been no more and no less attentive than the others in the party. Had it not been for the words I had heard pass between them, they might genuinely have met on the journey out but found each other neither sufficiently interesting to desire further company nor sufficiently dull to avoid it altogether. As it was, while Campion had described the layout of the temple, I had not been contemplating the glories of the ancient pharaohs but had been wondering exactly what sort of hold Campion had over Sky Benson. As he explained the development of the pylon, I had speculated on whether he had actually meant that a murder was planned or just that Miss Benson was acting in a way that would arouse such a suspicion. Nor were those my only thoughts; the relaxed-looking MI6 man in front of me had also been having an odd discussion with somebody who was also probably present in the group.

'I guess we'll be pretty expert on all of this by the end of the trip,' Purbright continued, fortunately unable to read my mind. 'Amazing stuff. Look at those paintings on the ceiling – over two thousand years old. You'd scarcely think it, would you?'

I looked up at the large stone slabs that formed the

ceiling. Some were well preserved. Others were cracked or decaying – explaining perhaps why the steps to the roof were temporarily out of bounds. But, where the old surface remained, the reds, blues and yellows were still surprisingly fresh, as though just decorated using a giant paintbox with just a few blocks of primary colour.

'You can get up onto the roof, I think,' said Purbright, following my gaze, 'if you pay some baksheesh to one of the temple guards.'

'It's closed off,' I said. 'There's a notice on the staircase, anyway. It all looks a bit precarious. I'm not sure I'd risk it.'

'Might be worth checking out,' he said. Purbright was clearly somebody who preferred doing to merely looking and shared Elsie's scepticism regarding health and safety warnings.

He had already departed, for the roof or elsewhere, when Herbie Proctor appeared from the entrance to the hall and joined me on the outside, in my small strip of shade by the columns. I pretended to be examining the hieroglyphs intently, in the hope he would pass me by without comment.

'You'll be able to read that stuff now, having listened to Campion,' said Proctor with a sneer.

'Not really,' I said, giving up the charade of doing so.

'Exactly,' said Proctor, leaning against the pillar. He was using a thumbnail to extract the last remains of his breakfast from between his front teeth. He held up the modest fruits of his labours to the light and squinted at it before adding: 'That man's a complete fraud.'

'I wouldn't go that far . . .'

'Oh, I would. "He of the Sedge and the Bee". What

sort of title is that? He hadn't got the first idea what those cartouches said.'

'I did wonder the same thing,' I said. I couldn't vouch for the hieroglyphs, but the Ptolemy numbering thing continued to niggle me. It felt odd siding with Proctor, but his suspicions echoed my own. I glanced round the courtyard to see whether any of our party was within earshot. I could see nobody, but of course anyone could have been concealed behind one of the numerous columns. 'Yes, he is acting oddly,' I agreed. 'He said something last night that I'm sure was wrong. He said this temple was constructed by Ptolemy II.'

Proctor nodded. 'They can't fool you, eh Ethelred? Ptolemy II my arse.'

For a moment I thought that, like Elsie, he was not taking my concerns seriously. I pressed on anyway.

'So, why should he be pretending to be an Egyptologist?' I asked.

'Why indeed, Ethelred? Why indeed? You see, I'm trained to pick up these things – in real life, where it counts. Of course, if this was one of your little books, he might just be a red herring – he might have some entirely innocent reason for playing at being a professor. But not in real life, Ethelred. When that sort of thing happens in real life, there's a reason for it. What you need in this business is cold logic and an instinct for danger. You have to be two steps ahead . . .'

The slab of sandstone, as I was later informed, was halfway to the ground before anyone spotted it. At that point two or three people had screamed helpfully, but it took far longer for us to react than for the rock to complete its descent and shatter against the flagstone floor. It was fortunate that standing still was a relatively safe option. I was aware only of something large hitting the deck not far from us. Whereupon a whole lot more people screamed. As the dust cleared I saw Proctor staring at me open-mouthed; then everyone within the courtyard and some from the hall beyond converged on us asking us if we were all right. My arm, I discovered, had been grazed by a fragment of stone, thrown up when the slab flew apart. Proctor appeared shocked and dusty, but unhurt. It was only once I had reassured everyone that I was fine that I thought to look up.

'It must have broken off from the roof, up there,' I started to say, though I couldn't have said exactly which part of the roof had given way.

'We need to clear the hall and get people over to the other side of the courtyard,' said somebody near me. 'Another piece could come down at any moment.'

There was general agreement on this point. Though the outer court was entirely open to the sky, and no part of it other than that adjoining the hall offered any threat of falling objects, most of us gravitated quickly to the far side – with frequent backward glances. There I met other members of our party, including Elsie.

'What happened in there?' she demanded, licking a large ice cream with three chocolate Flakes. 'Did you break something?'

'A rock fell from the roof,' I said. 'It just missed me and Herbie Proctor.'

Elsie nodded, though the rapidly melting vanilla goo was demanding the better part of her attention. I showed her my scratched arm, and received an assurance (between skilfully deployed licks) that I would probably live. Only when I pointed to the widely dispersed remains of the slab on the far side of the courtyard did she begin to take the incident seriously.

'You mean all of those rock bits over there?'

'It was still in one piece when it was dislodged from the roof,' I said.

'That's a bit of a coincidence, then,' she said with a frown.

'Meaning what?'

'Meaning that last night you get a death threat and today a rock almost kills you.'

'Oh, it couldn't have been the person who sent the text,' I said.

'No?'

'They're not even in Egypt at the moment.'

'You know that?'

'Absolutely. It must have been an accident. Maybe somebody who ignored the warning signs dislodged a loose stone. Herbie Proctor and I just happened to be in the wrong place.'

'It's not a very effective way of bumping somebody off, is it? You can scarcely get pinpoint accuracy.'

'Maybe you could warn somebody off?' I suggested.

'And you think that's what happened?'

'I suppose somebody *might* have wanted to warn Proctor,' I said. 'If he's been hired to guard this Raffles guy – wherever he is – wouldn't that have made him a target? Somebody could easily have dropped the slab of rock down into the courtyard where we were standing. Most people wouldn't have gone onto the roof with that sign there, so anyone who went up there would probably have been alone and unobserved. And with all of the confusion afterwards, it wouldn't have been too difficult to sneak away down that little staircase and out into the courtyard.'

'Did you actually see anyone up on the roof?'

'No,' I said. 'We were standing close to the wall, by that column over there. We wouldn't have been able to see anyone.'

'So, just an old, badly constructed roof?' asked Elsie.

'I guess so. After two thousand years, you could probably just put the whole thing down to reasonable wear and tear.'

Lizzi Hull found us at this point and, with no ice cream as a distraction, offered slightly more sympathetic remarks about the incident. She had abandoned her cap for a floppy sun hat, not dissimilar to that worn by Jane Watson – and indeed by many other ladies who were visiting the temple. After a while Sky Benson appeared, equally sympathetic, but currently bareheaded.

On the far side of the courtyard from us, officials were now hurriedly taping off the entrance to the hypostyle hall. I could see Proctor and another visitor pointing out to them, at a safe distance, where the stone appeared to have fallen from. It looked as though it was being treated as a health and safety issue rather than a crime. Eventually Campion too reappeared. The party was more or less complete and it was agreed that we should make our way back to the bus.

En route, I took Elsie to one side, on the pretext of wanting to take a look at the *mamissi*.

'I've just had a thought . . .' I began. 'The conversations we overheard last night – Sky Benson was saying that she didn't think she could go through with it. Campion was saying that, if the opportunity arose, they had to take their chance. Was that rock one of them taking their chance? Herbie Proctor was saying to me, just before the ceiling fell in, that he thought Campion was a phoney.'

'What? Are you saying that Campion could have overheard the conversation, worked out Proctor was onto them, dashed up to the roof and lobbed the slab down?'

I thought about it. The improbability of the unathletic Campion dashing anywhere, other than to the front of a queue, was the least of the possible objections. It would simply have taken anyone far too long to get up to the roof. Surely?

'I admit he would have had to have been pretty fast,' I conceded. 'Proctor had been standing there only for a minute or so.'

'Not him then,' said Elsie.

'Campion *is* a fake though,' I said.

'Are we also back to the very important Ptolemy numbering issue?'

'Yes, but without the note of sarcasm that you just employed. This is an important clue. My theory is that he's got the same guidebook as I have and that he is reading it up as he goes along, hence—'

'Ethelred,' she said. 'That's the biggest load of boll . . .'

Then she stopped suddenly, in mid-put-down. I turned and looked in the direction she was looking.

'Hello,' said Annabelle. 'It's so good to see you both enjoying yourselves.'

CHAPTER NINE

Elsie

'Hello,' said the scheming bitch. 'It's so good to see you both enjoying yourselves.'

I had been concentrating on explaining things, and Ethelred had been Ethelred, so neither of us had noticed a lady in a large floppy hat approaching us from an oblique angle. For a moment the three of us stood there, Annabelle smiling serenely, me frowning and Ethelred blinking. Of course, Annabelle wasn't just smiling. Every little nuance of dress and expression was carefully calculated – the cool, white linen blouse with three buttons open at the neck, the immaculate sand-coloured slacks with the large belt that emphasised her teensy little waist, the carefully understated touch of make-up that she'd probably been working on since two o'clock that morning, the more-in-sorrow-than-in-anger look in her eyes. Oh yes. Nor was my frown merely a frown – it said quite clearly: 'I'm onto your game, you bitch, whatever your game turns out to be.' Ethelred's blink was, obviously, just a blink.

'I think it's a little warmer today, don't you?' asked Annabelle, taking off her floppy hat to reveal her (dyed) blonde tresses to their full advantage. She gave me the sad half-smile again and I thought: 'Yes, Botox!'

'Hello, Annabelle,' said Ethelred finally. He leant forward awkwardly and kissed her on the cheek. The day was indeed quite warm, but I was afraid that Ethelred's lips might nevertheless end up stuck to her face, like when you kiss a deep-frozen tub of chocolate ice cream. (It happened once to a friend of mine.)

'What are you doing here?' I demanded, raising the question that seemed not to have occurred to Ethelred yet.

'I just felt like a little winter break,' said Annabelle. 'If you two can visit Egypt, why not I?'

'I thought you didn't want to come to Egypt?' I said. 'I thought you'd turned Ethelred down?'

She flashed a look at Ethelred that said quite clearly that he had told me too much for his own good. Ethelred went back to blinking, though slightly more nervously than before.

'I've decided that a trip on a Nile paddle steamer would be fun after all,' she said.

'Which one?' asked Ethelred, as if there genuinely was some hope that it was not ours.

'The *Khedive*, of course,' Annabelle cooed. 'It's the best boat on the river. I checked with the little man at the reception desk. There are apparently several cabins vacant. He has given me a nice one near yours.'

'That's nice,' I said.

'That's nice of you to say so,' she said.

I wondered whether we'd jointly achieved some sort of world record for using the word 'nice' sarcastically. Probably.

'So, you'll be with us for the rest of the trip?' said Ethelred, still hoping things weren't as bad as they looked.

'Every single day,' said Annabelle, confirming that they were. 'Now, I must run and take a look at the boat thing in the inner temple. I think we still have a few minutes before the coach returns to the *Khedive*. So *nice* to see you both.'

That's how it is with world records: no sooner do you set one than somebody else breaks it.

Ethelred was strangely contemplative as we drove through the streets of Edfu on our way back to the boat, our coach driver neatly avoiding horse-drawn carriages operating on the wrong side of the dual carriageway.

Once on board, Ethelred vanished to attend to his minuscule scratch. Annabelle, too, excused herself, saying that she had to unpack. I wondered what I should do next myself. My policemen had not only failed to report for breakfast but had opted out of the temple visit, so I thought perhaps I would update them on what had happened there.

'From what you say, it sounds like an accident,' said Inspector Mahmoud with a glance at his colleague. 'Not something we should get involved in.'

'You're sure you wouldn't like to contact the local police in case it's anything to do with the criminals?' I asked. 'I mean, I think it was an accident too, but you could talk to them and they would be able to carry out proper searches of the boat for clues . . .'

Mahmoud shook his head. 'The last thing we want

is that these people discover we are onto them. If we get uniformed policemen trampling all over the boat, we'll lose the best lead we've had for months.'

'And you still can't tell me who the criminals are?'

'There are two of them. We know that they have come out from London. One at least is already on this boat.'

At a time when good facts were hard to come by, it was reassuring to find that the number of criminals remained constant at exactly two, regardless of whose version we were listening to. A bit like Noah, I mentally paired off those who had boarded the boat. 'So that's Professor Campion and Sky Benson,' I said. 'There are the two American boys – but they've come from Kansas or somewhere, not London. There's Purbright, but he's clearly on his own. So is Proctor. So is the hat bitch. So's Lizzi Hull. So is *Annabelle*, *Lady Muntham*.'

I paused after this last name so that it could sink into their consciousness.

'Ah, yes, Lady Muntham,' said Mahmoud. 'She joined the *Khedive* this morning, having travelled down from Cairo. Do you know her?'

'A bit,' I said.

'She has a title. She is presumably very rich?'

'No,' I said. 'She is currently very poor. My ambition is to ensure she remains so.'

'She is famous?'

'No,' I said.

They seemed let down. Maybe meeting celebs was a perk of the job. Such charms as Annabelle possessed were all freely available for viewing between the hours of eight in the morning and eleven at night, but if they were looking for anything beyond that, they were going to be badly disappointed.

'We'll speak to her later.'

Reluctantly I agreed that we didn't yet have the evidence to put the handcuffs on Annabelle – and to be fair, there was only one of her. 'It must be possible to narrow things down a bit, though?'

'The two American guys travelled here via London,' said Majid, running through the passenger list. 'And they were in Cairo before they came to Luxor. They could be on holiday, like they say, or then again, maybe not. The CIA are checking them out for us.'

'Purbright is travelling alone,' said Inspector Mahmoud, 'but there is, of course, the gentleman who failed to join us at Luxor. He is down on the passenger list as "Smith", which we believe to be a fictitious and assumed name. He may well fit into the equation somewhere. We have been trying to find out about him too. We think he may be in the country and will join the boat later. Purbright and his missing friend remain our best hunch.'

'And Herbie Proctor?'

'I don't think so,' said Mahmoud. 'He doesn't quite seem up to . . . the crime we are investigating. You can vouch for Mr Tressider?'

'Obviously,' I said. 'Completely harmless. On the other hand, I overheard Professor Campion and Sky Benson having a rather strange conversation. He was trying to persuade her to do something she didn't want to do.'

'What exactly?'

'I'm not sure, but not the sort of thing you're obviously thinking, so you can wipe that grin off your face. I also heard Purbright talking to somebody.'

'And?'

'He wasn't too pleased to see them.' Even as I said it, I realised that this piece of intelligence didn't amount to very much. Majid and Mahmoud exchanged glances again. I was losing credibility as a detective.

'Can you remember anything they said?' asked Mahmoud. 'Purbright said something about it being a surprise to see this person but he couldn't throw them off the boat.'

'No, I suppose he couldn't. Throwing somebody into the Nile would certainly arouse suspicion. And then?'

'I couldn't hear the reply, but they stopped talking because . . . because they thought they might be overheard where they were.'

'And that was all?'

'Yes,' I said.

'You don't know if it was a man or a woman Purbright was talking to?'

'No,' I said. 'But maybe it was a woman.'

'Why do you say that?' asked Mahmoud.

'There was just this note of condescension in his voice,' I said. 'It's something men do.'

Mahmoud looked at Majid again and shrugged dismissively.

'Thank you,' said Majid. 'That is very helpful.'

I hadn't achieved much, but I'd achieved all they'd expected. Thanks, guys.

'What do you want me to do now?' I asked.

Inspector Mahmoud looked doubtful and seemed to be about to tell me I was released from my snooping duties, but Inspector Majid intervened.

'Maybe you could talk to Miss Benson,' said Majid. 'It would help to know a little more about her conversation with Professor Campion – and whether she subsequently spoke to Purbright. It may be that you can catch her off guard in a way that we cannot.'

This indeed was their problem. In spite of what Ethelred thought, the two of them were so obviously policemen that they might as well have sat there in full uniform saying 'Evening all' to passers-by. They were pretty lucky they had somebody like me to help out.

'Mind if I join you?'

Sky Benson put down her copy of *Snow on the Desert's Face*. 'Be my guest,' she said. It was already too hot for some of the passengers – certainly we were the only ones who had so far opted for a table and a comfy basketwork chair on the sun deck. Sky still wore no make-up but was now dressed in a T-shirt and shorts and sported a necklace of irregularly shaped pieces of coral that she must have bought in one of the shops in Edfu.

'Well, the visit to the temple was more exciting than I expected,' I said.

'I hope Ethelred is all right,' she replied. She seemed genuinely concerned. 'That bit of roof didn't miss him by much, did it?'

I nodded. 'Ethelred's fine – well, much the same as usual anyway. Were you in the hall?'

'No, I was outside in the . . . I'm not sure what its name is. I still haven't worked out what the different bits of the temple are called. Anyway, I just heard a bit of a crash, turned and saw a cloud of dust rising. You'd think they'd make sure these places were safe to visit, wouldn't you?'

'You didn't go up on the roof yourself?'

'With my head for heights? No thanks. Just the look of the stairs up there made me feel faint. Anyway, wasn't there a sign saying "No Entry" or something?'

'Yes, but only to stop you seeing the good stuff. How do you find travelling on your own?'

'It's fine. You get to meet people. Everyone seems very friendly.'

'And Professor Campion?'

'How do you mean?' She looked at me with an innocence that was almost as tacky as her necklace.

'What did you think of his talk this morning?' I asked.

'He's very good,' she said, but slightly cautiously.

'Where exactly is he a professor?'

'London,' she said. 'I think that's what he told me, anyway.'

'Do you know him well?'

'As well as you can know somebody after twenty-four hours.'

'You didn't know him before this trip then?'

'No, why do you think that?'

She was convincing – I had to hand it to her. If I had

not overheard her and the professor, I might have almost believed what she was saying.

'You were sitting together on the aeroplane,' I pointed out.

'Yes, that was quite a coincidence – being given seats next to each other, then finding out that we were on the same boat, I mean. We had a good old chinwag on the way out.'

'Do you also work at a university?'

'No, I'm a librarian,' she said. 'And you?'

'I'm a literary agent.'

'What fun!'

'You reckon? Did Professor Campion say why he was on this trip? As an Egyptologist he should have seen most of these temples before. It must all be a bit basic for him.'

'I suppose if you're really interested in that sort of thing, you can't get enough of them. You must find the same thing with books.'

'Not really,' I said.

'Or writers.'

'You'd be surprised.'

She picked up *Snow on the Desert's Face* again.

'You like Salome Otterbourne's books?' I asked.

'This one's better than *Under the Fig Tree*,' she said. 'But I really prefer detective stories.'

'That's interesting. Ever contemplated murder yourself?'

I'm not sure what I'd hoped she'd do. Breaking down and confessing that she was conspiring with Professor Campion to murder one of the passengers was perhaps a bit much to hope for.

'No,' was actually what she chose to say. But there was

quite a lot of contempt packed into that one short word. She opened her book and resumed reading at the place she had marked.

I had to concede that I had not been riveting company – leading questions fired at her in a staccato fashion, enlivened only by tacit accusations of mendacity. After a while she said she would go and get herself a coffee. She did not offer to get me one. She did not come back.

'Mind if I join you?'

We were likely to be playing this sort of game of musical chairs all the way to Luxor, but I'd hoped it would be a while before cruel fate landed me next to Herbie Proctor. Cruel fate had clearly decided that I'd avoided Herbie long enough.

'Yes,' I said. 'Actually I do mind, Mr Proctor. There are plenty of other tables. Go and sit at one of those.'

I'm normally quite good at making my views clear to authors, publishers, trick-or-treaters and the like; but I was obviously a bit out of practice with private detectives, because Proctor simply dumped himself in the chair, grinning crookedly, and stretched out his pale skinny legs. I noticed that they were covered with soft, almost white, hairs. They were the sort of legs that went well with long trousers. I wondered if the pink shorts were the only ones that he had. He would not have wasted money on a second pair without good reason.

'Close shave this morning in that temple,' he said. 'If I'd been stood a couple of feet to the left, I wouldn't be here now talking to you. You could say I bear a charmed life, Elsie.'

He was right. I could. But I decided, under the circumstances, not to bother.

'They can't kill me that easy,' he added, in case I didn't know what a charmed life was.

'Or Ethelred,' I pointed out.

'Him too, though obviously he wasn't the target.'

'You think the rock was aimed at you? You think it was the same people that you claim are after your client?'

'That sounds the most likely explanation, doesn't it? You see, anybody who wanted to kill a client of mine would have to get me out of the way first. That stands to reason. I thought nobody on board this boat except Ethelred – and you apparently – knew I was here to protect Raffles. The two things that I am really good at, Elsie, are client confidentiality and maintaining my cover. But when you've got something of a reputation as a private detective – well, people put two and two together. I obviously considered the possibility that the business this morning was due to a badly maintained roof – that's the problem with the ancient Egyptians, they just didn't know anything about building – but on reflection I think I can safely say that somebody was trying to get at my client by putting me out of the picture.'

So, Proctor not only thought that the rock was aimed at him, but seemed prepared to accept it as a well-judged compliment. Perhaps he felt that it was a good cause.

'Why *would* anyone want to kill your client, Mr Proctor?' I asked.

'Like I said, powerful people make enemies, Elsie.'

'Businessmen don't habitually get rocks lobbed at them – in person or by proxy.'

'You never can tell who might decide to bump you off. Could be a total stranger. Could be some left-wing nutter. Could be a member of your own family.'

'Your own family? Hang on . . . Raffles . . . Didn't somebody of that name murder his wife a while back? No, he must still be in prison.'

'The jury found him not guilty, Elsie. He left the court without a stain on his character.'

'In the strict technical sense I'm sure that's true but, if that's the man, he sounded a complete shit. Didn't he have links with organised crime?'

'The judge instructed the jury that any alleged links were irrelevant to the murder charge. And he still deserves the protection of the law . . . or me in this case.'

'I'm sure you are exactly what he deserves,' I said.

Proctor smiled, as though I could not have paid him a greater compliment.

CHAPTER TEN

I was not sure what Annabelle was doing in Egypt, but the text message she had sent gave a hint as to how she currently felt about me. I had a hunch that it would be best to stay out of her way for a bit.

I did however want to talk to Elsie's two 'policemen' and see why they had chosen to pull her leg so cruelly. From what I had seen of them so far, there seemed little to justify either Elsie's expectations or Purbright's concerns.

They proved to be in the saloon, drinking Egyptian coffee and watching the river from their comfortable, well-upholstered seats. I had not really talked to them properly up to that point, so we introduced ourselves. Elsie had referred to them almost interchangeably as Mahmoud and Majid as if, for all practical purposes, they were slightly differently branded versions of the same product. This was not entirely unfair. They were both, as far as I could judge, in their mid-thirties, both dressed in long-sleeved shirts with open collars, both clean-shaven. Quite ordinary-looking. Mahmoud was the taller, darker and perhaps somewhat the older of the two – when speaking English he had no perceptible accent of either class or region; only an occasional oddity of stress or vocabulary suggested something more exotic than the Home Counties. Majid was more slightly built and showed the first signs of losing his hair – his voice was that of somebody who had spent their entire life in London or its easterly semi-rural extensions.

That at least was how I saw them then. It was only later, as I got a chance to study them (and they me), that I realised that the similarities between them were fewer and the differences greater.

'We seem to be making better time now,' I observed. There had apparently been some temporary repairs done to the engines while we were at Edfu and we had speeded up a little.

'Yes, by the look of it,' said Mahmoud. 'We are nevertheless rather behind our original schedule.'

'You are in Egypt on holiday?' I asked.

'Yes. This is the country of my birth, but my family moved to Romford when I was two. When I speak Arabic, nobody here can work out my funny accent,' said Mahmoud. He laughed.

Majid's family had come to Britain from Morocco before he was born. They both worked in a bank in London and had decided to take a break in Egypt to get some sun. There was nothing about them to suggest they were policemen of any sort. Still, I thought that I should ensure there was no doubt.

'Have you always worked for a bank?'

'Pretty much,' said Majid. 'It pays the bills. Know what I mean? And you? Somebody said you are a writer?'

'Yes,' I said. 'I write crime novels. I doubt you would have heard of me unless you read a lot of crime. Maybe not even then.'

'On the contrary – we were told you are most well known,' said Mahmoud.

'I'm not Paul Fielder,' I said quickly. I still needed to clear that up with Purbright and had no wish to repeat the error with Mahmoud. On the other hand I liked to think that, as Peter Fielding, I had some small claim to fame. And I was aware that I had done little, if anything, since boarding the boat, that Elsie would classify as selling myself. I tried to think how I might 'big myself up', as I believe the phrase is. 'Of course, I do get invited onto panels at most of the crime conventions,' I added cautiously. On reflection, it didn't seem much of a selling point.

'So, folk back in the UK would have heard of you?' The question was posed in such a way as to suggest that, for Majid, I was at least as obscure as I had initially claimed.

'I'd like to think so,' I said. 'Well, crime fiction fans anyway . . .'

Mahmoud looked at Majid and nodded as if something was decided.

'We are indeed honoured to have a famous author on board with us,' said Mahmoud.

I looked at them to see if this too was just a leg-pull, but they seemed serious. I tried to look eminent but modest while I waited for them to ask me more about my writing.

'You weren't at the temple this morning?' I said after quite a long silence.

'Overslept, didn't we?' said Majid. 'They start these tours well early. We went for a walk round the market instead. There was something we needed to pick up. We'll be raring to go bright and early tomorrow for Kom Ombo.'

'It must have given you quite a shock,' said Tom.

'Not the sort of thing that happens every day,' said John. 'You must have upset somebody very much indeed. Did the police catch that woman?'

'Woman?' I asked.

Tom shrugged apologetically in response. 'John saw a woman climbing up the stairs to the roof a bit before the rock came down. He told the police, but since he couldn't give them much of a description, I don't think they took it too seriously.'

'You mean somebody from the boat?' I asked.

'Could be,' said John. 'I just saw a glimpse of somebody in a floppy hat nipping under the rope and haring off up the stairs.'

'You will see why the police took this piece of evidence so seriously,' said Tom. 'Three-quarters of the women there, and half the men, were sporting hats that would get you arrested by the fashion police if you tried wearing them on Seventh Avenue.'

'They'd be fine in Kansas, though,' said John.

'True,' said Tom.

We seemed to be drifting away from the idea of identifying the person who, arguably, might have tried to kill me – unless it actually was the Wicked Witch of the West. I vaguely remembered that she too had a floppy hat.

'But you saw somebody?' I persisted.

'Yes . . .' he said slowly. 'But there were people going all over the temple the whole time. Even if somebody up on the roof did knock that stone down, it may have been accidental. Or are there any women in floppy hats you know for certain you've upset lately?'

It was a good question. How many women currently wanted to kill me? I could only think of one – one who was, admittedly, now on the boat with me. But, if Annabelle was going to kill me, why would she have forewarned me of the fact?

'I don't think the stone was aimed at me,' I said eventually.

'Pretty fine shot if it was, though,' said Tom. 'For a girl leastways.'

CHAPTER ELEVEN

All day we had splashed happily along, while more untidy villages, date groves and rocky outcrops faded into the distance behind us. Sometimes the houses were the same shade of drab brown as the desert beyond; sometimes, for presumably good but ultimately unknowable reasons, their walls shone with yellow, green and blue paint. Sometimes the road and houses clung to the bank of the river, and trucks and motorbikes rattled past us, throwing up clouds of dust; in other places all signs of dwellings and transportation were discreetly concealed somewhere beyond the fields, where water pumps chugged and men in blue or grey *jellabiyas* hacked fitfully at the soil. Here and there solitary donkeys stood, like small allegories of sorrow, stiller than the quietly moving fronds above them; everything about their demeanour told you that they did not expect things to get better any time soon. Sometimes, for several miles, we would see nothing except the reedy bank and the date palms and the beige hills beyond. The one constant was the vast cloudless blue sky.

Occasionally the river split into strands around islands

or broad mud flats. The *Khedive* steered well clear of both. In plotting my own personal course around the boat, I too steered clear, as far as possible, of the obvious hazards. Even if Annabelle was not working on my death, I was concerned that she might nevertheless have a certain amount of unpleasantness planned, if and when we should find ourselves alone together. I was relieved that she seemed happy for the moment to keep her distance. Later that afternoon she appeared on the sun deck in a very brief (and I suspect expensive) bikini and occupied a lounger at the far end from where I was sitting. I glanced in her direction once or twice, but she gave no indication that she had noticed me. For a while she engaged in conversation with Purbright and, I must admit, as her laughter reached my end of the boat, I did feel just a slight twinge of jealousy. But eventually she wrapped herself in a towel, pulling it tight round her waist in a way that emphasised her slender figure, and went back to her cabin, looking straight ahead. I don't think she had even noticed me.

Towards the end of the afternoon, we were offered a tour of the boat. Most of the passengers accepted, the only ones to decline being Proctor and Campion, each claiming some task that would necessarily take priority. We first assembled amid the spotless stainless steel of the kitchen. Here we were reassured about hygiene and related matters. From there we proceeded to the surprisingly large and airy engine room, where an engineer stood in a sort of pit, oilcan in hand, nursing the ancient engines. He looked worried and was not talkative. Mahmoud and Majid were surprisingly attentive throughout, though I could not quite escape the idea that they were there mainly to watch Purbright and that Purbright was there mainly to watch them.

One small detail that we did pick up from the engine room during the tour was that the captain was not expecting to reach Kom Ombo that evening and that further emergency work on the engines would be required when we did. We were assured that we could still make up time afterwards and reach Aswan more or less as planned.

The landscape underwent subtle changes as the day drew to a close. At noon the river had sparkled with constantly dancing points of light and the horizon was lost in haze. Now the sun was about to set again and the river assumed a drab and mournful flatness. From competing minarets, gaudily lit with many coloured lights, the call to prayer sounded over the darkening, gently rippling water.

'I like it best in the evening, don't you?'

I had been joined at the ship's rail by Miss Watson. She had discarded the floppy hat, revealing her short hair – greyer than I had thought, but I doubted she would ever feel the need to dye it. In putting aside her hat she had also lost her rather vague manner. Her words were firm and precise.

'It's certainly a lot less exciting than this morning,' I said.

'Yes, I was sorry to hear that you had come so close to being squashed.' She paused, aware that this choice of words had been less than tactful. Then, perhaps deciding that she didn't much care what I thought, she added: 'Do you know if anyone saw who was up on the roof?'

'Was there somebody up there?' I asked.

'I understood that's what the police had been told.'

'Tom or John thought they saw somebody,' I said.

'That's who saw the person, was it?'

'One or the other. John, I think.'

'But he couldn't identify them?'

'No,' I said. I wondered whether to mention the floppy hat, but decided that that too would be tactless in view of her own choice of headgear. There had, as John said, been many floppy hats in the temple that morning, some more criminal than others.

'Elsie seemed to think that the new passenger – Lady Muntham, is it? – might have been up on the roof.'

'I don't think so,' I said. I hoped that Elsie had not been deliberately making trouble.

'Elsie said that Lady Muntham was formerly a pole dancer. Can that be true?' asked Miss Watson.

'Annabelle used to work as a model. Before her first marriage anyway. I don't believe she has ever been a pole dancer.'

'I suppose that Elsie could have made a genuine mistake about that?'

'Yes, I suppose she could have done,' I said.

'And what about you? I hear you're a writer,' said Miss Watson, thankfully moving the conversation on.

'Yes.'

'Do you write under your own name?'

'I write crime novels as Peter Fielding.'

'Paul Fielder?'

'No, Peter Fielding.'

She paused no longer than politeness dictated. Slightly less, actually. 'Sorry,' she said. 'It still doesn't ring any bells.'

'I also write as J. R. Elliot.'

'Crime as well?'

'Yes,' I said.

She shook her head. I decided not to ask whether she read romantic fiction. She didn't look the type. 'And what do you do?' I asked.

'I teach physical education.' She named a girl's boarding school on the south coast. It was well known and not far from where I live, though it was not one of the handful of schools that had seen fit to invite me to talk to small and rather reluctant groups of teenagers about crime writing. Judging by its reputation for sportiness, the status of a teacher of physical education there would have been quite high. 'There's not much call for my own sport, but I teach hockey and netball, and I organise the sailing.'

'You clearly have a range of talents,' I said.

'I was pretty good when I was younger. I represented Great Britain at the Olympics once, and twice at the Commonwealth Games. Almost got a medal at the Olympics. Probably would have got one if it hadn't been for that bloody letter.'

'Letter?'

'The one kindly telling me what my husband was up to while I had been spending my time training. Friends thought it better that I knew. No mobiles in those far-off days – it was a letter sent to my home address and then kindly forwarded, unopened, by my dear husband to the athletes' village, along with other bits and pieces. If he'd just left it for me to read on my return, I really think I might have got Silver . . . well, an outside chance of a Bronze, let's say. But you don't perform at your best when your mind is focusing on how best to cut off somebody's dick.'

I thought back to when my first, indeed my only, wife had walked out on me. Strangely I had never been able to be angry with her – or with my best friend, who had been the ostensible cause of Geraldine's departure. On the other hand, while I had understood and perhaps even sympathised with her inability to remain with me, I could not say that it had left me completely untouched.

'After Geraldine left me,' I said, 'I couldn't write anything for a year – maybe eighteen months. But you get over it.'

'You do, do you?' she asked. 'Maybe men are more forgiving than women then. In which case let me give you some advice: if you ever walk out on some poor woman, then watch your back.'

'Do you think so?' I asked.

'I know so,' she said. 'You can run, but sooner or later, we'll catch up with you.'

The second night's dinner was a formal affair, for which I wore the new white dinner jacket that I had sought and eventually purchased the previous week in Chichester. I was pleased to see that Purbright was also wearing something similar, though Mahmoud and Majid had opted for lounge suits and Proctor appeared in an open-necked white shirt, black trousers and cummerbund, which he described as 'Red Sea Rig'. The phrase suggested an earlier nautical career for Proctor, of which the current trip up the Nile was merely a logical extension. The two Americans apologised for the fact that they had been obliged to travel light, and they appeared, as usual, looking expensively casual. Campion was the last of the men to arrive, wearing the open-necked shirt and cotton trousers that might have been appropriate for the evening before. He scowled at my dinner jacket as though I was wearing it simply to show him up. Of the ladies, Elsie's costume was certainly the most imaginative, and had it been the fancy dress evening, it is likely that she would have won a prize. As it was, I saw Miss Watson raise an eyebrow at the brave combination of pink batik and orange paisley that Elsie had selected from her large suitcase as appropriate formal evening wear. Annabelle swept into the room, just as the first course was being served, wearing a figure-hugging, black silk evening dress with a very low-cut neckline and a single row of pearls. My gaze probably followed her a moment longer than it should.

'Your tie is crooked,' said Elsie to me reprovingly. 'And that dinner jacket makes you look like a spiv out of an Ealing Comedy. And . . . for God's sake . . . what's that stuffed in your pocket?'

'Just some interview questions I printed out before we left home,' I said. 'In case I couldn't work on them on the computer.' I tried shoving them further down and out of sight. 'I thought I might glance at them over coffee if I had a chance.'

Elsie briefly resurveyed me to remind herself of the worst aspects of my appearance and character. She shook her head and fingered the batik that she was wearing. 'It's a good job one of us has made an effort.'

Wine was included with the menu, but few of us seemed

to be drinking alcohol. Only Herbie Proctor entered fully and enthusiastically into the concept of unlimited free wine. It would be a cheap evening for the management.

'We decided that, travelling in a Muslim country, we would drink what the locals drank,' said Tom, indicating his *karkade* – the bright purple drink that I had previously seen Miss Watson drinking.

'In New York,' said John, 'we obviously drink nothing but Martinis. That's pretty much all that is available.'

'The Egyptian wine is surprisingly palatable,' said Professor Campion, putting down his glass. He had joined Proctor, though on a more modest scale.

'Not tried it before?' asked Proctor, possibly imagining he had asked a trick question.

'I meant *this* Egyptian wine is very good. Yes, we used to drink it all the time when we were carrying out fieldwork in Nubia.'

'I've been to Nubia,' volunteered Lizzi Hull. 'Did you do any work at Meroe?'

Campion shook his head. 'Another site entirely,' he said.

'Have you done any work in Palestine?' she asked.

'No. Not my area. And a little dangerous now, perhaps.'

'Palestine isn't all suicide bombers.'

'One or two would be more than enough,' said Campion archly. 'Though why anybody would want to be a suicide bomber escapes me.'

'Wait until somebody steals your country from you, and see how you feel then.'

This last remark implied that Campion had been personally responsible for the creation of the state of

Israel, which even Proctor would have been reluctantly obliged to admit was untrue. Around the table there were almost certainly all shades of opinion about Palestine but, being for the most part British, we were disinclined to say anything that might cause the remotest offence to each other. There could therefore have been a lengthy silence had Purbright not supported Lizzi by saying: 'I think people who can't understand why somebody would be a suicide bomber simply lack the necessary imagination. We've become a bit too comfortable in the West. In other places there are still causes considered worth dying for. You don't have to agree with the cause to empathise with somebody who feels that way.'

Annabelle looked in my direction and said: 'I can sympathise with anyone who has their home cruelly taken from them, by whatever means.'

Since, of the other passengers, only Elsie knew of the sale of Muntham Court, nobody was quite sure how to respond to this new contribution to the debate. Lizzi nodded supportively. Mahmoud looked uncertainly at Majid and shrugged. Fortunately Proctor decided that the least controversial thing to do was to bait Campion to breaking point.

'Which university exactly do you teach at, Professor?' asked Proctor, with what he may have assumed was guile. A genuine query would not, however, have given quite the same sarcastic emphasis to the word 'Professor'.

'UCL,' said Campion. He had not so much seen through as failed to notice Proctor's attempt at guile, and was now regarding him with a mixture of concern and contempt.

The mixture was slightly biased in favour of contempt, but that might yet change.

'I'm quite interested in Egyptology,' said Proctor improbably. 'Maybe I should Google the UCL Egyptology department and check out the course? I might sign up for it. I could check your own bit of the website too. I would imagine you're mentioned?'

You had to know Proctor pretty well to realise that he was trying to be subtle.

'If you wish,' said Campion with a discernible sneer. It was likely he had seen Proctor's antiquated phone and realised that the Google threat was not an immediate one. 'You're considering taking up archaeology as a profession, Mr Proctor?'

'I've always liked digging. I'm reckoned to be pretty good at it. *Digging.*'

'And what is your current line of work, Mr Proctor?' asked Campion.

'This and that,' grinned Proctor. If I had had teeth like Proctor's I would have grinned a little less and brushed a little more. Orthodontic work is expensive, but toothpaste was probably not beyond Proctor's budget.

'Sounds like Tom's old man,' said John, breaking off from another conversation. 'He just did a bit of this and that too. Or that was what he always told the jury.'

'They never managed to convict him,' said Tom. 'And at least he never worked for Nixon, like your father.'

'Dad said he only ever worked for Nixon in an ironic and postmodern way.'

'Shame he got three years for it.'

'That's what he thought too.'

Annabelle largely ignored me throughout the meal, though she talked in an animated fashion to Purbright, and laughed loudly at anything that he said that was even remotely amusing – and at quite a few things that were not. Once or twice I noticed that she laid a hand on his arm as she spoke to him, and left it there while he replied. At the far end of the table Lizzi Hull was having a fairly intense conversation in Arabic with Mahmoud and Majid. Sky Benson and Jane Watson had also found something in common that required discussion, though Jane Watson occasionally glanced in the direction of the Arabic speakers, as though she had caught a phrase or two that she understood.

Dinner had ended and we were all sitting round drinking a second or third cup of coffee, when Purbright nudged me and said: 'Fancy a stroll, old boy?'

I followed him out of the room, uncertain why he had selected me as his strolling companion. As soon as we were up on deck, however, it became clear that this was an extension of our earlier conversation. I would need to explain quickly that my links with MI6 were non-existent.

'You remember that I mentioned a colleague who had failed to show up?' Purbright asked.

'Yes,' I said.

'Well, he's shown up now. Dead, unfortunately.'

I decided not to ask whether he had been ill for a long time. It didn't sound like that sort of death.

'Shot on his way from Cairo to join me at Luxor. The group that we are monitoring is clearly monitoring us too.

In fact, it looks as though the balloon is about to go up,' said Purbright. 'Mahmoud and Majid have been keeping a pretty low profile so far, but now their people have shown their hand, we can expect some action.'

This was worrying, whatever role he foresaw for me. 'Do you know what they are planning?' I asked.

'Not exactly. The only firm piece of information that I have is that the party on board the *Khedive* had plans to meet up with some of their friends tonight.'

'How?'

'The others were going to join us by motor boat on one of the more deserted stretches of the river. Since the *Khedive* is making slow progress, however, my guess is that we haven't yet reached the rendezvous point.'

'And they are after you specifically?'

'Me? No, they want to blow up the boat. They are terrorists – probably linked to Al-Qaeda.'

'So how are you involved?'

'It's my job,' said Purbright. 'My colleagues in the Egyptian security service are trying to track down the people with the motor boat. I'm keeping an eye on Mahmoud and Majid. They were just a little too curious during this afternoon's tour of the kitchens, didn't you think? Planning where to put the explosive, no doubt.'

'If you say so. But why are you having this conversation with me?'

'If things go wrong, I need somebody on board I can rely on. As a former agent yourself . . .'

'I'm not Paul Fielder,' I said. 'I write crime as Peter Fielding. Similar names. Not the first time we've been confused.'

'Shit,' he said. 'I didn't think you looked like the photos. Too young for one thing.'

The 'too young' bit was obviously some compensation, though Fielder was probably now in his eighties.

'No,' I said. 'My Amazon rankings don't look like his either. Shall I just forget we had this conversation?'

He was nonplussed for a moment, then said: 'It's too late for that. And I still need somebody who can, if necessary, get a message back to the right people with our location. Do you have a piece of paper on you?' I pulled the *Southend Evening Echo* interview questions from my pocket. He scribbled something on the back and returned them to me. 'Keep this number until you need it.'

'OK,' I said.

He looked at his watch and frowned. 'Good man. Now, there's somebody else I need to talk to. If you don't mind, maybe you could stay here for the moment and we'll continue the conversation when I return. If you spot anything suspicious . . . well, maybe the best thing is just to come and find me. I'll be back here on deck in about ten minutes. But if anything goes wrong . . .'

'I am to phone the number,' I said. Even an ex-tax inspector could probably do that.

CHAPTER TWELVE

Elsie

The waiters were clearing away the coffee cups when Purbright (or Raffles) dragged Ethelred away for a quiet chat.

I hadn't quite made up my mind about Raffles (or Purbright). On the one hand, he seemed like a fun sort of guy – plenty of interesting anecdotes. On the other hand, at least if I trusted Herbie Proctor's version, he'd probably murdered his wife. My two policemen had suspicions about him as well.

I reckoned Ethelred would be safe with him for a while and carried on talking to the other passengers. Most had however decided it was time for bed. Beginning with Annabelle, one by one my dinner companions made their apologies and retired to their cabins or took a final stroll round the deck. Eventually my only remaining buddy was Herbie Proctor, who had partaken a little too much of the free plonk.

'Well, Elsie,' he said, successfully slurring both words. 'Just the two of us now, eh?'

The friendly smile alone was enough to make me decide

that it was time for me too to depart, unless Herbie wanted to clear off first. I tried this suggestion on him.

'Shouldn't you be watching over your client?' I asked.

Proctor was clearly a little bemused and, even if he had been sober, might have had difficulty in giving a clear answer. He looked thoughtful, as though trying to work something out.

'My client is quite safe,' he said eventually.

'In spite of the rock that you say was aimed at you?'

Proctor considered this. 'But they missed,' he said.

'Or,' I said, 'maybe it wasn't aimed at you. Maybe it was aimed at Ethelred.'

'Ethelred? Who would want to kill a third-rate crime writer?' asked Proctor.

'Second-rate,' I said. It wasn't really true, but as an agent you have to promote your writers actively. Herbie was however right in the sense that Ethelred was part of that class of living creatures that have almost no known predators. Nobody – even Annabelle – would really want to kill him. Accident still had to be the most likely explanation, but then again there had been that text message . . .

'Have we speeded up a bit?' asked Proctor.

'What?' I said. 'I can't hear you above that awful noise!'

'I said: We're going like a bat out of hell.'

I hadn't really noticed but, looking out of the window, I noticed that the bank did seem to be heading north a bit faster than usual. And the gentle throb of the ship's engines had increased to an unpleasant rumble that threatened to loosen my fillings.

'I thought we had to go slowly to avoid damaging the engines or something,' I said.

'What?' said Proctor.

'I said . . .'

But the noise had increased to a point where normal conversation was becoming impossible.

For a few minutes we behaved as if we were a rather unsuccessful mime act, mouthing and gesturing at each other. Then Miss Watson returned and said something to which both Herbie Proctor and I could only mime: '*What*?'

She waved a hand at us wearily and sat down at the table in a resigned sort of way. Then, inexplicably, she stood up again and ran towards the door. She turned and said something but I'm not sure how she expected us to hear her. Herbie Proctor actually had his hands over his ears and I was thinking of following his example. Miss Watson made her hands into a sort of megaphone and tried again, but she might as well have been reciting Keats, frankly.

Then the inevitable happened. There was an almighty crash and the sound of what was probably an old ship's engine breathing its last.

'. . .I said I heard a pistol shot, you cretins,' yelled Miss Watson, finally audible in the silence. Not a Keats sonnet after all then, or not one of the better known ones.

'It was just the noise of the ship's engine,' said Proctor, rising to his feet. 'Blowing up probably.'

'No, a moment ago, while we were still sitting at the table. I'm sure I heard a gun. We need to go and investigate.'

'You go then,' said Proctor. Coming from a private investigator I thought this was pretty wet, but Proctor only private-investigated for cash in hand.

'What if it's Purbright?' I asked.

'Raffles? Impossible,' he said. But he was now looking worried. A fee might be claimed eventually from a living client who had attempted to renege on a contract. Extracting a fee from a dead one might be trickier, especially when one of the key terms of the contract had been to keep him alive. 'You stay here. I'll go and check.'

'I'm coming with you,' said Miss Watson.

'I'm certainly not staying here alone,' I said.

The three of us did not have to go far. Just out of the door and round the corner, on a sheltered bit of deck, somebody in a white dinner jacket was lying face down. I know references to pools of blood are a bit of a cliché, but 'lake' was possibly overstating things and 'pond' didn't quite have the right ring to it, with its connotations of ducks and willow trees.

Just for a moment I thought it was Ethelred, then I caught a glimpse of the lined and leathery face. Miss Watson squatted down by the body, gathering up her skirt so that it did not trail too much in the pool/lake/pond thing, and took the wrist closest to her. It seemed unlikely that the victim would have much of a pulse on the grounds that you need blood inside you for that, but I guess somebody had to try it.

'He's dead,' said Miss Watson after a few moments.

So, there it was. Herbie Proctor had just lost a client. Careless, really.

CHAPTER THIRTEEN

Elsie

After that things started to happen quite quickly.

First Inspector Majid appeared from round the corner and came to an abrupt halt. He looked from me to Herbie to Miss Watson, and back to me.

'It wasn't us,' I said, though I wished that I hadn't sounded quite so much like a third-former caught behind the bike sheds with a couple of roll-ups.

'We heard a shot,' said Miss Watson, deciding to go for a more grown-up approach. 'We came to investigate.'

'About a minute ago,' said Proctor. 'While the engine was making all that noise. The trained ear, though, can always pick up a pistol shot. Miss Watson heard it too, I think.'

My own recollection was that Proctor had had his hands over his trained ears at the time, but Miss Watson seemed inclined to be quite charitable for once – we were, after all, in this one together. 'That's right,' she said simply. 'The three of us were in the dining room and we heard the shot. Whoever did it must still be close . . .'

Well yes, obviously, the killer could not have gone far.

We were on a boat – a boat that was, I noticed, now drifting back towards Luxor with the current, slewing slightly as it did so. I alerted Inspector Majid to this interesting fact, but he replied tersely that he was sure Captain Bashir had things under control. It seemed to me that the Nile had things under control but, as a policeman, Majid was perhaps rightly more concerned that we had a dead body on board.

Proctor too was primarily worried about the stiff in front of us. 'We'll need to question all of the passengers,' he said. 'I'd be happy to give you a hand with that, Inspector.'

Inspector Majid had, you will notice, said relatively little up to this point. Having now fully registered the material facts, he took matters in hand: 'Don't any of you touch anything, right? That includes you, Mr Proctor. Stay exactly where you are. And keep out of that pool of blood.'

OK, then, it was officially a pool.

The inspector, too, bent down to examine the body and, reaching the same conclusion that Miss Watson had done shortly before, stood up again. 'I'm going to have to contact my colleagues at headquarters. In the meantime, we'll need all of the passengers in the saloon.'

We shuffled back the way we had come and walked through the dining room to the saloon. The trip was accomplished in silence, not even Miss Watson deeming it appropriate to jolly things up. Proctor, thinking we might well be here for a while, quickly appropriated the most comfortable chair for himself. He was not however a happy private eye, clearly feeling that he should be helping with, or indeed leading, the investigation.

'I'm sure the police will invite you to assist them later in the process,' said Jane Watson. It was nominally a consoling remark, but in practice simply drew people's attention to the sad lack of trust that the local officers had for Herbie Proctor – which may well have been her intention.

'At least we know it wasn't one of us,' said Proctor.

'That is true,' said Jane Watson. 'I am happy to vouch for you, Mr Proctor. And for you, Elsie.'

'You'd better tell them about the death threats that Raffles had received,' I said to Proctor.

Proctor picked at an imaginary spot on the table with his fingernail. He was going to look pretty silly and he knew it.

'Raffles?' asked Miss Watson.

'The deceased – Mr Purbright as he was calling himself – had received a threatening letter,' explained Proctor.

'And you are saying that his real name was Raffles?' asked Miss Watson.

'That is correct,' said Proctor.

'And how do you know this?'

'He was employing me to . . . look after certain matters for him,' said Proctor. He had another go at the imaginary spot. Hopefully the table had a pretty solid veneer.

'Ah,' said Miss Watson. 'And had you formed any views as to which of the passengers might want him dead?'

'I had my eye on two of them,' said Proctor.

'Which two?'

'I can't tell you that,' said Proctor, as if clinging to some small vestige of professional pride.

'But two people working together?'

'Yes,' said Proctor.

'How terribly interesting,' said Miss Watson, as though

some long-held suspicion had just been confirmed.

We were at that point joined by the two Americans, both in pyjamas and silk dressing gowns. Tom had slippers to match his dressing gown. I would have to ask them where they shopped for nightwear. Those boys certainly knew how to dress for a crisis.

'Anybody happen to know what's going on?' asked Tom. 'We were told to come straight here. *Do not pass Go. Do not collect two hundred dollars.*'

'Mr Purbright has been shot,' said Miss Watson.

'*Raffles*,' said Proctor, though nobody much seemed to be paying attention to him. 'His real name is Raffles.'

Tom frowned. 'Shot? Here? On the boat?'

'Terrorists?' asked John.

'We don't think so,' said Proctor. 'We think that somebody followed him out from England.'

'That's terrible,' said Tom.

'Did the police get you out of bed?' I asked.

'Are you kidding?' said John. 'That dreadful noise got us out of bed. What was it?'

'They obviously decided to try to make up time and pushed the engines too hard,' said Proctor. 'We now have no engines at all by the look of it.'

We were joined by Professor Campion and, shortly after, by a worried-looking Sky Benson, who was accompanied by the purser. Annabelle arrived, still in her silk evening gown, but now with a pale pink cashmere shawl round her shoulders. Finally Lizzi Hull appeared in a tracksuit and her cap. She yawned and sat cross-legged on the floor, slightly apart from the rest of us.

'Is that everyone?' asked the purser, doing a quick headcount. 'No, we are still missing Mr Tressider.'

'Have you checked his cabin?' asked Majid.

'Yes,' said the purser. 'Also the dining room and the sun deck.'

'Do you know where Ethelred's gone, Elsie?' asked Majid.

'No, he went off with . . .' Then I stopped myself quickly. Yes, that was the slightly awkward bit. Ethelred had gone off with Purbright and Purbright had – no more than ten minutes later – been found dead in a great deal of blood. Of course, Ethelred had no gun. And while he had quite a good theoretical knowledge of guns, in practice I doubted he would have known which end to point and which end to hold onto. Anyone putting a gun into Ethelred's hands would have been well-advised to stand back or take cover – if they'd explained where the safety catch was, anyway, and nobody in their right mind would tell him stuff like that.

'He went for a walk round the deck,' I said.

I could see that Herbie was thinking hard, trying to recall the exact circumstances of Ethelred's departure. If anyone did remember that, then Ethelred suddenly looked like the prime suspect. Which was nonsense. On the other hand, where was Ethelred now? If he wasn't in the cabin or on the deck, where else was there a passenger could go? The boat was quite small but there was an awful lot of river out there. Had he decided to go for a midnight swim for any reason, would we have heard a splash with all of that engine noise?

'I'll go and look for him,' I said.

'No need. We are doing that right now,' said Majid. He sounded a bit grim. Ethelred's disappearance had not impressed him favourably.

Mahmoud now entered with Captain Bashir. The captain had the dissatisfied look of a man whose boat was now travelling sideways down the Nile when he had planned it should go forwards and up.

'Ladies and gentlemen,' Mahmoud began. 'As you will have deduced, one of the passengers has been shot. The time has therefore come for us to introduce ourselves to you properly: We are both Egyptian police inspectors. I apologise for not having mentioned this small matter before, but we needed to remain undercover. We have now called for reinforcements, who will be with us very shortly. In the meantime, we have no option but to hold everyone here. You are not under arrest, but since the murderer must still be on board, we have to treat you all as possible suspects. I had already asked Captain Bashir to make full speed to the next town but unfortunately . . .'

He smiled weakly at the captain, whose face remained every bit as grim as it was before.

'. . . unfortunately the engines proved incapable of effecting this. We are however completely safe and will be able to bring the boat under control very soon.'

The captain gave a short, but not especially happy, laugh. Relations between the policemen and the crew were not good. Without engines, there were no obvious means to stop us drifting sideways all the way to Alexandria, though getting back through the lock at Esna would be a challenge. I did not doubt that Captain Bashir had warned the policemen that it was inadvisable to run the engines too fast and that the captain was far from convinced that a ship drifting at a random angle was completely safe.

There was a shout in Arabic from outside on the deck. Captain Bashir looked at Inspector Majid, but Majid shook his head. The captain shrugged.

We were on one of the more deserted stretches of the river. I thought I could see the lights of a village in the distance, but for the most part the bank was black and unwelcoming. Only the moonlight revealed where the Nile flowed deeply and where the mudbanks lay. Interestingly, looking through the starboard windows, I noticed that we were slowly converging on a large bank at that very moment. There was another shout from outside, but a little too late to prevent what happened next, if (without an engine) it was preventable at all.

I must have sensed it coming and grabbed hold of one of the wooden pillars, as did the captain. The others were however all taken more or less by surprise, and both policemen were flung to the floor as our journey back to Luxor ended abruptly. There was a brief slithering sound beneath us and we were, for the first time that evening, moving neither north nor south.

Captain Bashir said something to Majid, which I assumed translated as: 'That's another fine mess you've got us into.' Majid did not reply, but Mahmoud asked the captain a couple of questions and got a couple of terse responses.

Lizzi translated for us in a whisper: 'The inspector asked where we were. The captain said we were on a sandbank. The inspector asked which sandbank. The captain said that up until now he hadn't needed to know the name of every bloody sandbank on the river. He gave him the name of the nearest village – it's some way off, apparently.'

Mahmoud had taken his phone out and now went onto the deck, away from us.

'Our colleagues ought to be here pretty soon,' Majid told us.

We all looked at each other but nobody said anything. I kept hoping Ethelred would walk in through the door, and that everything would be OK. But he didn't and it wasn't.

After a while we heard a boat's engine from a long way off. It proved, however, when it finally arrived, to be another Nile cruise ship. It slowed down and hailed us, and Majid went out and spoke to the ship's captain across the rail. There was a brief exchange and the other ship went on its way.

'Your colleagues are taking their time,' said Proctor. 'You might at least have asked that boat for a tow.'

'We are firmly stuck on the sandbank,' said Majid. 'The other boat was too small to pull us off. In any case, we have given our position to the local police. They are travelling here by fast motor boat from Esna. While we are on the sandbank, nobody else can board or escape. I shall need all of you to hand over your mobile phones – that includes the crew.'

'Well, at least we're safe in the meantime. No homicidal maniacs running around with guns,' said Proctor, reluctantly passing over what was clearly a valuable antique communication device. It seemed unlikely that it would function anywhere overseas – or in the UK come to that. I relinquished my state-of-the-art mobile (with superior apps). The others followed suit. Captain Bashir sent a message to the purser to begin a similar collection of phones owned by the crew.

It was at this point that Ethelred finally appeared. He looked haggard and his tie was now frankly all over the place. My relief at seeing him was tempered only slightly when he drew a gun from his jacket pocket and fiddled nervously with the safety catch, taking it off, then putting it back on, then finally taking it off. Seeming reasonably satisfied with what he had achieved so far, he pointed the pistol at the two policemen.

'I want both of you on the floor with your hands behind your backs,' he said. 'Elsie, find some rope now and tie them up.'

CHAPTER FOURTEEN

I had watched Purbright vanish round the corner. A minute passed very slowly. Nine to go. I continued to count them down. The breeze off the Nile felt cold, which is probably why I shivered.

If time was going at a snail's pace, however, the boat itself had suddenly started to pick up speed. The noise of the engines had increased perceptibly. I was surprised, bearing in mind how the captain had nursed the boat along up to this point, that he was risking going so fast.

We passed a small village quite close to the river. Bright neon lights, installed at various angles, incongruously lit up some of the buildings. A number of old men, sitting out in the village square, looked up as we churned along. One pointed. They had seen many paddle steamers over the years and they too clearly doubted the advisability of pushing an old engine so hard. But it was not their problem. They returned to their board game and their coffee.

By the time the ten minutes had finally elapsed, the village was just a few streaks of light beyond the stern, and the banks were dark on either side. Occasionally the

Khedive's floodlights would play on a nearby sandbank, as the captain steered a careful course. The noise from our engines grew deafening. I hoped somebody knew what they were doing. A sailor ran past me, heading for the bridge and looking as concerned as I felt. Instinctively I flattened myself against the wall, though who I was hiding from was not yet clear.

I took out the piece of paper. I was reluctant to make the call, only to have Purbright reappear, smiling, just as I did so. On the other hand, I felt foolish standing there doing nothing at all. With the engines reaching a crescendo, I unflattened myself and started to walk cautiously in the direction that Purbright had gone.

I passed the dining room, where (I could see through the window) a few people were still at the table, but there was no sign of the MI6 man, inside or outside. Then I stepped into a pool of blood. Just beyond it was Purbright.

He was face down, with an exit wound in the back of his dinner jacket, and he was very, very still. The deck must have sloped slightly in my direction, because the blood – quite a lot of it – was creeping towards me, dark red, almost black, in the moonlight. I had to get help for Purbright, preferably without getting shot myself. I looked straight ahead then, rather improbably, behind me, expecting to see . . . I'm not sure what. The light reflecting off the shining barrel of a gun? A crouching assassin? No – the deck was deserted. I thought for a moment that I heard footsteps going away but the engine noise was so bad that I couldn't be sure of anything. At least there were no footsteps heading in my direction. I knelt down. There was no sign of breathing. I took his wrist and checked his pulse. Nothing doing. I had a dead security service man on my hands, and saving the boat and everyone on it was now down to me, it seemed.

Then I noticed a bulge in Purbright's pocket, a bit smaller than a mass-market paperback and narrower at one end. To a crime writer this meant one thing and one thing only. I edged my hand slowly and cautiously into the pocket and made contact with warm metal. I had written about guns more often than I could remember. Normally however they were a loud bang somewhere offstage – or a brief *TFFFFTTT* noise, if a silencer was involved in the crime. Once my fictional detective had arrived, he (or the SOCO) got to examine the blood spattered on the wall and picked the gun up carefully on a ballpoint pen to examine it. I too examined the weapon now in my possession and wondered exactly what it would do to somebody if fired at close range.

'So, where's the safety catch?' I asked myself. Probably the little lever there – but which position was likely to be 'off'? Assuming that Purbright would have placed it in his pocket intending that it should *not* go off unexpectedly, I flicked the safety catch upwards and, with the gun held tightly in my right hand, carried on round the corner.

I had become slightly disoriented and was surprised, when I checked the lighted window on my right, to find I was looking again into the dining room. I had worked my way round the outside of the room, crossing from port to starboard. On the other side of the glass, Elsie, Proctor and Miss Watson seemed to be conducting some sort of animated dumbshow. Proctor was shaking his head from side to side, then Miss Watson suddenly stood up and headed for the far door. The others followed and passed from my view.

I continued walking, feeling an urgent need to move but not entirely certain where I was going. It was at that point that the engines finally gave up the unequal struggle. The boat slowed immediately and, for a moment, seemed to hang where it was, before beginning to drift back downriver.

My immediate priority had been to find somewhere to make a quick call to the number I had been given. In the silence I felt more vulnerable than ever – as if taking another footstep might give me away. My own cabin was some way off, but the one next to the dining room was very close and (I knew) empty, because Miss Watson had rejected it earlier. I speculatively tried the handle, expecting it to be locked, but the door opened smoothly and silently. I slipped inside and fastened the catch. I could make out, in the semi-darkness, a double bed, a chest of drawers, the wardrobe and the door to the bathroom. I moved across the room carefully, away from the window to a point where I hoped I could not be seen. In the silence, I dialled the number on my new mobile.

'Yes?' said an English voice. There was a pause that indicated I would get no more until I identified myself.

'Purbright's dead,' I said. 'What do I do?'

'Who is that, please?' Though I had presumably dropped something of a bombshell, the voice remained cool, measured, in control of itself.

'My name is Ethelred Tressider. Mr Purbright gave me

this number to phone if anything happened to him.'

'Why did he do that?'

'It's a long story. He thought I was . . . Well, he just did. I don't think we have time to go into it in that sort of detail.'

'Possibly not. Then just describe what has happened, if you don't mind.'

'We're on the *Khedive* – I guess you know that? We'd just had dinner. He went to meet somebody. I don't know who it was. He didn't return after ten minutes as arranged. When I followed him, I found him in a pool of blood.'

'You're sure he's dead?'

'Gunshot wound. Not breathing. No pulse. What would you say?'

'Did you see who shot him?'

'No.'

'Where are you?'

'The boat is somewhere between Edfu and Kom Ombo. The engines have given up and we're drifting with the current – sideways.'

'That's a big stretch of river, but we'll find you. Can't be that many vintage paddle steamers heading for Esna sideways. Anyway, it looks as though the terrorists have decided to bring their timetable forward. They'll move now to take control of the boat. We think that others will come out and join them.'

'And then?'

'They are aiming to make the biggest splash they can. They'll probably blow up the *Khedive* with everyone on board – it's a high-profile target. But we don't think that the two currently on the boat have the explosive with them. You'll be OK until they are reinforced.'

'Are you sure?'

'To be absolutely honest? No, not really.'

'What do I do then?'

'Where are you now – you personally, not the boat?' There were footsteps outside.

'I'm in what everyone thinks is an empty cabin, with the door locked,' I whispered. 'Hold on – somebody is trying the door handle now – no, it's OK, they've moved on.'

'You'll need to make your own judgement as to what you should do. I repeat: the terrorists will shortly try to take over the boat. The two who are on board will probably gather everyone together to keep an eye on them. Where could they do that?'

'The saloon probably – maybe the dining room.'

'OK. Wait a bit and see what develops. You'll need to disrupt their plans if you can. I'd say don't take any risks, but the fact is that doing nothing may mean that you just get blown up with everyone else. You probably don't have any absolutely safe options. The main thing is that we stop them making contact with their local counterparts. Hopefully we can locate you and get help for you within the next hour. We should already have a fix on this call. It's just a matter of getting a team to you. Are you armed?'

'Yes, I have Purbright's gun.'

'Do you know how to use it?'

'No,' I said.

'Then preferably don't even try. Otherwise, if your life is in danger, point it, squeeze the trigger slowly. Don't jerk it. Anything else?'

'Yes,' I said. 'Is the safety catch on when it's up or down?' I put the phone back in my pocket and slid down behind the bed. Looking across its smooth white surface I could just see out through the porthole onto the deck. Looking across its smooth white surface I could also see a small black object that my eyes had missed when I had first entered the cabin. I raised myself a little to get a better view. Resting in a slight indentation, and half wrapped in a standard-issue white cotton hand towel, was a gun. Either it was the murder weapon or the *Khedive* was a floating arsenal.

It was at that moment that the boat, which had been drifting peacefully downstream, hit (as I later learnt) a sandbank, and I was thrown against the bed.

For the next ten minutes or so I stayed where I was and tried to work out what Purbright would have done. Surprise was undoubtedly the key to it all, but what exactly would it take to surprise them? What was happening out there? As each minute passed, my own information about who was where and what was going on was getting more and more out of date. Occasionally a figure passed by the porthole. At one point I heard a boat's engine and crawled over to the porthole to get a better view. It proved to be another, smaller cruiser. I hoped they might send people on board to investigate but after a short exchange with us the other boat moved on.

It occurred to me that if the terrorists now had everyone gathered in the saloon, my absence would be very obvious and a more thorough search of the boat would begin. Just staying put wasn't much of an option. If there were currently only two terrorists, as Purbright had implied, and I could distract them for long enough, the passengers and crew should be able to overcome and disarm them.

Footsteps approached again and a key was inserted in the lock. I held my breath and aimed the gun at the door, ready to fire if necessary, but I had latched the door on the inside. After a few ineffectual attempts, the footsteps receded again. It would not take them long to work out that there had to be somebody inside the cabin. Time was running out. Unlatching the door, I cautiously went out onto the deck. It was deserted. The dining room too was empty. I noticed one of the crew members moving around – so the crew were not being held then? This seemed odd, unless they were all in league with the gang that had taken over the boat. It would obviously make everything far more difficult – indeed impossible – if we had a dozen or so crew to deal with as well as the two terrorists.

It was clear that the boat had come to rest on one of the larger sandbanks in this stretch of river – a sandbank boasting luxuriant reeds and grasses, together with a number of flourishing bushes. The *Khedive's* bows were still in the water, but the stern was firmly wedged in place, surrounded by driftwood and vegetation. The small tender which in happier times had rested on a platform just behind the paddle wheels, had been knocked sideways. One of the ropes that normally held it in place had parted company with it and it now hung at an angle. However we were all to leave the *Khedive*, it would not be on board the tender.

Over the ship's rail I could however see a motor boat

heading in our direction. It was still a long way off, but it was travelling fast. Whether it was the terrorists' reinforcements or Purbright's colleagues coming to the rescue, my course of action was clear. Gripping the gun firmly in my hand, I walked round to the door that led to the saloon. I opened it carefully. Elsie's two 'policemen' were standing facing the rest of the passengers, who were sitting round in a circle – Lizzi Hull on the floor, the rest in chairs. Captain Bashir was leaning against a pillar, looking very pissed off, over to one side.

If I was quick, I could save the whole lot of them. And myself. I pointed the pistol straight at Majid and Mahmoud.

'I want both of you on the floor with your hands behind your backs,' I said. 'Elsie, find some rope now and tie them up.'

CHAPTER FIFTEEN

Elsie

'Ethelred, you pillock,' I said. 'These guys are policemen. Purbright, whoever or whatever he is, is dead. The police want everyone to remain here until their colleagues arrive.'

'I know Purbright's dead,' said Ethelred, the gun still pointing at the two inspectors.

'Do you? OK, then you'll understand we need to let the two police inspectors get on with their job of finding out who killed him. If, following your helpful advice, I tie them up, then I'm going to spend the next thirty years in some Egyptian jail. So, I'd rather not if it's all the same to you. Where the hell did you get that gun anyway?'

'It's Purbright's. These two aren't policemen any more than I am. They told me they were bankers.'

'We're working undercover,' said Majid. His voice was a bit muffled because, taking no chances, he was keeping his face to the floor. 'Obviously I couldn't tell you we were with the police. You can check our warrant cards if you wish.'

'You mean the fake warrant cards?' sneered Ethelred.

'I'm hardly going to be taken in by those, am I?' I couldn't help feeling that the less he said now, the less stupid he would look in about ten minutes' time.

Mahmoud turned slightly. 'Could you please just put the gun down, Mr Tressider? You've made a mistake – that's all. Things are very tense and we understand that you may have got hold of the wrong end of the stick. We are keen that, for your sake and ours, you don't do anything stupid. Just put the gun on the floor and come over and join the others.'

'Who,' I asked Ethelred, 'told you that Inspector Majid and Inspector Mahmoud were terrorists?'

He paused. 'I phoned a number that Purbright gave me before he was shot.'

'And who did you speak to?'

'They didn't say,' said Ethelred.

'But they specifically said that the terrorists were posing as policemen?'

'No,' said Ethelred. 'They just said there were terrorists on board.'

'OK – let's get this right. You are threatening to shoot two inspectors from the Cairo police force on the grounds that some guy you've never spoken to before, and whose name you don't know, told you they *might* be terrorists?'

'You're twisting what I say,' said Ethelred, but you could see he was beginning to doubt whether you should believe everything the Voices tell you. He turned and addressed the room more generally. 'Who shot Purbright if not these two?'

Hmmm. I went through possible suspects. Proctor and Jane Watson had been with me when the shot was fired. In which case that left everyone else. Annabelle? Campion? Sky Benson? The two nice Americans? Campion and Sky Benson had been planning something. But . . . hey! . . . it wasn't my problem to solve. The police were here and they could sort it all out, if Ethelred would just let them get up off the floor and start sorting.

'We don't need to know that,' I said. 'Point the gun somewhere else for a moment, or better still give it to a responsible grown-up, and then Inspector Majid and Inspector Mahmoud can start questioning everyone.'

'Which of you two bastards shot Purbright?' demanded Ethelred, in a way that he would probably regret when his words were read back to him by the prosecuting counsel.

'We are not even carrying guns, Mr Tressider,' said Inspector Mahmoud. 'You may search us if that would reassure you.'

'No, of course they're not carrying guns,' said Ethelred to the rest of us. 'They threw the gun onto the bed in the empty cabin next to the dining room.'

'If we are terrorists taking over the boat,' said Majid, 'why would we throw away our only gun just as we might need it?'

'Good point, Inspector. Tressider is talking complete crap, as usual,' said Proctor. 'Ethelred, just give them the bloody gun and come and join us.'

'If not them, who shot Purbright?' Ethelred repeated.

On the one hand, this was Ethelred being tedious

and repetitious. On the other, it was still a relevant consideration. One of us, passengers or crew, must have shot Purbright, because we were on a boat, and nobody could have easily joined us or left us. Allowing the policemen to get up and do their job was probably going to take us further than Ethelred waving a gun around, but in the end what he was saying was true. The final result of any investigation would be to reveal a killer in our midst. The important question was, in the meantime, did we feel safer with two policemen guarding us or one crime novelist? The Home Office, who have a bit of experience in these matters, tend to employ policemen.

'Mr Tressider, unless you wish to convince us *you* shot Mr Purbright, will you please put down that gun?' asked Mahmoud.

'No,' said Ethelred.

It was a bit of a stand-off. Ethelred continued to point the gun. The chugging of the outboard engine was now very close indeed.

'Ethelred, I think you should let them get up and hand over the gun,' I said. 'It won't look good if you are still pointing it at them when the other police arrive.'

'Elsie, get some rope,' said Ethelred. 'Look – you can use those curtain ties over there.'

Well, the point had come for decisive action. A writer in jail was no good to me.

'OK,' I said. 'Let's tie these bastards up. I'm no good at knots though. You get the rope. I'll cover them with the gun.'

'Good plan,' said Ethelred.

I got up and walked over to him. He passed me the gun. Honestly, if I wasn't such a good agent, I'd seriously consider becoming a hostage negotiator.

CHAPTER SIXTEEN

I passed her the gun.

We were back in business. I reckoned if I could get these two immobile, I could hold off the motor boat with a few shots if necessary. Purbright's people could then take over when they arrived.

'You two stay there,' I said to Mahmoud and Majid. I selected three or four of the curtain cords and turned round to check that the terrorists were behaving themselves. It transpired that they now had the gun and were pointing it at me.

'But . . .' I said.

'I'm sorry, Ethelred. It was for your own good,' said Elsie.

'You idiot,' I said. 'You've given the gun to the terrorists!'

'She's given the gun to the *police*,' said Proctor.

'Thank goodness,' said Campion, who seemed to feel it was payback time both for making him lecture to the group and for the dinner jacket business.

So it wasn't just Elsie then. The passengers seemed united in making sure the boat was blown out of the water.

I looked from one to another to see if there was the slightest indication that anyone believed me, but Campion had apparently spoken for them all. There was general relief that the only weapon immediately available was now in the possession of crazed suicide bombers.

'Well done, Elsie,' said Proctor.

'If you would now like to take a seat, Ethelred,' said Mahmoud, the gun still aimed between my eyes, 'we can then wait calmly for our colleagues to arrive.'

I turned to the others. 'Listen to me,' I said. 'Their "colleagues" are bringing explosives to blow up the boat.'

'You're a laugh a minute, Ethelred,' said Majid. 'You should do stand-up – honest. Actually, you will be pleased to learn, we're not currently planning to blow anything up. So, let's all wait patiently for just another couple of moments. Thank you. Inspector Mahmoud, would you kindly go and ensure our local colleagues know where we are?'

I was speculating on what it would feel like to be killed in an explosion when Tom said casually: 'You guys really are from the Cairo police, then?'

'This is what we have been trying to explain to you all for some time,' said Majid.

'You've been liaising with the British police over this?'

'Scotland Yard,' said Majid.

'That would be with SCD 5, I guess?'

'That's right,' said Majid.

'Cool,' said Tom.

He stretched and yawned as though bored with the topic but, when Majid was not looking, he flashed me a glance

161

that suggested he did not think I was a total moron after all. Viewed one way this was good, but viewed in another way, it was very bad indeed. If Tom knew the Met well, and SCD 5 was something like HR or catering, that would explain his current expression. But that in turn confirmed my hunch that we were all about to find out how being blown up felt.

We heard an outboard engine being cut as the motor boat glided alongside.

'If you could all just stay seated for the moment,' said Majid, a little nervously.

Majid's full attention was now on Tom. I reckoned we had about thirty seconds to get the gun back before the others boarded and we were hopelessly outnumbered.

I stood up very slowly. I hadn't tried a rugby tackle since I was at school, but Majid was close enough that I'd be able to check very soon whether I still knew how it was done. I was pretty sure that Tom at least would join in on my side. I was about to spring when a hand grabbed my arm. It was Proctor. Majid heard the noise and turned back to me. Tom now got to his feet and seemed to be about to tackle Majid himself, when we heard steps outside. Mahmoud had returned. With him were two men carrying machine guns. They did not look much like police – local or otherwise.

'I think you should all resume your seats,' said Mahmoud, 'while we sort things out.'

'I don't know where you're from,' said Tom, 'but you've never had any dealings with the Met. A lot of my legal practice concerns children and I happen to know that SCD 5 is a child protection unit. You certainly haven't talked to them about counterterrorism. So, who are you?'

'How many times do I have to say it? We are policemen. As far as this SCD thing is concerned, my colleague must simply have misheard you,' said Mahmoud.

'I don't think so.'

The other passengers were looking from Tom to Mahmoud and then at me. Doubts were beginning to form in their minds but, sadly, about five minutes too late.

'We shall need to question you all one by one, beginning I think with you, Ethelred. Perhaps you would like to accompany us downstairs? A little privacy would be helpful.'

'I'm happy to be questioned here,' I said.

'You may be, but we are not,' said Mahmoud. One of his 'local colleagues' pointed his machine gun in my direction. 'Would you be so kind as to follow me?'

With Mahmoud ahead of me and the other three behind, we descended the stairs to the lower deck, where the motor boat was tied up.

'Now, Ethelred, we are going to take a little ride.'

'Where to?' I asked.

'It will be more convenient to question you ashore. In the meantime, a boat has been sent for to pull the *Khedive* off the sandbank. Your friends will be quite safe.'

'So, it is only me that you wish to question?' I asked.

But Mahmoud merely smiled and ushered me towards the boat.

The first part of the journey remains a confused memory since I was, for some reason not explained at the time, temporarily blindfolded. There was a short delay while something else was loaded into the boat – perhaps the same thing that was later dragged along the boat and dropped into the Nile with a gentle splash. We were well clear of the *Khedive*, and heading rapidly upstream, when I was again permitted to observe proceedings.

'You're not from the police, are you?' I said, blinking and trying to make out any landmarks on either bank.

'What do we have to do to convince you, Ethelred?'

'A straight answer – yes or no.'

'We've told him enough,' said one of the Egyptians.

'You've told me nothing,' I said. 'So, it would be a reasonable assumption you *are* terrorists.'

'You are jumping to conclusions,' said Mahmoud.

'I've been in touch with the British security services – they said there were terrorists on board the boat.'

'Anything else?'

'That you were planning to plant a bomb.'

'Us? How interesting.'

'Have you planted a bomb on the boat?'

'Of course not.'

'You shot Purbright. Why should I trust you or believe you?'

'That wasn't us either,' said Mahmoud. 'Somebody else shot Purbright.'

'Who?'

'Somebody on the boat. If not you . . . then somebody else who must still be on board. Perhaps the same person who tried to kill you and Mr Proctor at Edfu.'

'Are you serious?'

'You should be grateful, Ethelred,' said Mahmoud with a smile. 'Here you are enjoying a nice boat ride with us instead of being back on the *Khedive* with a murderer who, if what you are saying is true, may be about to strike again.'

The man at the tiller, perhaps impatient with my questions, gave the throttle a savage wrench. The bows rose suddenly in the water, throwing me back hard against the seat. I held on for dear life as the boat raced northwards, into the night.

CHAPTER SEVENTEEN

Elsie

'Well, at least we're safe now,' said Campion, though any threat that Ethelred had posed had always been mainly to Ethelred.

We listened thoughtfully to the sound of the outboard engine dying away. For a while nobody spoke.

'Have they all gone then?' asked Proctor eventually. 'I thought they were going to question Ethelred here on the *Khedive*.'

'They have obviously taken him to the nearest police station,' said Campion. 'That seems to me an entirely proper procedure.'

'But they've just cleared off and left us here on the sandbank?' said Proctor, who was perhaps less concerned about procedure.

'They're not policemen,' said Tom again. 'They won't be going near any police station if they can help it. Hell – if I'd just asked them that question a minute earlier . . .'

'Inspector Mahmoud said that Inspector Majid had misheard,' said Campion, carefully stressing the rank of both gentlemen. 'In any case, you can hardly expect the

Cairo police to be au fait with every single Scotland Yard unit. Let's look at this sensibly. Ethelred comes in here brandishing a gun like a maniac, and accuses the two policemen of murdering Purbright. The policemen act sensibly – to ensure none of us gets hurt, they lie down on the floor and try to reason with him. They even offer to let him search them. That's scarcely how a terrorist would behave, is it? Ethelred's been acting oddly the whole trip in my humble opinion. Who do you want to believe?'

'All the same . . .' said Tom.

'The policemen can't be the ones who killed Purbright,' said Campion. 'It's ridiculous. I'm sure it was an accident, but Ethelred must have fired the gun.'

'That's true about the policemen, that is for sure,' said Captain Bashir, unexpectedly. He didn't seem happier than any other captain to have his boat on a sandbank with no working engines. He could therefore have been excused the tiniest grudge against Mahmoud and Majid. If he was now about to defend them, at least nobody could accuse him of being unduly prejudiced in their favour. So we listened to what he had to say. A pin dropping could have been heard from one side of the boat to the other. (Having no working engines helped.) 'If the shots are fired at the same time that the engines fail, then it is impossible that either of the two gentlemen is the killer. They both come to the bridge and tell me they are policemen. We have to get to Kom Ombo as fast as possible and make contact with the authorities. I protest – we are going as fast as we can – but they give me no choice. When the engines blow, we are still on the bridge, still arguing. So, neither of them leaves until well after the shot was fired.'

Campion looked unconvinced, but Proctor was eyeing us all suspiciously, trying to work out who had done him out of his fee plus reasonable receipted expenses.

'When do you think somebody will come and pull us off the sandbank?' asked Sky Benson, raising a practical issue that had been on my mind as well.

'We have only Mahmoud's assurance that anyone has been sent for. If those guys are *not* police, then we may have a long wait,' said Tom.

'We can phone the nearest police station ourselves,' said Campion.

'Good idea. Anyone manage to hang onto their mobile?' asked Tom.

Nobody had.

'Any other way of communicating?' Tom asked the captain. 'They took the phones and the ship's radio,' he said. 'They are thorough.'

'Then, Captain Bashir,' said Campion, 'you must launch the ship's tender and get help. I am sure that the policemen will already have radioed ahead, but it may reassure those like Tom who doubt it. For my part, I shall go and see if I can retrieve the gun that Ethelred claims was in the cabin by the dining room. After that, Captain, I should be grateful if you would question the crew. I shall question the passengers to set people's minds at rest that it was *not* one of us. If the opportunity arises, we shall hail a passing boat and ask it for assistance.' It was the sort of speech that Purbright might have made and just got away with. Delivered in Campion's petulant whine, it did not carry a great deal of authority. The captain in particular looked pissed off at being ordered around on his own boat. Proctor sniggered. Sky Benson made a point of looking out of the window, though there was nothing to see except the black river and a few bright stars. Still, objectively, it was not such a bad plan for a group of people stranded in the middle of the Nile with a killer amongst them and no means of communicating with the outside world.

'You mean, launch the tender onto the sandbank that we are currently stuck on?' asked Captain Bashir with an air of disdain.

'Certainly. And then push it into the Nile,' said Campion, as if they did little else at the UCL archaeology department.

'Using the one undamaged winch to get it clear of the tree that it is in?' asked the captain.

'I am sure that it could be manhandled by four or five of the crew . . .' Campion began; but nothing in the captain's expression suggested to him that it would be worth completing the sentence.

'Who says you get the gun anyway?' asked Proctor, deciding that he might as well nitpick as not. 'You could be the killer as easily as . . .' He looked round the room trying to spot a more likely killer, but neither Ethelred nor the two policemen were there. I too wouldn't have trusted Campion with a gun, though. I hadn't forgotten his late-night conversation with Sky.

'I think the gun should be handed over to Captain Bashir,' I said. Other than Tom and John, he was the only one left I trusted entirely.

'It would be quite safe with me,' said Campion. He clearly saw himself in the role of a natural leader and was disappointed that we couldn't see it too. 'In any case, we have all agreed that the most likely killer is Ethelred. He burst in here threatening everyone. He did have a gun, even if he doesn't know how the safety catch works. I repeat: I'm not saying it was deliberate. The way he was waving that thing around, it is much more likely to have been a tragic accident. But the police quite clearly suspect him and I say they are right to do so.'

'I don't think so,' said Tom. 'In fact, the second gun more or less clears him.'

'Does it?' asked Proctor.

'I'd say it does. Ethelred would scarcely require two guns so, if there really is a second gun in that cabin, somebody else on board the boat has been using one this evening.'

'But even if it belongs to one of us, why would anyone leave a murder weapon lying around?' I said. 'The obvious thing is to throw it into the Nile. Nobody would have heard the splash with all that noise. So, why leave it somewhere that even Ethelred could find it?'

To that question, as to so many others, there was no obvious answer. John was in any case wrestling with another problem. 'Tom,' he said, 'are you sure about this child protection thing? Couldn't you be misremembering? Hell, all these initials . . .'

'Or maybe Inspector Majid misheard you?' said Proctor. 'There was quite a lot going on at the time.'

'Why don't I just go and get the gun?' said Campion, returning to his role as natural leader.

'No,' said Proctor. 'I think we should stay put and each state clearly where we were when the shot was fired. Then we'll decide who gets the gun.'

Proctor and Campion tried staring each other out, but it was pretty shoddy work. Neither was what you would describe as an impressive starer.

'Tell you what,' said Tom, pointedly ignoring them both. 'I'll start. John and I had both turned in for the night. We were sitting in our respective beds, reading, when the engines began to get noisy. So we decided to take a look.'

'There were crew running everywhere,' continued John, 'mainly heading for the bridge or the engine room. Everyone could tell the engines weren't going to stand the strain. A couple of waiters came out on deck to find out what was going on, then went back in again. Ethelred was standing up near the stern, looking out for somebody or something. I didn't see any gun. Anyway, we went back towards the bridge. Inspector Mahmoud was there with the captain, then after a while Majid came and joined him. Most of the crew seemed to end up there too, trying to find out what was going on. Everyone was fairly cross with everyone else, and they were all shouting a lot, so we just snuck off back to the saloon. The deck was fairly deserted by then – I don't remember seeing Ethelred at all at that point. Eventually the noise got really bad, the engines blew and we came to find the rest of you. And here we still are.'

'So Mahmoud and Majid were not together on the bridge the whole time?' asked Proctor.

'They were both on the bridge when the engines blow up,' said Captain Bashir. 'That is when you heard the shot, isn't it?'

'Yes,' said Proctor. 'And when I heard it, I was here with Elsie and Jane Watson. So the shot was definitely not fired by me or Elsie or Jane.' He was keen we were clear on that point, as indeed I was quite keen myself. Jane Watson just shrugged. It took more than a murder to make her worry what people thought about her. 'What about you, Professor Campion?' Proctor continued. 'Where were you when the shot was fired?'

'In bed,' said Campion.

'Any witnesses to that event?' asked Proctor.

'Scarcely,' said Campion.

Proctor smiled. Campion was not going to be the one who got to fetch the gun.

Sky Benson half raised her hand. 'I was also in bed,' she volunteered. 'Alone. No witnesses of any kind.'

'This is a complete waste of time,' said Campion, seeing the way things were going. 'Most of us won't have witnesses as to where we were. And we don't need them because *none of us did it*. But we do know that Ethelred went off with Purbright. And we do know he had a gun. From what Tom and John say, it sounds as though he was later lying in wait for him on deck, at almost exactly the time the shot was heard.'

'One of the crew did see him,' said the captain. 'He is trying to hide, for sure. He is – what do you say? – flattening his body against the wall.'

'What more proof are you after?' Campion was pathetically triumphant. 'The only reason nobody actually saw him fire the shot was that everyone was in bed or had gone to the bridge or the engine room to find out what was happening. It's obvious. The police have taken the right man away. We are all safe. Let us now just go back to our own beds and sleep. Help is undoubtedly on its way.'

Most of us might have been inclined to go along with the idea of sleeping, but Herbie Proctor had an announcement to make.

'Some of you may not know,' said Proctor, 'but I am a private detective.' It was quite touching that he thought he still had any part of his cover intact. We let him continue. 'I was hired to guard Mr Purbright. He'd had death threats. Purbright is not his real name. His real name . . .' Proctor paused very unnecessarily for effect: '. . . is Raffles.'

Nobody could think of anything to say in reply to this, but there was a gentle thud as Sky Benson dropped her copy of *Snow on the Desert's Face* onto the floor.

'Sorry,' she said.

Tom was looking puzzled. 'You mentioned the name Raffles before. Why do you think that's what he was really called?'

'He was employing me to protect him,' said Proctor.

'Nice work in that case,' said Tom. 'What were you protecting him from?'

'There had been threats against him,' said Proctor.

Campion was frowning. 'I vaguely seem to remember somebody of that name was tried for murdering his wife? You are not, surely, saying that this was the same man?'

'Yes, but he was found *not guilty*,' said Proctor irritably.

There were more puzzled looks – this time exchanged between Sky Benson and Campion.

'What exactly makes you think he is Raffles?' asked Campion.

'He'd contacted me. I'd arranged to meet him on the boat,' said Proctor.

'I'm losing track of this a bit,' said Tom. 'Why should Ethelred want to kill this Raffles person? Even if Raffles does sound a rather unsavoury character. Did Ethelred even know that Purbright was really Raffles?'

'Yes,' said Proctor. 'I told him. But the killer can't have been Ethelred. Whoever killed Raffles tried to kill me earlier today at the temple – that's obvious. Ethelred was with me then, so it can't have been him.'

'Well,' said Campion, 'I can see that, if people knew you were guarding Purbright . . . or Raffles or whatever you want to call him . . . they might have felt they should get you out of the way first.'

Proctor had lost a client rather publicly, but it clearly assuaged his professional pride a little that he himself should also be a target. He nodded sagely.

'Precisely. While I was around it would have been difficult for anyone to kill my client,' he said, puffing out his chest to the limited extent it would puff.

'Except that they did kill him,' said Tom.

'Yes,' said Proctor, implying this was only a slight flaw in his theory.

'Well, that does put a very different complexion on things. So, let's start from here: who would want to kill Raffles?' Tom continued.

'Plenty of people,' said Sky, wrapping her dressing gown more closely around her. 'At least, I would imagine so. He may have been found not guilty but he got off on a pure technicality.'

Campion seemed keen to get us back to his idea of spending the next few hours asleep. 'Look,' he interrupted, 'this isn't getting us anywhere . . .'

'You know about the trial, Sky?' asked Tom.

'I thought everyone did,' she said. 'For a couple of weeks it was in all the papers, and on television. It was a really dreadful case. I felt so sorry for the children.'

All of that was probably true, though there had been plenty of dreadful cases since then, equally well reported, and my own recollection of the Raffles case was now patchy at best. I vaguely remembered that the children had had to be called as witnesses.

'Well, maybe we are getting somewhere,' said Tom. 'If there are a lot of people out there who think Raffles was guilty, then maybe one individual might have decided that justice would be done by bumping him off?'

'Two people,' said Proctor. 'The letter said it was two people.'

'So you're saying they might have found out he was travelling to Egypt, booked on the same cruise and waited for their chance?' Tom asked.

Proctor nodded.

'But why would anyone take that sort of risk?' asked John.

'I don't know,' Tom replied. 'Perhaps if it was your sister or daughter who had been killed by him? Then, what if you chanced to find out that this Raffles guy would be here, on this boat, without the sort of protection he might have in England?'

'Very picturesquely described I am sure,' said Campion,

'but not very likely, is it? We are going round in circles. The police think that Ethelred killed Mr Purbright – or Mr Raffles if you all prefer. That's good enough for me.'

'They are not policemen though,' said Tom.

'Just as I say,' continued Campion. 'Round and round in circles. The majority of us are happy to believe the police.'

'I'm not sure you have a majority,' said Tom.

Campion folded his arms and looked round the group, defying us to vote against the proposition. 'Well, my vote is certainly for Ethelred. How about the rest of you?'

'I really have no idea,' said Jane Watson. 'You can scarcely solve a murder case by each of us putting crosses on a ballot paper.'

'Quite,' said Annabelle.

'Absolutely,' said Lizzi.

It was a shame that the vote had been called off because I had been planning to rig it in favour of Annabelle, Lady Muntham, by some devious method yet to be explained. But I just said: 'I'm sure it wasn't Ethelred. Or my two policemen.'

Campion looked miffed that public opinion was not as much in his favour as he had hoped. As with most of the other suggestions that evening, it had not taken us as far as it might have done.

Still, my Annabelle theory had its merits, and I needed to run it past somebody that I could trust. I beckoned to Tom and we found ourselves a secluded corner of the saloon, away from the others – and especially away from Annabelle.

'There's another possibility,' I said in as low a voice

as I could manage. It was a weird idea, but no weirder than some of the others. 'What if the stone *was* aimed at Ethelred after all, not Herbie? And what if the shot that killed Purbright was aimed at Ethelred too?'

'Who would want to kill Ethelred?' asked Tom.

'He'd received a death threat,' I said. 'There was a text message from somebody saying they were going to kill him.'

'Who sent it?'

'He just said it was a friend.'

'So, who are his friends?'

'He doesn't have many, to be perfectly honest. But there's Annabelle . . .'

'The Annabelle who has just joined us?' asked Tom. 'Does she know Ethelred?'

'A while ago,' I said, 'a mate of Ethelred's – Sir Robert Muntham – died and left his house, Muntham Court, to Ethelred.'

'And where does Annabelle fit in?'

'Annabelle is Lady Muntham – Sir Robert's widow. He had, frankly, good reasons for leaving her as little as he could get away with – two-timing bitch.'

'I can see that might have pissed her off,' said Tom, 'but you say she is a *friend*?'

'She decided that the best way of keeping the house was to get her hands on Ethelred. Ethelred is not, sadly, well versed in the ways of evil two-timing bitches – he rather seems to like them in fact – and I thought for a while that he might be about to go along with the whole thing. But just before he left for Egypt he finally saw reason and put Muntham Court on the market. Annabelle would have taken it as a clear signal that her original plan was pants and that she needed another one.'

'Just out of interest, if Ethelred dies, does the house revert to Annabelle under the will?' asked Tom, echoing thoughts I had already had.

'I don't know,' I said. 'I guess there could be something in it about Ethelred having to survive Sir Robert by a certain time, failing which the bequest might go elsewhere.'

'And you think she has joined us to bump Ethelred off? Surely not?'

I thought about this. Purbright's shooting was the work of somebody who was very desperate, very pissed off, a very cool customer . . . *and probably an ex-pole dancer.* Into how many of those classes did Annabelle fit? Four at least. But would she really have mistaken Purbright for Ethelred?

'Ethelred and Purbright were both wearing white dinner jackets,' I said. 'Annabelle saw them leave the dining room together. She followed, gun in hand, lay in wait, and then shot the wrong one. She panicked and dumped the gun in the empty cabin, which Miss Watson had failed to lock properly that first afternoon after faffing around over her choice of bunks.'

'Having previously tried to kill Ethelred at the temple by toppling that stone?' asked Tom.

'It was a strange coincidence that she showed up precisely then,' I said. 'And she matches the description of the lady in the floppy hat seen heading for the roof.'

'Interesting theory,' said Tom.

'Yes,' I said.

'If so, Purbright was simply in the right place in

178

the wrong clothes – the sort of dreadful fashion faux pas anyone might make. Maybe the question is now irrelevant – but do you think Purbright really is this Raffles person? That would certainly be an ironic twist – to get accidentally bumped off by one of the few people who didn't think you deserved it.'

'Was he Raffles? Only in Herbie Proctor's imagination,' I said. 'The police reckoned Purbright was actually the one who was out to kill Raffles.'

'Majid and Mahmoud actually mentioned Raffles by name?'

I tried to remember what they had said; it all seemed a long time ago. 'Kind of,' I hedged.

'Curiouser and curiouser,' said Tom. 'In that case, the potential murderer is himself bumped off. But where is the real Mr Raffles then? More to the point, where is Ethelred?'

I was wondering that too. I just had to hope my nice policemen were guarding him well.

CHAPTER EIGHTEEN

Q: Our readers are always interested in how writers work. Describe the room you are writing in now.
A: I am in a small hut somewhere in the Nile Valley. It contains a wooden bed, on which I am now sitting, and an old table that may have been painted blue at some point in the distant past. The walls are completely bare. The door seems to be locked. There are bars on the windows. There is a single light bulb hanging from the ceiling. I can't see any way of switching the light on or off from inside the room. That's about it, really.

Q: Do you have a regular writing routine?
A: I tend to get up early and write, particularly if I can't sleep for any reason. It's currently two o'clock in the morning, for example.

Q: What books are on your bedside table at the moment?
A: The Koran.

Q: Have you travelled much?
A: Yes. During the past few hours I have been on a Nile paddle steamer, a fast motor boat and then a pick-up truck with bad suspension. Finally I had a tricky walk, while blindfolded for the second time today, with a machine gun prodding me in the back. I'm hoping that somebody will soon tell me where I have travelled to. And why. Yesterday I was on a coach travelling to Edfu temple – though that seems a very long time ago now.

Q: I realise we aren't a great tourist destination, but have you ever visited Scunthorpe?
A: You've no idea how much I would like to be there with you right now.

'It's good to see you hard at work,' said Mahmoud, locking the door again behind him.

'Just some questions for a newspaper in Scunthorpe,' I said, looking up. 'All publicity is good publicity.'

Being able to do something as mundane as answer interview questions was strangely reassuring. It seemed unlikely that anyone had ever been murdered while writing for the *Scunthorpe Telegraph*. Or not recently.

'That is exactly how I feel about my work as well,' said Mahmoud. He had remained standing – a position of advantage, as it now seemed to me from my rickety wooden chair.

'And what is your work?' I asked, looking up at him. 'You are not expecting me to believe that this is police headquarters?'

Mahmoud looked around the room as if seeing it for the first time. 'You are right. This is not police headquarters. It is however a convenient place for us all to be in at the moment. It may not have the amenities of a British police station and perhaps the Police and Criminal Evidence Act doesn't apply here – but, as Tom would say, I have a feeling that you are not in Kansas any more.'

'So why am I here?'

'Other than because you shot Purbright, you mean? That would seem reason enough.'

'I didn't shoot Purbright. You know that perfectly well.'

'You went out on deck with him.'

'Yes.'

'You were the only passenger not to come to the saloon as requested.'

'Yes.'

'You had a gun. You threatened to shoot us.'

'I didn't shoot Purbright,' I repeated. 'I didn't lay my hands on the gun until after he was dead. And what motive could I possibly have had?'

'You would say that, wouldn't you?'

He was right there, of course. I would say that. I have after all written many scenes in which the murderer is obliged to deny a shooting or a stabbing in almost exactly these terms. What usually followed was a grilling in which they were slowly worn down – in the case of my Master Thomas historical mysteries, by foul means as often as fair. As the motor boat had sped away from the *Khedive*, it had struck me that I might experience some discomfort, and possibly boredom, before I was ransomed. Death had at that point seemed unlikely – why should anyone wish to kill a second-rate, or even third-rate, crime writer? But death, and perhaps a fairly unpleasant one, was surely something that I had to allow for? Twice I had placed Master Thomas in a position in which he faced being tortured to death unless he revealed information that he simply did not have. Master Thomas had remained quite perky, even in the malodorous dungeons of Bramber Castle. His answers to questions had been confident – insouciant even – in the face of the most blatant threats. My voice, I noticed, had a tremor in it even at this stage. It's much easier to write insouciance than do it.

'I'm the least likely person to have shot Purbright – we were on the same side. Whoever killed him, it wasn't me.'

Mahmoud suddenly whacked a large fist into the palm of his hand and smiled when I involuntarily jumped at the sound. I expected him to follow up this action with some remark along the lines that he had ways of making me confess. What he actually said was slightly different.

'What a pity,' said Mahmoud. 'You see, Ethelred, we had rather hoped that you had shot him. It would have made things much more straightforward for us and, from your point of view, it would scarcely be something that we would hold against you. As it is, what you say presents us with a problem, because *we* certainly did not kill him. And that means we have to ask ourselves who else is on board the *Khedive* and why they should have chosen to kill a member of your security services.'

'And his colleague,' I said. 'Somebody had already killed Purbright's colleague.'

'Ah yes, the colleague,' said Mahmoud. 'Since we were

on the boat at the time, that, you must concede, could scarcely have been down to us.'

'But you know about it nevertheless?'

'The killing of the Egyptian security service man? He was travelling down from Cairo to join the boat. We think he knew that he was being followed. That is why he did not take the express service from Cairo to Luxor, but travelled by local train, changing twice. He was at a small station, not so far from Luxor, when he was shot. Apparently he had just finished a phone call. His final words were: "I understand. I'll watch out for the woman." Do you know who he might have been referring to?'

'No,' I said.

'So,' said Mahmoud, 'you will appreciate our problem. Was the woman, in effect, on their side – another member of the security service of one country or another – and he had to make contact with her? Or was she a threat that he had to guard against? If so, did the woman kill your friend Purbright?'

'So Purbright *was* with MI6? And you *are* Al-Qaeda or something?'

'It's a murky world that you have just entered, Ethelred. Things are not always what they seem. Let us just say that we are as sure as we can be that Purbright had been sent to watch us and interfere with our plans if he could. Did he mention any of that to you?'

'I don't remember,' I said.

'You aren't very good at lying, are you? Your face gives you away. What puzzles us is why he clearly took you into his confidence in the way he did. You were scarcely likely to

184

be of much value to him. Then, out of the blue, somebody shoots him. You say it wasn't you. And we say it wasn't us. So, we have to conclude that there was somebody else on the boat who found it inconvenient to have Mr Purbright on board with them. The question is: who? And for us it is a more urgent question than you may think. When exactly did you last see Purbright alive?'

He smiled at me reassuringly, the previous threat temporarily shelved. Mahmoud was, to give him his due, quite able to play both good cop and bad cop without help from Majid. It seemed better to keep him in good cop mode and at least appear cooperative. In any case, I too wanted to know who had shot Purbright.

'You know the answer to that too,' I said. 'I last saw him alive just before he was shot. He told me he had to speak to somebody and that I should wait for him.'

'And that person was?'

That was a question that had of course been at the back of my mind for some time. Who had Purbright gone to see, and why hadn't he wanted to tell me who it was? He had after all taken me into his confidence more generally. Was it the same person Elsie and I had heard him talking to the other night? And, thinking about it, Purbright had glanced at his watch before telling me that he would be away for ten minutes. So, the meeting had certainly been prearranged. But he hadn't seemed worried. Mildly irritated perhaps, but not in fear of his life. Except, he *had* given me the phone number just in case . . .

'I don't know,' I said rather lamely.

'This time, I think you are telling the truth. But perhaps

together we can find out what actually happened. It really is in both of our interests. Did Purbright think he was in danger? Could he have received the same warning as his Egyptian counterpart?'

'I think Purbright may have known something. He gave me . . .' I paused. The phone number was written on the back of my *Southend Evening Echo* interview and, more helpfully, would still be in the memory of my mobile phone, which had been taken from me as soon as we had arrived at our present location. 'He certainly led me to believe that he might be in danger,' I said.

'Did you hear the shot?'

'No, there was too much noise.'

'But a pistol shot is quite loud, would you not agree? And you were very close?'

'Yes to both of those questions,' I said. 'Perhaps the killer used a silencer?'

'No, three people apparently heard the shot quite distinctly – so the killer did not use a silencer. Perhaps Purbright was shot further away from you – and closer to them – and he subsequently managed to stagger back that far?'

'I don't know,' I said. The main objection to the staggering hypothesis was that there had been plenty of blood around Purbright's body, but I couldn't remember seeing any anywhere else on deck. Had there been blood on the wall behind him? It had been dark and I hadn't checked – at the time, examining blood spatter patterns had seemed a lower priority than checking whether the killer was still at large. The balance of probability was that Purbright had collapsed and died pretty much where he was shot, but I couldn't be absolutely sure.

'Were you aware of anyone – one of the passengers or crew – taking an undue interest in Mr Purbright?'

'No,' I said. 'But the stone at the temple may have been aimed at him.'

'But, if that was not an accident, the rock was surely intended for you or Mr Proctor?'

'I was there with Purbright a few moments before.'

'So the stone could have been aimed at Purbright by somebody who had not realised he had moved on?' asked Mahmoud.

'Your guess is as good as mine,' I said.

'On the contrary. You were there at the temple. Majid and I were back at the boat. Your guess would be considerably better informed. If the shooting was the second attempt on Purbright's life, that would indicate a determined and rather reckless assassin, would it not?'

'If you say so.'

'But, Ethelred, you didn't see anyone up on the roof?'

'No.'

'What do you know about Lizzi Hull?'

'Nothing really.'

'She is well informed on Middle Eastern matters.'

'She said that she could understand why somebody might choose to be a terrorist – that's miles away from actually being one.'

'I agree. Then Miss Watson? Miss Benson? Lady Muntham?'

'You are ruling out the men? On the basis of a chance remark, overheard at a railway station?'

'Not entirely, but we have to look at probabilities. We don't have very long, to tell you the truth.'

'You don't suspect Elsie?'

'No.'

'Tell me,' I said, 'why was it only Elsie that you told you were policemen?'

'There's nothing so convincing as allowing a story to come out bit by bit from an apparently reliable source.'

'You were counting on her not to keep it a secret?'

'Of course. Did she not tell you straight away?'

'Yes,' I said.

'But, in the meantime, we are still no closer to identifying the killer. And before you accuse us again, I repeat that it is in our common interest that we believe each other for a moment.'

'Does it really matter to you who killed him?'

'Oh yes, it matters to us. And to you. You see, it affects how we deal with the small problem of the *Khedive* and those who are still on it.'

'The *Khedive* is hardly your problem. They'll already be towing it off the sandbank,' I said.

'On the contrary. I doubt that will happen until the morning,' said Mahmoud. 'We still have our options open.'

'You mean you might go back and blow it up?'

'You really are convinced we are terrorists, aren't you?'

'Yes,' I said.

Mahmoud smiled. 'I'll leave you to work on your interview.'

But somehow, in spite of his consideration in leaving me alone, I couldn't quite interest myself in the *Scunthorpe Telegraph* any more.

It was perhaps half an hour later when Majid came to see me.

'I am sorry that you are not being treated as well as I would like,' he said.

I reassessed the good cop/bad cop thing. Majid was not, after all, completely redundant in the scheme of things. Mahmoud had worried me. Maybe Majid would now set out some proposal that would offer me a hope of safety and secure my agreement to participate in whatever plan they had dreamt up.

'I can't say I'm comfortable, but I can't complain at being mistreated,' I said.

Majid shook his head grimly: 'I thought Mahmoud would have said something to you. There's been a change in plan.'

'So what is the new plan?'

'You are his new plan. You don't need to blow up a boat with thirty or forty people on it to get publicity. There are plenty of other ways of grabbing the world's attention for a few days. A video of the death of a famous writer, for example.'

'You mean me?' I asked. I hoped he didn't.

'That's Mahmoud's preference – but we don't always get everything we wish for in this life.'

'Meaning what?'

'Listen,' said Majid, dropping his voice to an urgent whisper. 'Things are not quite as they seem.'

'In what way?' I asked.

'Keep your voice down. I really *am* with the Egyptian police,' said Majid.

'And the others?'

'As you have already guessed, they are part of a group of very dangerous extremists.'

'Any particular reason why I should believe you aren't part of the group too?'

'I can understand why you might be cautious. But the risks I shall ask you to take are small ones compared with the risk that I am running myself.'

'I guess I would have to agree with that. If that's the truth, you're taking a big chance telling me all this.'

'I'm taking a big chance being with the group at all. Mahmoud is beginning to suspect. It's time for me to – what is the phrase you use? – come in from the cold. But first I need to get you back to the *Khedive* unharmed.'

'How?'

'We'll come to that in a moment.'

'But I still don't understand why I am here. What was the change of plan? What does Mahmoud intend to do with me?'

'The original plan, as you seem to know, was to blow up the *Khedive*. Security's tight these days, so we weren't going to risk bringing the explosive on board with us and keeping it in our cabin. Our role was to suss out where the explosive would go – and to make sure that our friends got on board with the goods. Then we hit a problem. The boat was going too slowly to make the rendezvous. Mahmoud also thought that Purbright was onto the plan and that we simply didn't have time to delay everything by the day or so that was needed. He was ready to abandon the whole operation, but then Purbright was shot.'

'And that meant you were free to act?' I asked.

'It meant that there was probably somebody else on board who was on our side – though we couldn't be sure which organisation they came from. We had no wish to blow up one of our own people. So there was a change of plan, while we tried to contact other groups and see whether they had operatives in the area.'

'But,' I said, 'up to that point, Majid, you were intending to simply go along with Plan A, which entailed blowing us all up. Couldn't you and Purbright have simply overcome Mahmoud?'

'Not without destroying my cover. There's much more at stake here than just the *Khedive*. In any case, the boat would have been safe. It would have been my job to set the timer. That's my field of expertise. This time, the bomb would have unaccountably failed to detonate. These things happen.'

'And the change of plan?'

'Kidnap was always Plan B. And we had discovered that we had a celebrity on board.'

'Who told you that?'

'Your agent told us. You are a very famous writer. Mahmoud decided you would make the best hostage. Grainy footage of your death, filmed in some anonymous location, would have quite an impact.'

'So, I'm about to be beheaded on camera because my agent's attempts at PR finally worked?'

'Not necessarily. That, as I say, was Mahmoud's idea. The group as a whole is still divided on the best way to exploit this opportunity. Others see your fame as a good reason for keeping you alive. If you could be persuaded as to the rightness of their cause, you could be valuable to us. Let's say for the moment that the majority view is that you are too important to allow you to be blown up or shot . . . or beheaded. Let's say that they have a role that somebody like you might play and, while that is the preferred option, there is a good reason for keeping you alive and unharmed.'

'And this role is dependent on my fame as a writer?'

'Oh yes. Think about it. We could execute anyone and it would still be news. But the other plan depends on your being somebody the public will listen to.'

'And if I were, say, perhaps slightly less famous than my agent has been claiming . . . ?'

'It might tip the balance in favour of Mahmoud's plan.'

I considered this question from a number of angles, including what they might do if they felt it necessary to check out my sales figures.

'Do you think the group reads a lot of fiction?' I asked.

'Not that much,' he said.

'Good,' I said. 'Just tell them I taught Dan Brown all he knows.'

CHAPTER NINETEEN

Elsie

At two o'clock Captain Bashir returned to say that he had been able to speak to each of the crew members. All could be accounted for at the time the shot had been heard. Those in the engine room had been working desperately to save the boat, and had no time to go wandering round. The waiters and cooks had mostly been together, putting everything away after dinner – some had gone to the bridge to find out what was happening. Short of assuming a conspiracy by the crew as a whole, none of them could have fired the gun.

'So, it comes back to it being one of us,' said Tom. 'One of us must have killed Purbright.'

'*Raffles*,' said Proctor.

'If the dead gentleman in a white dinner jacket is Raffles, we do at least have a fairly clear motive for murder,' said Tom.

'And if he isn't?' asked Campion.

'In that case, I guess we'll end up coming to the wrong conclusion, which might be dangerous for all of us, if the killer is still here.'

Sky Benson looked distinctly uneasy at this and Campion shot her a disapproving glance.

'Did you want to say something, Sky?' asked Tom.

'No, she doesn't,' snapped Campion. 'Leave the poor girl alone.'

We all looked at Sky, but she just shook her head.

'OK,' said Tom, turning back to the rest of us, 'so let's say somebody here shot Raffles, having followed him out here from England for exactly that reason.'

Nobody wanted to do anything as high-profile as denying this, but nobody seemed up for admitting it either.

'Of course,' said Proctor, 'you'd have to be pretty crazy to try shooting anyone on a boat from which you couldn't make an escape. Unless you were thinking like a suicide bomber.'

Slowly, one by one, we remembered an earlier conversation. Eventually Lizzi Hull broke the silence.

'Why are you all looking at me?' she asked.

'Well, you did say that you could understand why somebody would be a suicide bomber,' said Tom.

'You may not have noticed,' said Lizzi, 'but nobody has been blown up. Anyway, I said I could understand why somebody would do it, not that I had similar plans myself.'

'So where were you when the shot was fired?' asked Proctor.

'Like most other people, I was in my cabin.'

'Had you heard of the Raffles case?' asked Tom.

'Sky said it was very well reported,' said Lizzi.

'And did you think he was guilty?'

'The case sort of collapsed,' said Lizzi. 'I can't remember why. The papers had to be careful what they said, but the Internet chat rooms were full of people saying it had to be him. They never arrested anyone else, did they?'

'But you're not saying what you thought,' said Tom.

'I'm not sure I thought anything,' said Lizzi. 'I was probably in Juba or Ramallah or somewhere at the time, so I'd have missed a lot of the coverage. He seemed a pretty unpleasant sort of person. I'd have felt sorry for his wife, whether he killed her or not. And for the children, as Sky said. If that is Raffles out there on the deck, I couldn't say I was unhappy about it.'

'That's a point – where is the body now, anyway?' asked Proctor.

It was a thought that had occurred to me once or twice. Presumably the local police would want the crime scene left untouched and he was still lying where he fell.

The captain, who had been listening to much of this in silence, rubbed the stubble on his chin. 'They take it,' he said.

'Who?' asked Proctor.

'The policemen. Inspector Mahmoud tells the others: "Put it in the boat." He says they will make examination at the police station.'

I'm no expert, but I thought back to the various manuscripts of crime novels, publishable and crap, that I had been obliged to read over the years. Not even in the most improbable of them had the police grabbed the body after a cursory glance and carted it off with them as a keepsake. There were spatter patterns and fingerprints and shoe prints and cartridge cases and . . .

'That can't be right,' I said.

'Go look yourself,' said Captain Bashir.

'So, there's just an empty pool of blood now?' I asked.

'They say I can hose the deck down.'

'And did you?'

'Of course,' said the captain. That was the *Khedive* for you: nicely coiled ropes, starched linen, clean decks.

'The Egyptian police probably just do things differently,' said Campion.

Proctor nodded, but the others looked doubtful.

'So – whoever they are – they've got Ethelred and Purbright,' said Tom.

'Ethelred and *Raffles*,' said Proctor. 'Wherever they've taken them,' I said.

I looked out of the window at the Nile. There was a lot of it and, at the moment, it was mainly very, very dark.

CHAPTER TWENTY

Q: *Do you make use of your personal experiences when writing your books?*
A: No, but I may in future.

Q: *What's the funniest thing to have happened to you this week?*
A: Yesterday somebody tried to kill me by dropping a rock on my head. It's all gone downhill a bit since then.

Q: *What do you do when you get stuck and can't see where the plot will take you next?*
A: I usually send one of my characters on a road trip of some sort. They head off in search of clues. You never know what a change of scenery will throw up. Where I have two main characters this can create problems, of course – for example, having sent one off somewhere, how on earth do I get them back together again?

'Still writing, Ethelred?'
'I have little else to do, Inspector Mahmoud.'

'I think you may dispense now with the title of "Inspector". Plain "Mahmoud" is fine. Titles are unnecessary between friends.'

'So we're friends, are we? I got the impression we were on opposite sides. Hence my being imprisoned in a hut in the desert.'

'That does not mean we cannot observe the usual courtesies. When Richard the First was ill, Saladin sent him ice from the mountains to cool his drinks. I am not sure that Richard the First ever returned the compliment, but that is perhaps irrelevant in this context. While you are our guest, you will be treated with proper consideration.'

'I'd prefer to continue to call you "Inspector" but to be released. Preferably with my head still on my shoulders.'

'I have good news for you then. We may be about to grant your wish,' said Mahmoud. 'I said we still had a number of options, and one is to return you to the *Khedive*.'

This was not an option mentioned by Majid. There had clearly been further discussion.

'And what have you decided to do?' I asked.

'Just that – you are to be returned.'

'Still writing, Ethelred?'

'No, Majid. I've done all I can. Mahmoud says I am to be returned to the *Khedive* in one piece. I don't understand. I thought my fame as a writer was all that was keeping me alive.'

'How good exactly is an Amazon ranking of 15,239?' asked Majid. 'That is by the way the best ranking of any of your books – paperback or hardback.'

I tried not to show too much pleasure that there were only 15,238 books that were selling better than mine.

Majid looked at me slightly pityingly. 'Dan Brown's bestseller is, conversely, listed as number three. You have clearly taught him well, Ethelred, but sadly you must at the same time have neglected your own work.'

'The sales of my German translations are much better,' I said.

'Unfortunately,' said Majid, 'they checked those too.'

'American?'

He shook his head sadly. 'We also looked at your recent reviews. The most complimentary we could find read: "People who enjoyed this author's previous novels will enjoy this one."'

'*The Times*?' I asked.

'*Sunderland Herald*.'

'Ah,' I said.

'Hence the change of plan. As a hostage, your value is virtually zero. But we are a democratic body, and the majority decision is that your death is of virtually no value either. Mahmoud is not very happy with this, but then he is not very happy about the mission in general. Our enquiries have failed to reveal the operatives of any friendly organisation on board the *Khedive*. He therefore regrets not leaving at least a token amount of explosive behind when we took you away. He also feels that your agent was less than truthful. You won't be surprised to hear that Mahmoud's vote was for disposing of you in much the same way that Purbright was disposed of.'

'How was he disposed of?'

'Mahmoud decided that his body should not be left on the *Khedive* lest it should provide clues as to who the killer was – he still thought at that point that there was a friend on board. The body is therefore now somewhere at the bottom of the river. But you will be freed unharmed. And as a gesture of goodwill, we shall take you back to the *Khedive* ourselves.'

'To the *Khedive*? You won't just leave me at the nearest town?'

'Mahmoud sees himself as a latter-day Saladin,' said Majid. 'Since he has no choice but to return you, he'd like it to be seen as a bold and chivalrous act. He'll sweep in under the noses of his enemies and sweep out again unharmed.'

'But that's crazy,' I said. 'The security services – British and Egyptian – will be there by now. Forget sweeping in and sweeping out. You won't make it within fifty yards before we're all gunned down.'

'Not if the people on the *Khedive* know that you are with us and that we are trying to return you. Anyway, I have my own reasons for indulging Mahmoud. I have to get some papers to MI6 in London. Your people know who I am and that I am working undercover.'

'Then they knew you were on board?'

'No. I wasn't able to tell them that. Nor could I risk making any sort of contact with Purbright – Mahmoud was watching me all the time. But these papers are important. I need you to carry them onto the boat for me.'

'Won't I be searched before I'm allowed to leave here?'

'I'll make sure that doesn't happen. I just need you to confirm things are OK at the other end.'

'I could phone Elsie,' I said. 'No, hold on – you took all of the phones.'

'Can you alert your people in any other way?'

I thought about this for a moment. 'Yes, I have a number I can phone. If you let me have my mobile back.' I gave him a brief description that would narrow it down to two of the phones in his possession.

'Good,' said Majid. 'I'll arrange for that. You'll need to choose your words with care – Mahmoud will be listening to everything you say.'

'You're sure he isn't now? Could this room be bugged?'

'I don't think so. This is just a temporary base. The group doesn't stay anywhere longer than it has to.'

'But if they have overheard . . . Mahmoud, you say, still wants me dead. If the others knew what we were saying now, surely that would give him his excuse to shoot me and dump me in the river?'

'Probably. I have to admit, he would still prefer you didn't make it to the *Khedive* intact. So, I'll be watching your back all the way.'

'Fine. Well, you'd better give me those papers now. I can stuff them into my pocket. If I ditch the interviews, they won't notice anything different. I'll still have a pocketful of A4.'

'It would be a bit obvious if you tried to stuff what I plan to give you in your pocket. It is a whole briefcaseful.'

'You're kidding? A briefcase? I can't see how that can be done.'

'I shall take the briefcase in the boat with us. As you transfer to the *Khedive*, I shall throw it to you. Once on

201

board, just hand the case over to them. They're expecting it – just not by this route.'

'But isn't there a danger – indeed, isn't there a stone-cold certainty – that Mahmoud will see you do it? Even if I manage to get safely on board with it, that's your cover blown for good.'

'That will not be a problem,' said Majid. 'It will be fine if they see me. My intention in fact is that Mahmoud should see me.'

'Why?' I asked.

'Because I'm going to tell him that there is a bomb in the briefcase,' said Majid.

CHAPTER TWENTY-ONE

Elsie

At about three o'clock a truce of sorts was declared on board the *Khedive*. Proctor and Campion had largely run out of snide comments to direct at each other. Tom had conceded, reluctantly, that Majid might have misheard him – though he still did not seem entirely convinced himself. Any offence that Lizzi might have taken at being accused of suicide bombing had been forgotten or at least put to one side. But nobody felt quite safe enough to return to his or her own cabin. By mutual agreement, we decided to sleep, as best we could, in the saloon. Herbie's annexation of the most comfortable chair now revealed itself to have been not merely the slimiest but also the wisest move of the whole evening. The rest of us were left to compete for the seventh- or eighth-best sleeping places. Annabelle had used her dubious charms to get Professor Campion to give up his spot on the sofa, and was currently curled up, covered by her shawl.

The waiters, released from suspicion, now bustled about serving coffee, tea and biscuits to those who needed sustenance to get them through the night. They alone seemed cheerful.

Tom, however, showed no inclination to rest. He winked at me, and we went quietly out on deck.

'Sorry. It gives me the creeps to know I'm in there with a murderer,' said Tom.

'It's not that much better out here,' I said. 'There's nowhere much to get away on a boat like this.'

'That's what makes the whole thing so odd. It's not what a normal person would do, unless they really didn't care about being found out. Maybe we still have a terrorist here on the boat. Or somebody who had wanted to kill this Purbright or Raffles so much and for so long that they were prepared to risk it.'

'Nobody seems to fit either of those categories,' I said. 'The fact that Lizzi Hull says she could understand why somebody would be a suicide bomber doesn't make her one. Sky Benson is worried about something but I'm not sure her hand is steady enough for murder. Campion is desperate to get the gun back for some reason but doesn't strike me as a cold-blooded killer. Of course there's still Annabelle. Maybe she should be locked in the bilges or the lee scuppers or whatever the nastiest bit of the boat is, just until we've worked out who did it.'

'Well, *somebody* certainly fired the gun,' said Tom, ignoring my very good suggestion.

'Do you think it's still there in the cabin?' I asked.

'I doubt that Majid and Mahmoud had time to collect it. Captain Bashir has bigger problems on his mind . . .'

I looked at Tom and he looked at me.

'Why don't we go check?' he said. 'Just in case.'

* * *

It was a short, artificially nonchalant stroll round to the cabin next to the dining room. Tom tried the cabin door and it opened. The gun was indeed still there in the middle of the bed, half wrapped in a white hand towel. Tom leant over and inspected it.

'Baikal Margo,' he said, being careful not to add his fingerprints to available evidence. 'Russian. Semi-automatic. Nice and accurate, and this is the version with the shortened barrel – easier to conceal. Maybe not what you would expect a terrorist to use – it's a bit old and only carries five rounds. Interesting choice of murder weapon. I still don't understand why anyone would just dump it in the cabin though. Why not try to get rid of it properly? And, thinking about it, here's another odd thing: no silencer. If you were planning to kill somebody on a boat like this, you'd pack a silencer in your suitcase, wouldn't you?'

'Maybe they threw the silencer overboard?' I suggested.

'Then why not throw the gun too? But the shot was heard from some way off – so clearly no silencer was used. It would seem that whoever used this was not worried about guns being noisy. After all, they had no way of knowing that the engines would blow just as the shots were being fired. And we had two policemen on board.'

'You're back to their being policemen?'

Tom shook his head. 'No, not really. It's true they didn't act like terrorists. They didn't plant explosives on the boat before saying goodbye. But they didn't act much like policemen either. And they have gone off and left us all stranded. Actually, taking Ethelred like that doesn't make much sense whatever they are. Nor does taking the body.

Maybe taking Ethelred away is some sort of elaborate ploy? The real killer relaxes his guard, Majid and Mahmoud come back, and this time they catch the right guy.'

'That's a bit far-fetched,' I said. 'Why would they think that would work?'

'Yeah. I guess I'll believe that was the plan only when they return with Ethelred,' said Tom. 'Kidnappers who did that would either be stupid or very devious indeed.'

CHAPTER TWENTY-TWO

I dialled the number that Purbright had given me earlier. Once again the call was answered immediately with a simple 'Yes?'

'It's me,' I said. 'Ethelred Tressider.'

'Don't worry, Ethelred. Keep your head down. Our people are close to the boat. They should be with you in ten minutes or so. If you have a view of the river, you might be able to see them.'

'I'm not on the boat any more,' I said.

'Where are you?'

'I don't know. I've been taken to somewhere out in the desert. Mahmoud and Majid are with me.'

'Are you a hostage?'

'I guess so.'

'They let you keep your mobile?'

'They've returned it to me so I can make this call.'

'They know you are phoning us? I'm not sure I like this. What are they up to? Are they in a position to track where you are calling to?'

'I hadn't really thought – but there doesn't seem to be any high-tech equipment out here.'

'That doesn't mean there isn't any. You should assume you're being listened to at all times, as a matter of course.'

'Two of them are standing beside me.'

'Then we'll keep this very short, please. What do they want?'

'They want to return me to the *Khedive*. I'm not such a useful hostage as they thought. I have to pass on the message to you that your men should not fire at us as we approach.'

'Anything else?'

'They want to speak to you.'

'OK, but make it quick.'

I looked at Majid and Mahmoud.

'I will speak to them,' said Mahmoud.

'No, leave it to me,' said Majid, intercepting the phone.

For a moment Majid and Mahmoud glared at each other and, with a sinking feeling, I realised that Mahmoud might already be onto Majid. He wasn't going to be allowed to pass on any coded messages – or he would have to be very clever if he did.

'Hello,' said Majid. He listened for a moment and then said: 'Yes, that's right.'

Mahmoud was clearly still unhappy, but Majid shook his head and turned away from him.

'We have a Mr Tressider in our possession,' said Majid into the phone. 'We're going to let you have him back, as a gesture of goodwill. I need your word that you will allow us to approach the boat without undue let or hindrance. It's cold out on the river at this time of year and he would wish to come in as speedily as possible, as I might too under the circumstances. We will approach quickly, drop him off and then depart as rapidly as we can.'

Majid listened again and eventually said: 'You have understood me precisely. Given those kind assurances, we shall set out now. My colleagues will be trusting you to keep to your side of the bargain. You should be aware that they will be well armed, just in case there is anyone who thinks it would be a good plan to fire on our boat before or after the handover.' He terminated the call abruptly and handed me back my phone. 'Sorted,' he said.

'We are almost ready,' said Mahmoud. 'Please do not leave anything of value behind. You will not be coming back here, ever, and it may be difficult for us to forward items to you.'

It was perhaps ten minutes later. The small group that had brought me out had been reassembled to take me back. I was to be blindfolded again for the first part of the trip.

Mahmoud had been sent – or had elected to come – to fetch me. Again I got the impression that he suspected Majid and was trying to keep me away from him until we were on the boat.

It was odd. At first, the two of them had seemed, both to Elsie and to me, almost interchangeable. Only gradually had I got to know them. Mahmoud was not only the taller, but also the suaver, more urbane of the two. But behind the courteous exterior was a hardened and utterly ruthless terrorist. Majid conversely was more taciturn, slightly diffident, with a pleasant, almost shy, smile. Underneath there was steely resolve here too, but I could detect none of the cruelty that I was now sure Mahmoud was capable of. It was reassuring that I had Majid on my side. I would not have trusted Mahmoud, whatever he had told me. It amused me to think that, once back on the *Khedive*, I would be able to give MI6 a very good description of Mahmoud – one that would ensure that he could not operate openly again in Egypt or the UK.

'Do you think you are really going to get away with this?' I asked.

'In the short term, you had better hope we do,' said Mahmoud. 'For the next hour or so, your safety and ours depend on much the same factors. Later perhaps not, but later we must all look after ourselves.'

'Just in case neither of us makes it, I'm mildly curious to know: *did* you shoot Purbright?'

'No,' said Mahmoud. 'We did not shoot Purbright. Any other final questions?'

'Also just curiosity, really: what made you get mixed up with terrorists?' I asked.

Mahmoud gave me a smile that might have meant anything. 'I wish I could remember,' he said eventually. 'It must have seemed like a good idea at the time. Still, on the plus side, you don't need to buy many ties.'

CHAPTER TWENTY-THREE

Elsie

'So, this is where you all are!' Miss Watson, brandy glass in hand and slightly unsteady, in spite of the lack of any motion at all on the part of the *Khedive*, approached the spot that Tom and I had located for continuing our confidential chat. We had left the gun where it was, but were still speculating on who might have had the skill to use it.

'Good evening, Jane,' said Tom, with his usual politeness. He and I might have been discussing Keats for all he gave away.

'Bloody awful evening,' she said and leant against the rail.

'They're serving brandy now, are they?'

'You know what the crew are like. It would take more than a murder to disrupt normal service. They'll probably whip you up some scrambled eggs if you're feeling peckish.'

Tom yawned and rubbed his hands together. 'It's getting pretty chilly out here,' he said. 'I'm going in to get some coffee. Are you going to join me, Elsie?'

I was about to agree that coffee would be good, when Jane Watson put her hand on my arm and said: 'You go ahead, Tom. We girls will stay here and chat a bit more.'

When Tom had gone, I said to her: 'So what do we girls chat about then?'

Jane Watson tried to take another gulp of brandy, but discovered it had all gone. 'They talk about what bastards men are,' she said. 'There are other things, but that's generally a good start. Don't get involved with them.'

Most of the men I meet on a regular basis are authors, so I am not subjected to a great deal of temptation in that respect. Still, I wasn't planning to disagree with what was basically good advice.

'Tom seems nice enough,' I said.

'Don't get your hopes up. He's gay,' she said.

I hadn't thought too much about it, but (now I did) I had to admit he probably took too much interest in classic Broadway musicals.

'Maybe,' I said.

'And, just because he's gay, it doesn't mean you can trust him. He's still a man.'

'I feel safe enough with him,' I said.

'Really? Isn't Tom's father supposed to be a New York mobster – a bit like this Raffles guy?'

'John says so – but it's only a joke, surely?'

'Tom says John's father was a Nixon aide – that's true, or there was a Nixon aide with that surname. It's not all joking with those two.'

'You're not saying they were mixed up in the shooting?'

'You know where I was when the shot was fired, and I know where you were, but can we trust anyone else on this boat?'

'But Tom's so nice,' I pointed out.

'The most devious people are,' said Miss Watson.

I thought again of Annabelle, there in the saloon slumbering the sleep of the undetected. I was wondering whether to tell my new buddy Jane all about it when she pointed to a dark spot in the middle of the river that was heading towards us at some speed.

'It looks like the good guys are finally coming to rescue us,' she said.

Or the bad guys were coming back to finish us off, of course. That too was a distinct possibility.

CHAPTER TWENTY-FOUR

I had, as I say, been blindfolded for the journey from the hut to the boat. This time the trip had been short, suggesting that our arrival had been by a deliberately circuitous route, either to avoid police surveillance or simply to add confusion as to where I had been. Since one bit of desert looked much like another, the subterfuge appeared redundant – at least to me.

Seven of us were now squeezed into the boat, all heavily armed, except for one crime writer. Majid nonchalantly lowered an old attaché case into the boat at the last minute. Mahmoud's attention was at that moment on the Nile and the first tinge of dawn on the horizon. But it seemed impossible to me that the case would be unnoticed for the whole trip or, even if it was, that it could be passed to me without everyone seeing clearly what was being done. This game of bluff and counter-bluff was complex. What had Mahmoud already been told? What was really in the case? I thought I could trust Majid. But if I couldn't, then I was pretty much dead anyway. I simply had to trust him.

Majid said something to Mahmoud in Arabic and got a short and acerbic response. One of the other men laughed at the exchange, but the rest looked grim. Mahmoud cast off and pushed the boat away from the bank. The boat's engine again roared into life and we were away.

Travelling downstream now we made much faster time than we had before and the *Khedive* was in sight very quickly, still wedged sideways on in the middle of the river. We slowed when about half a mile away to allow Mahmoud to scan the decks with his binoculars.

'We do indeed have company,' he said. 'There seems to be a boat tied up alongside the *Khedive*. But otherwise there is no sign of life. I have no wish to get gunned down doing a good deed. I want you to phone the number you had again and make sure that our deal remains valid.'

As before my call was answered quickly and briefly.

'It's Ethelred,' I said.

'Where are you?'

'Within sight of the *Khedive*.'

'Good. We assumed that was you out there. Can you talk freely?'

'No,' I said.

'OK, I understand.'

'But if you can see us, that means you are already on board the *Khedive*?'

'Yes. Tell your friends to approach slowly and tie up against our own boat, then transfer you across. After that, they have three minutes to get out of range before we open fire. We don't trust them hanging around the *Khedive*.'

'I'll pass that on.'

'Just you, Ethelred, and the clothes you stand up in. Nobody and nothing else? Got that? I said: Have you got that?'

'Yes,' I said. 'I've got that.'

The sky was beginning to glow red on our right-hand side as we covered the last few hundred yards. All over Egypt tourists would be getting up for early-morning starts to view temples or be carried by balloons over the desert. They would be getting breakfast. They would know that the bags they were carrying contained only a guidebook, water bottle and floppy hat.

From the motor boat, the decks of the *Khedive* appeared deserted. On the lowest deck at the stern of the boat, where the crew had their quarters, some greyish washing flapped briefly, then wrapped itself damply round the iron rail. Even more briefly, a window on one of the upper decks caught the redness of the rising sun, then darkened again. Our guys were giving little or nothing away. Half the Egyptian police force might have been on board with machine guns and grenades, or it might just have been the man I had spoken to. The passengers and crew had been told to keep out of sight. The bulk of the ship, of no nameable colour in this half-light, slowly rose above us as we drifted into its cold shadow and tied up. I briefly had a chance to admire the ornate ironwork from a new angle.

I was aware of the stillness of a morning that had only just emerged from being night. The loudest sound was the water slapping rhythmically against the hull of the *Khedive*, and the other boat chafing at its mooring. From a long way away I could also hear the inevitable sound of a donkey braying and a dog's bark in response. Then there was silence from the bank and once again just the lapping of the Nile, held up momentarily on its long, fluid journey northwards.

There was still no sign of anyone, but the transfer from our boat, across the one already tied up there and through the door ordinarily used for boarding passengers, looked simple. In a moment I would know whether it actually was simple or whether it involved me getting a bullet in the back.

'OK, Ethelred,' said Mahmoud. 'You are free to go. We have enjoyed your company, even if you have not perhaps enjoyed ours. We have also kept our side of the bargain. I hope you will urge your friends to keep to theirs.'

I stood up and worked my way carefully down the boat. Every movement seemed to make it rock one way or the other, and I had no wish to fall into the Nile and drown just as safety was in sight. Majid was standing at the point where I had to climb over the edge, as if to assist me. I placed one foot on the side and stepped up, balancing for an instant before dropping down into the slightly smaller motor boat that I had to cross. As I landed, I turned and found the firm angular shape of an attache case thrust into my hands. I looked at Mahmoud, but once again his attention was diverted at the critical moment. Clutching the case to my chest I nervously skipped two steps across the boat and sprang through the open door of the *Khedive* to be met by a tall guy in a white linen suit. Behind me I heard an engine cough into life and a shouted farewell from Majid.

The guy in the suit looked at me. 'What the hell is that bloody thing in your hands?' he demanded.

'The case? It's OK. Your man Majid gave it to me to deliver,' I said.

'We don't *have* a man Majid,' said the guy in the suit. I looked at him and he looked at me, but I said it first. 'Shit,' I said.

CHAPTER TWENTY-FIVE

Elsie

The arrival of the first boat had been the only bit of good news for some time. The arrival of Ethelred and the second boat was a bit of a downer by comparison, but that still lay in the future when the security service boat drew alongside, at a time when dawn was still the merest smudge of pink across the horizon.

There were six of them in the little rubber boat – two British, four Egyptian – and they went about their business checking the *Khedive* for explosives and reassuring everyone that it was almost over.

'We're expecting the terrorists to return at any moment with Mr Tressider,' said Masterman, the senior of the two Brits, and therefore the person tasked with saying reassuring things to us in a condescending manner. 'When they do, we shall arrange for his transfer to this boat with the minimum of fuss or formality, and hopefully without resort to weapons of any kind.' Masterman bore only a passing resemblance to Purbright. Both had the sort of confidence that you presumably need for a life in espionage. He was however taller and distinctly heavier; if they'd been to the same parties, then he'd been tucking into his main course while Purbright was still toying with cocktails and working out whether thirty minutes was enough time to seduce both the hostess and the hostess's daughter. Masterman had missed his true vocation, running an empire, by some fifty years. But he was quite at home in a crisp linen suit, organising the defences of an old paddle steamer stranded in the middle of the Nile. Kitchener would have been proud of him. Had he received slightly different advice at the careers office, one could have equally imagined him ending up as the headmaster of some rural prep school, adored by the parents, but giving no quarter to those who handed in their work late or to a wayward shirt tail or an undone shoelace.

The group now gathered around him in the saloon viewed the situation with varying degrees of trepidation, but few of us doubted we now had the man for the job. He spoke in generalities, giving no more than hints as to which organisation we were up against or who he reported to in London. His Egyptian counterpart, a genial man with a carefully clipped moustache and well-pressed army uniform, was happy to confirm that we had firepower on board to stop any number of terrorists. He seemed to harbour a secret hope that Masterman was wrong about not having to resort to violence, but otherwise they were pretty much of one mind. His short speech concluded, the two of them nodded to each other, then turned again to us.

'Questions?' asked Masterman, in the manner of one who believes they have covered everything well enough. The cough from Herbie Proctor's direction would probably therefore have come as an unwelcome surprise.

'If they're on their way,' said Proctor, his nasal whine more than usually pronounced, 'why not get us off the boat first using that rubber dinghy thing you arrived in? The nearest town would be good but, if not, that bit of bank over there looks safe enough.'

'Nearest town is miles off,' said Masterman, with studied patience. 'I can't afford for us to be stranded here ourselves while we wait for our boat to return. We don't know for certain what the terrorists will do, and we need all our options open, I'm afraid. As for putting you ashore right here – which we could do – I don't mind personally, but the next town's as far away by road as it is by river. It's a long walk in the dark and we can't offer you any protection while you attempt it. For all I know, there may well be some bad hats already stationed on the bank to cover an escape. Don't worry. We're as sure as we can be that there's no explosive on the boat. If there's shooting later – and there shouldn't be – just keep your heads down. They'll be aiming at us, not at you.' A patronising little smile accompanied the last sentence.

'It's not *their* bullets I'm worried about,' said Tom. 'Purbright's killer is still on board. Mahmoud and Majid were both with Captain Bashir when the shot was fired.'

'Is that right?' asked Masterman.

'Yes,' said Jane Watson. 'We heard it.'

'Many things can be mistaken as shots,' said Masterman, 'at least by the inexperienced.' Having put the gym mistress in her place, he turned as if to talk to the Egyptian officer.

'So, you're saying I'm wrong?' demanded Jane Watson.

'That would seem the most likely explanation, wouldn't it?' said Masterman with studied politeness.

'You are the second most arrogant man I have ever met.'

Masterman did not regard this as breaking news. 'That does not mean I am in any way mistaken,' he said.

Jane Watson lapsed into silence. Annabelle flashed her a sympathetic smile. If they had had a gun between them, Masterman would have needed to watch his back.

'Thank you all for your patience,' said the Egyptian officer, stroking his moustache. 'If there are no other questions, I must ask you, please, to remain here until you are told otherwise.'

So our little group was back together again – minus Ethelred and minus Purbright, but otherwise intact.

'Well, aren't we having an exciting evening?' said Miss Watson drily.

'The Cairo bit of your trip was certainly a lot quieter,' said Tom.

'Cairo?' asked Miss Watson. Her mind still seemed for a moment to be elsewhere – possibly in a place where people like Masterman could be legally strangled and dumped into the nearest river.

'We met you and your friend in the museum, remember?' said Tom in clarification. 'In case you can't recall him, he had a big moustache and an army uniform.'

'Sorry, I keep forgetting that we met you there. Of course – Ahmed and I went to the museum. We saw you there. You said hello.'

'I don't think your friend liked us much,' said Tom.

'You'd just interrupted a conversation. That's all. He was giving me some advice.'

'Local knowledge is always good,' said Tom.

'Yes, isn't it? Ahmed told me where to go and what to do when I got there.'

'Including this boat?'

'Yes, he told me about the boat. Of course, he wasn't to know how things would turn out. I've known Ahmed for ages. We both competed in the same Olympics, way back. We've stayed in touch – met up from time to time. He's divorced now, a bit like me – well, he's divorced, I'm separated. We had a lot to talk about this time.'

'He looked like a tough cookie.'

'Yes, he is a bit. But beneath all that . . .' Miss Watson looked at the empty brandy glass she was still clutching. 'He's a good friend. If his information about this trip missed out one or two vital points, that wasn't his fault. He certainly wasn't to know we would all end up here on a sandbank.'

'I still say they should evacuate this scrapheap and take us in their boat to Kom Ombo,' said Proctor testily. 'Unless the professor wishes to manhandle the ship's tender off those bushes for us.'

Campion, who had perhaps now had a chance to examine the ship's stern and the small boat hanging diagonally from it, decided to ignore the latter option. 'They couldn't do it in one trip,' he pointed out. 'There are too many of us.'

'They could get some of us away,' said Proctor.

'Who?'

'We could draw lots for who goes first,' said Proctor.

'Not women and children then?' asked Miss Watson.

'I don't see that many children,' said Proctor. 'The

grown-ups should draw lots equally. Fair's fair.'

'I'm happy to let the ladies go first,' said Tom. 'I just don't think we're going to be given that option for all of the reasons we've already heard. And I don't think we should split up with a killer in our midst. Always a mistake – check out almost any B horror movie if you don't believe me.'

'But Masterman said it was Mahmoud or Majid,' said Proctor. He still wasn't quite sure how it had happened, but he was coming round to the idea that the loss of a client by terrorist action might be excusable.

'Only if you don't believe Jane's version of events,' said Tom.

'He doesn't think that girls know anything about firearms,' said Miss Watson. 'Maybe he's right. I'm obviously confusing a pistol with a rolling pin. Silly me.'

'You heard the shot too, Herbie,' said Tom.

'Yes,' said Proctor. 'That's right. I heard the shot.'

'And you, Elsie?' asked Tom.

'Actually, I might confuse a pistol and a rolling pin,' I admitted. 'I never cook anything that won't fit into the microwave. But I'd trust Jane on this.'

'Well, that's at least two people who were here against one who was miles away,' said Tom.

'At least,' said Campion, 'you now know that Mahmoud and Majid were not policemen.'

He implied that he had known this all along, which wasn't the way I remembered it. Of course, it also meant Ethelred had been right, which was a serious flaw to any theory. I also still had a reasonable doubt that I wished to introduce.

'I don't want to throw in further complications,' I said.

'But how do we know what Masterman is saying is true? How do we even know that Masterman is actually from MI6?'

'But he's a colleague of Purbright's,' said Campion.

'Except Purbright is really Raffles,' said Proctor, who was now beginning to have doubts about his doubts. Without some fixed point on which to tether our theories we were going to drift around indefinitely.

It struck me that in a perfect world the good guys would arrive in white boats and the bad guys in black boats – that way you'd be certain what you were getting. As it was, we were probably with the good guys and the bad guys were probably out there . . .

'So,' said John, 'you mean maybe we should all try to rush these guys when they least expect it and wait for the real police to return . . .'

This was getting too complicated for most of us. Somebody had to throw us a lifeline. That person proved to be Sky Benson.

'He's not Raffles,' she said. 'Purbright is really Purbright. Masterman is therefore really Masterman. And I'd rather you didn't try rushing anybody who might start shooting anywhere near me.'

'Are you sure?' asked Tom.

'Yes. One hundred per cent. Purbright looks nothing like Raffles. There's no chance of it being Raffles who was shot.'

'So you know what Raffles looks like?'

'Absolutely.'

'Well, it would have helped if you'd said that earlier,' said Tom. 'But at least we now know.'

'Hold on,' said Proctor. 'Raffles was my client, but *I*

225

didn't know what he looked like. And it wasn't through want of trying. There was nothing on the Internet. At the trial they imposed reporting restrictions because they didn't want the children identified. You can't get a picture of Raffles anywhere.'

'Well . . .' said Sky.

'It is perfectly clear to me,' said Campion. 'Since there were no photos, Sky must have seen an artist's impression or something at the time. I think we should just accept that Purbright and Raffles are different people. Let's leave the poor girl alone.'

'There were no artists' impressions either,' said Proctor. 'Or nothing good enough to identify anyone. How on earth is Sky supposed to know him?'

Sky paused as if on the verge of some significant revelation. What she eventually said was: 'I'm a librarian.' As revelations go, it was not a big one.

'He used to come into the library,' Sky added, getting into her stride. 'To borrow books.'

'What sort of books?' demanded Proctor.

'Romantic novels,' said Sky.

Proctor had not been embarrassed that his client had narrowly avoided conviction for murder, but this shameful disclosure left him, for the moment, with nothing to say.

'OK,' said Tom quickly. 'Purbright is Purbright and Raffles is Raffles. So we won't try violence on anyone for the moment.'

'There's something else,' I said. 'Raffles was, it would seem, definitely planning to join us on this boat. Isn't that a bit of a coincidence under the circumstances?'

'Loads of people come into the library,' said Sky.

'Coincidence or not, we've been lucky to avoid his company,' said Campion. He looked around the group, defying us to contest this statement. 'Unless we are suggesting that Sky killed Purbright, and I for one am not, I can't see this is getting us anywhere at all.'

I looked at Tom and he looked at me. He seemed to be thinking the same thing. Everything pointed to my policemen being, very sadly, a couple of terrorists. And to Ethelred being right. But there were still a few things that needed to be explained.

Tom and I again gravitated to the far side of the saloon, where a whispered conversation could be conducted in the reasonable hope of secrecy.

'I'm not calling Sky a liar,' said Tom, 'but isn't it just too much of a coincidence that she knows Raffles and now turns up on the same boat that Proctor is expecting to find his client on? And can you recently recall seeing somebody as nervous as Sky is now?'

Ethelred was once up for a very minor literary award, and had shown a similar propensity to drop and knock things over, right up to the moment that they announced he hadn't won it. But there was of course more to Sky's unease than that.

'Sky and Campion were plotting something,' I said. 'I overheard them talking the other evening. Campion was saying that they had to go through with it now – or something to that effect. Since then Campion's been on pins every time Sky opens her mouth, as if he's afraid she'll give something away.'

'So the pair of them could, on some sort of tip-off, have travelled out to Egypt in the hope of being able to get a better chance to take a potshot at Raffles here.'

'Sky has to be in disguise,' I added. 'The whole no-make-up, cheap-jewellery thing always seemed a bit overworked. Nobody over the age of sixteen would wear a necklace like that except for a bet.'

'Good point. Why didn't I spot that? Damn, I'm losing my good taste. Anyway, Raffles gets a warning letter and calls in Herbie Proctor. But Raffles chickens out and doesn't show up.'

'That doesn't sound like Raffles – not from Proctor's description,' I said.

'No? Well, accepting now that Purbright never was Raffles, perhaps Sky and Campion are still expecting the real Raffles to join the boat later – at Aswan, say – and decide it would be safer to get rid of Proctor first, or at least warn him off. Sky goes up to the roof of the temple in her floppy hat and lobs the rock down.'

'But,' I said, 'they'd have no reason then to shoot Purbright, being the only ones on the boat who were absolutely sure he wasn't Raffles.'

'That's the one minor flaw in my theory,' Tom conceded.

'And where does Campion fit in, anyway? Even if we accept that Sky supplies Raffles with romantic fiction, what's Campion's interest in all this?'

'I'm certainly not letting it drop anyway,' said Tom. 'Maybe Ethelred will have some answers when he gets back.'

We looked out through the window. There was another

boat approaching. Seven men in a white motor boat. And they were heading our way fast.

'Stay away from the windows!' said Proctor. 'We were told to keep our heads down.'

Tom was crouching and I decided it might be a good idea to crouch too. The white boat was now sliding silently alongside. I could see Ethelred, quite clearly, starting to get awkwardly to his feet, then the boat disappeared out of our line of sight.

I stood up, hoping to be able to catch a glimpse of it from a better angle, but all of the action was going on somewhere I couldn't quite see.

'Get *down*,' hissed Proctor.

'It's OK,' I said, still standing. 'The white boat is leaving. It's swinging round and back off up the Nile. Everything's going to be OK. We're safe!'

At which point there was the most enormous explosion.

CHAPTER TWENTY-SIX

'Shit,' I said.

The guy in the linen suit paused for a moment. We were both calculating how long we had. The terrorists would not detonate the bomb while they were still moored to the *Khedive*. So, ten seconds to cast off, then fifteen seconds maybe to get clear of us before they pressed the button?

The case was ripped from my hands and flung through the open door in a broad arc that took it twelve feet or so above the smooth waters of the Nile. There it seemed to hang, improbably suspended in mid-air, before it started to tumble, end over end, and down into the murky depths. I saw the white motor boat speeding away, then all was hidden by a vast plume of water as the briefcase, perhaps still drifting slowly towards the bottom of the river, exploded with a roar.

'So,' I said as the guy in the suit helped me to my feet, 'Majid isn't on our side then?'

'Doesn't look like it.'

The ringing in my ears was so bad I had to ask him to repeat that, which he did. 'He told me he was,' I said.

'We'll have to add "deceiving a member of the Crime Writers' Association" to the list of charges then. I wouldn't like to be in his shoes.'

'No,' I said.

The chandelier above our heads was still swinging gently, the glass lozenges brushing against each other with a tinkling noise that was in a different key from the noise in my ears. The overall effect was a bit like Stockhausen. I've never liked Stockhausen.

'George Masterman,' said the guy in the suit, holding out his hand, this time to shake mine.

'Ethelred Tressider,' I said.

'Yes, we know that,' said Masterman. I suspect that most things he said sounded dismissive, but he had put just that extra bit of effort into his last remark.

'I'm sorry to have put you to this trouble,' I said.

He grunted. He was sorry too. 'A tip for you, Ethelred. If we tell you not to bring anything with you, we mean just that. It's not like when the girly at the airline check-in desk asks you if you've packed all your bags yourself. You could have killed everybody on the boat.'

'He said he worked for the Egyptian police.'

'Don't believe everything people tell you.'

Masterman purported to work for MI6. He seemed to think that I *should* believe that, the crisp linen suit presenting an irrefutable argument in his favour.

'Is everyone on board OK?' I asked.

'They're fine. Maybe we should join them?'

* * *

Fortunately I had not expected a hero's welcome when I found my way back to the saloon.

'You moron, Tressider,' said Proctor. 'When did you join Al-Qaeda?'

'I didn't know it was a bomb,' I said.

'What did you think it was?' asked Proctor. 'A ham sandwich?'

There were obviously many other things the case could have contained other than a bomb or a ham sandwich, but I felt the mood of the meeting was too much against me to point this out.

'I thought it was just a briefcase,' I said.

'Yeah. A ticking briefcase,' sneered Proctor.

'Actually,' I said, 'bombs rarely tick. This one was designed to be detonated remotely by—'

'Thank goodness the security services were on board,' said Professor Campion. 'That's all I can say.'

'Are you sure you don't have any other bombs with you?' asked Proctor, backing away in mock terror. 'Have you checked your pockets?'

'Look,' said Tom. 'Ethelred's had a pretty tough time out there. Had things gone differently, the world of literature might have lost one of its stars tonight. Maybe we should show him a bit of sympathy?'

'He's an idiot,' said Campion. 'And the world of literature would hardly have missed him.'

'True enough,' said Elsie. 'Still, give the poor lad a break, eh?'

'Yes,' said Annabelle. 'I think we should give Ethelred a break.'

And Elsie, for some reason, glowered at her.

* * *

I ended up sitting with Elsie out on deck, watching the sun come up. She had filled me in on what had transpired in my absence.

'Well,' I said, 'that looks like that. We know who killed Purbright. It was Mahmoud and Majid. They were clearly not policemen. And, whatever they told me, they clearly needed him dead. Masterman says a tug is on its way from Aswan to get us floated again. We'll be in Kom Ombo in time for lunch. They'll do running repairs there to get us to Aswan.'

'But *do* we know who killed Purbright?' asked Elsie. 'Mahmoud and Majid are accounted for at the time the shot was heard.'

'But Masterman says Jane Watson was mistaken.'

'That's only because he is a pompous prat,' explained Elsie. 'I was with Jane when she heard the shot. I believe her.'

'Did you hear it?' I asked.

Elsie paused and considered. 'There was an awful lot of other noise,' she conceded, 'but Masterman wasn't even *there*. How does he know? How do we even know who Masterman is?'

'He's MI6,' I said.

'What proof do you have?'

'I spoke to him via the number that Purbright gave me,' I said. 'Also he hasn't tried to blow us up lately, unlike your so-called policemen.'

'Good point,' said Elsie. 'It could have been Annabelle of course.'

'Why?'

'In mistake for you.'

'Hardly,' I said.

For a while we sat there, the horizon now a broad flash of crimson that merged slowly into the last blue-grey strands of night.

'Why did Annabelle initially refuse to come on this trip?' asked Elsie.

'She changed her—'

'How about the truth this time?'

I sighed. 'You know that I am planning to sell the house?'

'Yes. You told me ages ago . . . hold on, you hadn't told her, had you?'

'Not until last week,' I said.

'But you have a buyer.'

'More or less,' I said.

'So didn't Annabelle notice would-be purchasers tramping through her sitting room?'

'The market for houses that size isn't like the market for flats,' I said. 'The agents advertised it discreetly to a small number of potential clients. I had arranged for the agents to visit Muntham Court when Annabelle wasn't there to take video footage. Most of the likely buyers were overseas anyway.'

'But to tie up the deal they would have to see it?'

'It's been known for sales to take place without that, but yes, in this case, they wanted to.'

'So Annabelle would have found out . . . unless she was away for a while. In Egypt, for example.'

'Yes,' I said. 'That's a fair summary.'

'So you booked a trip for the two of you on the *Khedive*?'

'At first she wasn't keen. Then she noticed that the word "luxury" was mentioned twenty-seven times in the brochure.'

'That woman is *so* shallow,' said Elsie.

'We were all set to go but—'

'But she found out?'

'The buyers turned up ten days too soon. They thought it would be OK to bring the appointment forward a bit.'

'So, was it OK?'

'Annabelle and I had a long discussion about it afterwards,' I said.

'I bet. And then you decided that you'd come to Egypt anyway?'

'It seemed prudent,' I said.

'Ethelred,' said Elsie. 'If you were to die before the sale goes through – and heaven forbid that my signed first editions should appreciate in value in such a sad manner – what exactly happens to Muntham Court? Does Annabelle get it back by any chance?'

'Yes,' I said. 'It's complex but—'

'"Yes" is fine,' said Elsie. 'And the message threatening to kill you was from Annabelle?'

'It wasn't intended to be taken literally,' I said. 'She probably sent it – well, round about the time she realised I actually had gone to Egypt on my own. Think of it as a reflex reaction. Anyway, I can't see Annabelle chipping her nail varnish firing a gun, can you?'

I could tell that Elsie desperately wanted it to be Annabelle who had killed Purbright in mistake for me. That Annabelle might kill me was still very much on the cards, but she'd be more subtle than a bullet fired at close range. Of that at least I was certain.

* * *

The Nile was very still. On its surface lay an impressionist view of green banks and distant brown hills. It was day, but the last damp traces of the night still hung in the air. Out in mid-river, sensibly avoiding running aground, were three small fishing boats. The men on board were going through a routine of beating the water with long poles, then dragging it with nets, then beating again. They waved. I waved back. In the distance I heard a diesel engine cough into life as a pump started its work for the day. There was a cruel normality to everything I could see or hear or smell. It was difficult to believe that any of the previous night's events had actually occurred, were it not for the fact that the *Khedive* was stranded on a grassy bank and that Purbright was not there and would never be here or anywhere else again.

Most of the passengers had retired to their cabins to catch up on their sleep. I was wondering whether there was any point in my not joining them, when I saw Annabelle appear from the stairway. Her suitcase must have been almost as capacious as Elsie's, because she wore yet another perfectly pressed outfit – this time an off-white linen skirt and blouse. Her hair was tied back with a bright pink scarf. She looked in my direction and smiled. Instinctively I glanced behind me, but then realised that I was for some reason the object of her pleasure. She confirmed this by coming over and standing next to me at the ship's rail.

'Sorry,' I said, for no better reason than because it was the way I began most conversations with Annabelle.

'I think you've been very brave,' she said, placing her hand gently on my arm.

I wondered which of my actions she was referring to. Probably not the bit where I hid under the bed. I tried to look brave but modest.

'Are you all right?' asked Annabelle.

'Yes, I'm fine.'

'You seemed to be pulling some sort of face.'

I tried to look brave but normal. 'I'm just tired,' I said. 'I didn't get much sleep.'

'Nor did we,' said Annabelle, in the tone she usually used about my snoring.

'Sorry,' I said again.

Annabelle seemed to be heading for a snort of derision, then checked herself and took a deep breath. She gave me a tight-lipped smile.

'Thinking about it,' she said, 'you saved the *Khedive* and everyone on it.'

'Did I?'

'Oh yes. Most certainly. You cleverly got the terrorists away from the boat by . . . by . . . being frightfully clever. Then you spotted that they had put the bomb in the briefcase. Cleverly. You shouldn't be so modest, Ethelred.'

Though I felt this was much closer to the truth than Herbie Proctor's earlier assessment of my conduct, there was nevertheless something in Annabelle's tone that put me on my guard.

'I wouldn't go that far,' I said, this time avoiding pulling any sort of face.

'I admire bravery in a man,' said Annabelle. 'Particularly the man that I am planning to spend the rest of my life with.'

Just for a second I wondered whom she could have met on the boat who had impressed her so quickly. Then I realised that that wasn't quite what she had meant. But I had been led to believe that particular deal was dead in the water.

'Me?' I said.

She pulled me closer to her, encircling my arm with her own. 'When they . . . when they took you away last night, I suddenly realised I might never see you again.'

'When we last discussed the matter, Annabelle, that was your preferred option. You did mention meeting up again when hell froze over, but I didn't put it in my diary.'

'One says things in the heat of the moment,' said Annabelle. She was looking over the river and into the distance, as though seeing a future that was still shrouded for me.

Out on the Nile, the fishermen were hauling in a net that kicked and pulsated with its slippery silver contents. Their early-morning work, using age-old techniques, had borne fruit.

Annabelle rested her head on my shoulder. 'Sorry,' she said. 'I'm so sleepy.'

'Me too,' I said, without thinking.

'Maybe we should go back to our cabins and have a nap before the day really begins,' said Annabelle, though she did not release my arm as a necessary preliminary.

'Good thinking,' I said.

'They've given me quite a large cabin,' said Annabelle. 'It has a really comfortable double bed.'

'Mine too,' I said. 'Brilliantly comfortable.'

'Your place it is, then. Get your coat, Ethelred, you've pulled.'

'But . . .' I said.

This too was an arrangement that I had imagined had been terminated. Since our last conversation in England had precluded ever meeting again, I had assumed it must rule out sleeping together. Apparently not.

'You mean a lot to me, Ethelred,' said Annabelle, giving me a little kiss on the cheek. 'Of course, you have your faults, as you must be aware. You can be rather pedantic. You are self-pitying to an extent that I had not believed possible. Your demeanour is usually that of a lost puppy. You think that it is endearing, possibly even normal, to wear a twenty-year-old Barbour jacket that is fit only for the compost heap. You snore. You refuse to accept the idea that you are going bald. Your idea of disposing of dental floss is to put it on top of something else then forget about it. You refuse to eat any marmalade that isn't the colour of treacle. You are, under most circumstances, completely spineless. You cannot remember when your own birthday is, let alone other people's. You go on and on and on and on and on about wanting to write a great literary novel, but you never do write one. You do not trim the hair in your ears. You neither wear nor throw away your old ties. You squeeze the toothpaste tube at the *top*, for God's sake. You are completely under the domination of your literary agent, who you should have sacked years ago. You see the best in everyone. In spite of that, you have no friends with whom any sane person would wish to associate. You are untidy. You have no ambition. You apologise all the time, regardless of whether you have done anything wrong.'

'Sorry,' I said. Then: 'Were you going to add a "but"?'

'*But* in spite of all of that I still love you,' Annabelle concluded graciously.

I'd hoped Annabelle might have noticed one or two good points to list in the credit column. Maybe she'd tell me about those later, perhaps in that distant future she had been contemplating.

We walked back down the stairs together and along the gloomy corridor to my cabin. For some reason I found myself checking that Elsie had not observed us. Annabelle was right in that respect, however: I did need to stand up to Elsie more.

Once we were safely in the cabin Annabelle drew back the curtains as though to check that my view was not better than I deserved. Outside, the men were at work again on the water, beating away with their sticks and convincing the fish that being caught was the wisest option. She slowly closed the curtains again and turned to me, a significant glint in her eye. She slipped off her shoes and started to approach me with stealthy steps.

'Of course,' I smiled, as she wrapped her arms round me, 'all of this makes no difference to my decision to sell Muntham Court.'

'Meaning what?' She unwrapped her arms and took half a step back. There was no note of seduction in her voice any more. None at all.

'Meaning, we can't possibly afford to keep it on.' I had started to unbutton my shirt, but I too stopped, my fingers still holding the fabric.

'And you still think I get no say in this? In spite of the fact that this is our future we are talking about? In spite of the fact that Muntham Court is currently my home?'

'We talked it through logically when we were in Sussex . . .'

'*Logically* . . .' she sneered. There was something about the word that displeased her.

'If we try to hang onto it, the cost of maintaining it will bankrupt us within a year.'

'Something will come up. We could run the house as a conference centre in the meantime.'

'We went through all of this before. I explained it all to you. We'd have to employ staff. We'd have to make alterations to the building to meet health and safety regulations. We'd have to advertise. And there's Wiston House just down the road catering for conferences already. We'd just be bankrupt even faster.'

'I bet you can't go bankrupt faster than a year whatever you do,' said Annabelle, probably correctly. 'And if you're going to go bankrupt it might as well be for a lot as a little.'

'Annabelle, I'm *not* doing it,' I said.

'You are completely useless,' said Annabelle, possibly summarising, or more likely adding to, my list of faults.

'If you would just think it through sensibly,' I said.

She didn't like the word 'sensibly' either. 'Just get out of my cabin,' said Annabelle.

'It's my cabin,' I said.

'Then get out of your cabin,' said Annabelle.

'OK,' I said. 'Sorry.'

I wondered whether it was too late to ask her what my compensating good points were, but decided that I'd probably missed my chance. I turned towards the door. As I was leaving my cabin I noticed that Annabelle had failed to draw the curtains completely. Through the gap I could still see the fishermen pulling in the last of their net. One fish, luckier than the rest, had managed to flip itself up into the air and over the side of the boat. From where I was, I observed a small splash and saw the fisherman turn briefly towards the escaper. Then, without further delay or comment, they resumed their work.

CHAPTER TWENTY-SEVEN

Elsie

It was mid-morning by the time the two tugs arrived. Lines were attached, with much shouting and many elaborate nautical precautions, and we were eventually inched carefully away from the sandbank and into deep water. After some repositioning of the cables, the tugs set off upstream, with the *Khedive* following in their wake, ignominiously at the wrong end of a tow rope and with various bits of greenery still decorating the stern, but at least now pointing in the right direction. There was no question of running our own engines until a number of parts had been replaced.

We visited Kom Ombo temple in the late afternoon. Campion led the party once again. After a fraught twenty-four hours, the only danger we were in was an encounter with a particularly aggressive guide leading a group of Germans around the same site. Campion, having positioned us in one of the few shady spots for his talk, found himself having to compete with a loud commentary in German a few yards away. We retreated to another part of the temple and the

Germans moved into our shade. After what we had been through, none of us felt like a fight.

As at Edfu, the party eventually split up to pursue our own inclinations. This time I stuck by Ethelred's side. There was no sign of rocks falling from anywhere, but I reckoned Ethelred could be trusted to be right underneath if any did fall. And I had no wish to give Annabelle a chance to take him to one side. It wasn't only the possibility of her killing him that I was worried about.

Ethelred was however for some reason rather moody. We might have continued in silence round the entire temple complex if his phone had not rung.

'Yes?' he said. Then he was quietly attentive for a long time as somebody told him something. 'I see,' he said eventually. 'I don't think there are crocodiles in this stretch of river though. Really? OK. Thanks for letting me know. I assume I can tell the others? Good. I'll see you in Luxor then.'

'On behalf of the others,' I said, 'who was that?'

'That was Masterman. The Egyptian police intercepted the terrorists' boat yesterday on its way back to wherever they were going. There was a bit of a fight and Mahmoud and Majid were both killed. Masterman says he's certain that one or other of them shot Purbright, but now we'll never know for sure which of them it was. Anyhow, as far as the Egyptian authorities are concerned, the case is effectively closed. They'll be issuing a press statement later today saying that the terrorist group who killed the British secret service man were swiftly and effectively brought to justice. Masterman wants to meet up with me when we are back in Luxor, but otherwise we are free to enjoy the rest of our trip in whatever way we wish. Oh, and they've recovered your iPhone, along with everyone else's.'

'Have they found Purbright's body?' I asked.

'No. Masterman doesn't think it will ever be recovered – he mentioned crocodiles, but really there aren't any below the Aswan dams. Even so, I can see that, unlike Osiris, he may never show up now.'

It was a grim conversation to be having in the warm winter sunshine, with flocks of tourists milling around, snapping each other and having fun.

Ethelred seemed to cheer up slightly after the call, his cheerfulness mainly taking the form of trying to interest me in ex-pharaoh-related stuff. After a bit, I decided retaining my own sanity was more important to the world of publishing than Ethelred's possible death or seduction at Annabelle's hands. The reading public were hardly going miss the odd crime writer. So Ethelred was allowed to wander the temple by himself.

I was therefore alone when I found Tom sitting on the remains of a column. He was deep in thought, but I reckoned he would be curious to learn of the fate of Mahmoud and Majid anyway.

'But you're still not convinced they were the killers, are you?' I concluded.

'No,' he said. 'Whoever it was, he or she is still with us on the boat. I'm certainly going to be locking my cabin door tonight and I would suggest you do too, or we may find ourselves in the position of being People Who Know Too Much For Their Own Good.'

'Except,' I said, 'that that isn't really how serial killers work. Serial killers kill basically because that's what they enjoy doing. Think of it as a vocation – a bit like writing but more respectable. They rarely need to do it because their subsequent victims know too much. Most subsequent victims know too little – that's how they become subsequent victims.'

'The terrorists who took Ethelred were convinced that they had fellow travellers on board the *Khedive*.'

'They were not entirely truthful with Ethelred on some other matters. That could have been a ploy too.'

'It fits in with what they actually did though, doesn't it? Why they didn't blow us up at first, but then changed their minds?'

'I guess so.'

'Then we need some means of getting the real killer to give themselves away.'

'How?'

'Let's see what we can do over dinner,' said Tom. 'Isn't that how Agatha Christie would have done it?'

Dinner had been announced in the programme as a fez evening and nobody had thought fit to countermand it. The men had acquired in the market at Kom Ombo, with mixed success at bargaining and a consequent wide range of prices, almost identical fezzes, the single noticeable difference being that some were red with black tassels and some were blue with yellow tassels. They had however been obtainable only in one standard size, which clearly had not fitted all. Proctor's rested on his ears, while Ethelred's perched on top of his head at one of the most rakish angles I have seen. Ethelred, I noticed, seemed to have trimmed the hair in his ears, for no apparent reason. Annabelle had purchased a *jellabiya* somewhere. Its general shape was authentic enough, but the plunging neckline indicated that it had not been made for the local market. It was all strangely frivolous attire for a boat that had so recently been touched by death – and indeed for the evening that Tom had planned.

We were midway through the meal when Tom tapped his wine glass and made an announcement.

'I think we should drink a toast,' he said, 'to our departed fellow passenger, George Purbright.'

'Is that the right way to remember him?' asked Proctor. 'Shouldn't we have a minute's silence or something?'

'Oh yes, I think an alcoholic tribute would be entirely fitting,' said Miss Watson.

There was a general murmur that might have passed equally for approval or disapproval and most of us drank.

'Perhaps we should also drink to the British and Egyptian security services,' said Campion, 'for having tracked down his killers.'

'Except they haven't,' said Tom.

'But Ethelred said—' began Campion.

'Masterman believes that Mahmoud or Majid fired the gun,' said Tom, 'but I don't.'

'I hoped,' said Campion, 'that we had finally got away from the ridiculous idea that it was one of us.'

'It's not so ridiculous,' said Tom. 'Let's begin with the gun. It was one that was good for target shooting, but not what a terrorist would carry. And you'd have expected a silencer.'

'Not as accurate with a silencer,' said Proctor.

'How accurate did it need to be?' asked Tom. 'He must have been shot from a few yards away. Purbright had arranged to meet this person, whoever it was. And in any case, Majid and Mahmoud were on the bridge when the shot was fired.'

'Masterman says not,' pointed out Campion.

'Well, there are people who could have committed the murder, whether the shot was fired when I think it was or a little earlier,' said Tom. 'You could, Sky. I still don't buy this idea that it was a pure coincidence that you showed up on the boat that Raffles had been planning to join.'

'Of course it was a coincidence,' said Sky indignantly. 'Anyway, why should I shoot anyone? Unpaid library fines? And Purbright wasn't Raffles – I've told you before.'

'We have only your word for it. Perhaps you haven't been truthful about that – any more than you have about what you do.'

'She's a librarian,' said Campion.

Tom didn't even bother to look in Campion's direction. 'You see, Sky, there are two possibilities,' he continued. 'Either by some amazing coincidence Raffles booked the same cruise as his librarian or, for some far less improbable reason, you have pitched up here deliberately on his boat. If you were me, which would you believe?'

'I met him at the library,' said Sky, but she didn't sound that convinced.

'OK, Sky, what's the Dewey Decimal code for Social Science?' asked Tom.

Had I been Sky, I would have just brazened it out and said '49' or whatever the first number was that came into my head, because my guess was that Tom didn't know either. Sky looked, however, like a cornered rat – a rat that was beginning to feel that it should have read up on the Dewey Decimal Classification system.

'Right then, let's get to the bottom of this,' said Proctor, playing a rather scruffy and flea-ridden terrier up against Sky Benson's rat. He narrowed his eyes and twitched his nose. 'Why did you follow my client here? Why did you want to kill him?'

'Nobody has killed Raffles,' said Sky.

'Well, somebody has killed somebody,' said Tom. 'Do you want us to turn you over to the police as the most likely suspect or do you want to tell us how you know Raffles? The truth this time.'

'I bet she's never met Raffles,' sneered Proctor. 'I bet she's making the whole thing up.'

There is a point at which even the mildest and most tolerant of rats will round on the terrier and bite him on the nose. 'I was *there* at the trial, you moron,' said Sky. 'I saw that man's odious face every day for two weeks, spouting one lie after another. I saw how his barrister hoodwinked the jury – or enough of them anyway. If that had been Raffles lying out there on the deck, that would be justice. It's just a shame that it wasn't him. And it's a shame that there are people like you, Mr Proctor, who would actually work for somebody like Raffles and try to protect him.'

Proctor found himself to be a scruffy terrier whose rat had unexpectedly bitten him on the nose. His doggy instinct was still to pick Sky Benson up by the neck and give her a good shake – but more cautiously this time.

'I'm sorry,' said Sky to nobody in particular. 'Of course, I don't really wish anybody dead . . . even him.'

Campion decided it was time to intervene. 'OK,' he said. 'I think that's conclusive. Sky clearly does know Raffles and we can legitimately accept her identification. Now perhaps we can move on . . .'

'Not so fast,' said Proctor, unwilling to be deprived of his rodent. 'In what capacity were you attending the trial?'

'Does it really matter?' asked Campion.

'Not many people have to sit in on a whole trial. Witnesses don't. I doubt if you were the judge. So what were you?'

'I was a member of the jury,' said Sky. 'OK? Satisfied now?'

'And you found him not guilty?'

'A majority were certain he was guilty, but three had doubts. We couldn't return a verdict. The CPS decided not to go for a retrial.'

'Don't they give you extra time for things like that?'

'The foreman of the jury screwed up,' said Sky. 'Just when it looked as though we might be able to return a majority verdict, the judge called us back into the court again and asked whether we had reached an impasse. The foreman said "yes". The judge dismissed us. We were all too gobsmacked to say anything there and then. Afterwards we went to the judge's chambers, but were told it was too late. You can't un-dismiss a jury. It would have to go to retrial – but it didn't.'

'The foreman stitched you all up?'

'The foreman said afterwards that he didn't know what an impasse was and didn't like to admit it in court. From his point of view the right answer was a fifty-fifty guess and he got it wrong.'

'So, you decided that you would exact justice of your own, and murder him quietly here on the Nile,' said Proctor.

'Of course not,' said Campion unexpectedly. 'That wasn't the plan.'

'And how do you know?' asked Tom. 'Were you on the jury as well?'

'No,' said Campion. He exchanged glances with Sky and shrugged. 'I'm a journalist. I covered the case for my paper.'

So they were in it together, exactly as I remembered predicting from the start. Allowing for Ethelred being right about the policemen, that made it one all.

'After the trial, we didn't know how to handle things,' said Sky. 'The judge had said there was nothing more he could do. We thought maybe we could talk to a journalist, so we did. But you can't report on what went on in a jury room. So, between us we came up with a scheme.'

'Precisely – to murder my client!' Proctor exclaimed with slightly more drama than was justified at this stage.

'As I have already explained, that was most certainly not our intention,' snapped Campion. 'And if it had been, we certainly would not have chosen somewhere like this. You'd have to be crazy. No, the plan was to get a confession out of him. Raffles is basically a loud-mouthed drunk. We reckoned that sooner or later he'd be confiding to some drinking companion how clever he'd been to get away with it. When he did, we wanted to be there with a concealed microphone. The problem was how to gain his confidence. We were able to find out where he did his drinking, but a casual approach in a pub would have looked too suspicious. On the other hand, you get talking to all sorts of people on holiday. And the bar often stays open late. I have access to various sources of information . . . Eventually, using one of the slightly less ethical ones, we picked up Raffles' name on a passenger list and were able to do a bit of detective work that led us here. So my editor paid to send two of us, armed with recording devices, on the *Khedive*. Sky volunteered to come with me, though she has since had some qualms about the whole thing.'

'I doubt he would have recognised me,' said Sky. 'I've dyed my hair and without make-up I do look quite different. And he'd obviously never heard me speak . . . It was just the thought of having to talk to him at all that turned my stomach. But we discussed it on the first night on board and I realised I would have to go through with it if he did join the ship at Kom Ombo or Aswan. Otherwise I'd have let the whole group down.'

'And my editor,' said Campion, who clearly had a slightly different agenda after all. 'He wouldn't have been pleased either.'

'So you're not a librarian?' asked Ethelred, with a tinge of disappointment.

'No, I'm a pole dancer,' said Sky.

'So there you have it,' said Campion. 'That was our plan. Blown now, of course – thank you very much, Tom –

as I shall have to explain to various people when I get back to England. But that was our plan.'

'I didn't think you were a professor of Egyptology,' said Proctor. 'You were pretty stupid to think nobody would find you out.'

'I'm a bit rusty,' said Campion haughtily, 'but I do have a degree in the subject. I can at least still read the hieroglyphics.'

'Yes, I realised that,' said Proctor. He looked round the group, hoping none of us would remember his sarcastic comments at the temple and that none of us would regard him as a total dickhead in retrospect. I gave him a big smile to show that the thought had never crossed my mind.

'I have had to rely quite a lot on the guidebook for information about each site though,' Campion added.

Ethelred flashed me a smile that might have been Ptolemy-Eye-Eye related. Whatever. It still didn't make it two one.

'You did well, Professor,' said John. 'You certainly had me convinced. Anyway, with two of you to identify him, we can at least be sure now that Raffles and Purbright are different people.'

'If Purbright was really Raffles,' said Ethelred, 'he wouldn't have had the number to phone the security services. Or, if he did, I can't see why he would have got me to phone it. To make Purbright Raffles, he'd have had to have a whole back-up team of fake security service people.'

Pretty much our conclusion earlier, though the bit about the phone numbers gave it more weight. That seemed to clinch it for most people anyway.

'Why did the two of you send threatening letters, then?' I asked. 'That was hardly going to make him open up.'

'We didn't,' said Campion, puzzled.

'I didn't say the letter was threatening,' said Proctor. 'Just that he'd been told to watch out – that somebody was after him. Could one of the other jurors have not liked the plan and felt that they ought to tip him off?'

'Yes, there were three, as I said . . . And maybe the foreman wasn't being stupid after all – juries have been nobbled before now. It looks as though we were sabotaged before we even set out,' said Campion with a sigh. 'What a waste of time and money.'

'So where is Raffles now?' I asked.

'He must have missed the boat,' said Proctor. He seemed slightly happier. A missing client could be tracked down and perhaps persuaded to pay a cancellation fee.

'So Purbright was always Purbright,' continued Ethelred, 'but it *is* true that the terrorists themselves thought that it was somebody else on the boat who was sympathetic to their cause.'

Again all eyes turned to Lizzi Hull. 'Hold on,' she said. 'I've already been through this – having some sympathy for the Palestinians is not the same thing as having sympathy for terrorism.'

'You were talking a lot to Majid and Mahmoud,' said Tom.

'To practise my Arabic,' said Lizzi. 'And they seemed nice people.'

'You're not the lady that the Egyptian security services were looking out for?' asked Ethelred.

Lizzi looked puzzled. 'I hope not,' she said. 'Look, I

travelled out in the same plane as most of the rest of you. I went through the same scanners. You can't get a pair of nail scissors through airport security these days. If it's any of us, then it must have been somebody who had a chance to stop off in Cairo or somewhere and acquire a gun.'

'Which way did you come in?' I asked Annabelle in an offhand manner.

'Yes, Elsie, it was via Cairo,' she said. 'I changed planes there. I certainly wasn't travelling direct on the charter flight. But I wouldn't know where to buy a gun in Cairo, even if I'd had the time. Anyway, why would I want to kill Purbright?'

'You didn't. But you might have shot him in mistake for Ethelred. They were both wearing white dinner jackets. It would be an easy enough mistake to make in the dark.'

'Why should I want to kill Ethelred?'

'You threatened to kill him – you sent him a text message.'

'How do you know?'

'Ethelred told me.'

Annabelle flashed another venomous glance at the crime writer on the other side of the table. 'Things like that are not to be taken literally,' she said.

'But if Ethelred died, you'd get Muntham Court back?' asked Tom.

I doubt that Ethelred had any real plans to mend bridges with Annabelle, but if he did, then that question sealed it for good. He had revealed one too many family secrets.

'That is scarcely something that it is appropriate to discuss here.' She spat her words like machine-gun bullets.

I think Ethelred may have actually ducked. 'In any case – you and John travelled here from Cairo too, didn't you?'

'Yes, they did, and so did I,' said Jane Watson. 'Where are we supposed to have got a gun from anyway?'

'I've no idea,' said Proctor. 'What were you doing in Cairo anyway, Miss Watson?'

'As I thought I had already explained, I was visiting an old friend, Colonel Ahmed,' said Miss Watson. 'A very respectable gentleman, who would I am sure vouch for my conduct while there.'

'So,' said Proctor, turning to John and Tom, 'what were you both doing in Cairo?'

'Just the usual sights,' said John. 'The museums and the rest of it.'

The museums. Where they had met Jane Watson. And Jane Watson's friend had not been pleased to see them. Did Colonel Ahmed know something about Tom and John? Or had they just interrupted a private conversation?

'You seem familiar with guns, Tom,' said Proctor.

'A bit,' conceded Tom. 'I belong to a gun club in New York.'

'And you were prowling around the boat when the shot was fired.'

'That's true,' said Tom.

'So you're as much a suspect as anyone.'

'That's true as well.'

'But I'm not a suspect of any sort,' said Proctor smugly. 'I have two witnesses as to where I was when the gun was fired.'

'I have a theory about that too,' said Tom. 'What if a

silencer was used for the murder – a silencer that was later thrown overboard? What if we were all mistaken about hearing a gunshot when the engine was about to blow up?'

'Rubbish,' said Proctor, reluctant to lose his alibi so soon after recovering his client.

'It sounds reasonable,' said Ethelred, thoughtfully.

'A fat lot you know about guns,' sneered Proctor. 'This stuff about a silencer is pure conjecture. And I was with Elsie and Jane when the shot was fired.'

'I'm not suggesting we're all equal suspects,' said Tom. 'As Mr Proctor so rightly points out, for example, not everyone here knows about or can handle a gun. So I thought we might try a little experiment. I have here in this bag the gun that was used – nobody collected it from the cabin, so I took the liberty of doing so myself. I've removed the bullets obviously. What I'd like each of you to do is to take it, aim it at somebody round the table and press the trigger.'

Lizzi Hull shrugged. 'Sounds interesting. I'm game, if it will actually prove anything.'

Campion looked doubtful. 'Surely the killer will just deny all knowledge of how to fire a gun? I can't see the point of this at all.'

'I agree,' said Proctor. 'All the killer has to do is to say they've never fired a gun in their life and then pretend they can't even operate the safety catch. Still, I'm willing to play along if that's what you wish.'

'I hate guns,' said Annabelle. 'Count me out – either as the shooter or as the target. Every time I see a gun, I shudder.' She put her carefully manicured hands up, as if to fend off the possibility of being made to touch the murder weapon.

'Me too,' said Sky. 'I wouldn't go near one.'

'You have my assurance,' said Tom blandly, 'it will be quite OK. It's unloaded. I'd just like to see each of you take the gun, aim and pull the trigger.'

Jane Watson however had had enough. The gym mistress spoke and spoke firmly: 'You are clearly a complete idiot. Do you not know the first rule of handling a firearm? Never point a gun at anyone – loaded or not. And don't mess with the trigger unless you are actually proposing to shoot something. Frankly, Tom, I am surprised at you. You are a danger to everyone on the boat. If that's how New York gun clubs operate, I for one never plan to go near them. I forbid you even to take the gun out of the bag.'

Tom looked suitably abashed. 'Well, since you put it like that, Jane, I guess we'll have to cancel that particular game. Shame though.'

'Aren't there fingerprints on the gun?' asked Ethelred, more concerned with detection than gun safety.

'Wiped clean,' said Tom. 'You could eat your dinner off it. OK, guys, I'll just put it under my seat and we'll get back to polite chit-chat.'

'Do it carefully, and whatever you do don't drop it,' said Miss Watson.

'It has an automatic firing-pin safety,' said Tom.

'So it does. I'd still prefer that you didn't drop it, though,' said Jane.

And with exaggerated care, Tom placed the bag under his chair.

* * *

After dinner, Tom, John, Ethelred and I were the last four left at the dining table.

'Well, Jane Watson certainly put you in your place,' I said.

'Yes,' said Tom. He did not seem too worried.

'What surprises me,' said Ethelred, 'is that the police – the real police, I mean – left the gun where it was.'

Tom reached under his chair again, pulled out the plastic bag and placed it on the table. Then he put his hand into the bag and removed a portable hairdryer.

'Nice,' I said.

'I never travel anywhere without it,' said Tom. 'I have such difficult hair. As for the Margo, the police obviously gathered it up straight away. I just wanted to see how people reacted to my suggestion that we should pass the weapon around.'

'And?' I asked.

'Some were clearly pretty nervous of being anywhere near a gun. Some were quite touchingly willing to take my word for it that the gun was not loaded – suggesting they hadn't spent much time around firearms.'

'Anyway,' I said, 'Jane's intervention stopped the experiment halfway.'

'I wasn't planning to let people use my hairdryer in earnest,' said Tom. 'It can overheat if you're not careful – there would have been a real danger of split ends. No, I'd gone as far as I'd planned.'

'But we're no further forward than before,' said Ethelred.

'On the contrary,' said Tom. 'I'm pretty sure I now know exactly who shot Purbright. I don't know if it was the same person who dislodged the stone at the temple, narrowly missing Ethelred and the good Mr Proctor in the process – I'm beginning to feel that may have been an accident after all. But a number of things are a lot clearer – Masterman was clearly wrong about Jane Watson not knowing what a gunshot would sound like, for example. No, the murderer gave herself away this evening. The problem – and it's a big one – is that the motive completely eludes me. I wish I had a little more by the way of solid evidence and I wish I could tell you *why* she shot him. But I'm as certain as I can be about what happened.'

'She?' I said.

'That's right,' said Tom.

'Who?' asked Ethelred.

'Since I can't prove it, maybe that's all I should say – but, yes, the killer was a member of the deadlier and more ruthless sex.'

CHAPTER TWENTY-EIGHT

'Well,' said Elsie, once we were completely alone, 'who exactly is Tom saying is the murderer?'

I sighed. 'Isn't it obvious? He means Annabelle.'

Elsie nodded a little too quickly for my taste. It was almost unthinkable, but it was the only logical conclusion. She did however raise one small objection. 'Tom's little experiment suggested that Annabelle wouldn't go near a gun. Doesn't that throw a spanner in the works?'

'My guess is that Tom wasn't fooled any more than I was. Two of her previous husbands have been keen on grouse shooting. She'll have held a gun more often than most people on the boat. She certainly knew better than to point the gun at somebody. But she pretended she hadn't used one. That bit of play-acting was pretty much what convinced me and is probably what convinced Tom too. No, it seems quite clear what happened. She picked up a gun in Cairo as she passed through – I don't know where of course. The first attempt to kill me was at Edfu – just after she arrived. John saw somebody in a floppy hat climbing the stairs to the roof. Then, after dinner the other night, she saw me go off with Purbright and decided to have another go. Maybe she used a silencer and the shot was earlier than we think – I know Tom now has Jane Watson down as an expert on pistols, but she could still have been mistaken. If so, the silencer was disposed of almost straight away. Or maybe the shot was fired when we first thought. Actually it doesn't matter much. Both things are possible and, either way, Annabelle's whereabouts are unaccounted for at the time Purbright was killed.'

'Was she that desperate? I mean to try to kill you?' Elsie asked.

'I think so. Tom said he couldn't quite see the motive – but he doesn't know how passionately she wanted to continue to be Lady Muntham of Muntham Court. That's why she got Robert to buy the house in the first place. Once I'd sold it, that would be that. In the end she would probably have stooped to any trick. I too find it hard to believe she would have gone quite that far but nothing else makes sense . . .'

Elsie put her hand on my arm. 'Look on the bright side. You might have married her. As it is you've got away with just a few scratches from that rock. And a kidnapping. And a near miss at being blown up. And looking like an idiot for bringing the bomb on board. I'd call that lucky myself.'

'I do wonder,' I said, 'whether Annabelle and I might not have been happy together, under slightly different circumstances.'

'Ethelred, pet, no ex-pole dancer is going to make you happy.'

'She's too old to be an ex-pole dancer,' I said. 'It didn't really catch on until the nineties.'

'At last!' said Elsie. 'Welcome to the real world.'

I drained the last of my coffee. The waiters had finally gone to bed. Doubtless they would clear away the remaining cups in the morning.

'There's nothing to be done,' I said. 'The police think it was Mahmoud and Majid.'

'We could tell them anyway,' said Elsie. 'I can't see what we've got to lose. And it would be fun.'

'It would be a complete waste of time,' I pointed out. 'You've met Masterman. He doesn't seem like somebody who changes his mind. He'd rather have Purbright's family know that he died in the line of duty than that he was collateral damage in a lovers' tiff. And the Egyptian authorities have already issued a press release with the official version of events set out. They might find it slightly awkward if the men they've shot hadn't killed Purbright. Anyway, as Tom says, we've *no proof*. You know who it was. Tom knows who it was. I know who it was. That's the end of the story.'

'And what are you intending to do for the rest of the trip? She's tried to kill you twice. Are you planning to let her keep taking potshots until she gets lucky?'

'She's disarmed – unless she plans to kill me by blowing me dry. And I'll stay away from any unstable ceilings.'

I was eating alone. Elsie had decided that she had seen enough dawns to last her for the trip and that she would take the risk of any egg shortage that might occur towards the end of breakfast service. Miss Watson was however only a few minutes behind me, and sat down at my table. Her selection of fruit from the buffet was placed in front of her with a flourish by a smiling waiter.

'I'm not quite sure what I'll do,' she said, 'when we are back in England and breakfast does not get transported for you from the counter to your table. I suppose we could reintroduce fagging at my school and get the smaller girls to fetch and carry. I rather think they might actually enjoy that. We could persuade the parents that it was part of some history project. Were you ever a fag, Ethelred?'

'Not of any sort,' I said.

'Your agent said something about your having attended a boarding school in Sunderland.'

'No,' I said.

'I have to say,' said Miss Watson, changing the subject, 'that I found Tom's performance last night very odd. What on earth was it all about?'

'He thinks he knows who killed Purbright,' I said.

'But the police are convinced that it was Mahmoud and Majid, surely?'

'Tom thinks otherwise.'

'Does he have any proof?'

'None that he's shown me.'

'I wouldn't necessarily trust all that Tom says.'

'No?'

'No.'

'Elsie said that your friend in Cairo was not keen on him.'

'Colonel Ahmed? I suppose that's right.'

'Why?'

'I'm not sure.'

'What does Colonel Ahmed do, exactly?'

'Something terribly secret.'

'But what?'

'When it's terribly secret, you don't get told.'

'No, I suppose not,' I said. 'But you mean that Tom and John might be spies or terrorists or something?'

'If I had to pick an obvious suicide bomber amongst our little group, it probably wouldn't be them. Still, I wouldn't place too much trust in what they say either.'

'No,' I said. 'I'll bear that in mind.'

'My two nice Americans are not spies,' said Elsie.

'That's not what I said,' I pointed out.

'You did, more or less.'

'I just said that Miss Watson's friend obviously suspected them of something.'

'Or just didn't like Americans.'

'Miss Watson knows more than she is saying,' I said. 'I don't know whether Colonel Ahmed told her something in Cairo or she saw something on the night – but she is giving us a definite steer not to trust Tom's theories.'

'She was with me when the shots were fired,' said Elsie, 'so she can't have seen anything I didn't. And if Colonel Ahmed is her friend and knew the boat was full of spies and terrorists, wouldn't he have warned her not to travel?'

'Perhaps,' I said.

'OK,' said Elsie. 'Maybe the police are right. Maybe Tom's wrong. Maybe Mahmoud and Majid did shoot Purbright. I'd still put my money on the rock being a present to you from Annabelle, but I'll never prove it. At least you are free of her. You were always far too much under her

265

control. You need to stand up for yourself more. Just make it clear to her that she's history.'

'Whatever you say,' I said.

We had, I felt, gone as far as we ever would to uncover Purbright's killer. There seemed no way forward. Which in a sense was odd. I had a strange feeling at the time that I already had all of the information that I needed and that Tom had spotted something in the conversation over dinner that I had missed.

It is possible, even on quite a small boat, to keep clear of some people most of the time. I succeeded in exchanging no more than a few words with Annabelle until the *Khedive* limped into Aswan. By declining the optional excursion to Abu Simbel, I avoided her completely on the first day. On the second I was not so lucky.

The suq at Aswan is a long road that runs parallel to the Nile but one block inland. The shops on each side, open-fronted, spread surreptitiously onto the thoroughfare and press in on you with offerings of fake designer T-shirts, belts, cheap gods and heaps of rice, soap and saffron. The smell of spice alternates with that of leather and jasmine and occasionally drains. The shopkeepers greet you as the friend they hope you will become. No rejection on your part, however final, dims their optimism in this respect. It does not pay to linger for more than a few seconds outside any shop at which you do not plan to spend money.

I had just completed the purchase of a black and gold statuette of the god Thoth, his pen poised above a writing tablet. I was about to exit the dark, narrow little shop, still blessed with many reasonably priced deities of all shapes and sizes, when I found my way barred. I could not leave without pushing past Annabelle, who had chosen that moment to enter and purchase that or some similar divine being. For my part, I had no wish to retrace my steps and buy (say) Horus or Osiris, though the shopkeeper had already pressed upon me the many advantages of acquiring one or the other. I had in any case already hesitated too long to be able to pretend that I had not seen her.

'Good morning, Annabelle,' I said.

'Good morning, Ethelred. I didn't see you at breakfast. I can scarcely believe sometimes that we are travelling on the same boat. You are quite elusive.'

'No, I just breakfasted early.'

'How wise. I did however run into Elsie back there by the spice shop.'

'Did you?'

'Don't look so worried. Yes, we've just had a lovely little chat. Could I ask you to tell her a couple of things though?'

'Of course.'

'The more important is that you should get it into her head that I have never been a pole dancer. I have no idea where she got that idea from, but I would not know how to dance round a pole, even if you gave me one.'

I confirmed that I had no plans to do this. 'And the second thing?' I asked.

'The less important thing is that she seems to be working on the theory that I have been wandering round the deck of the boat carrying a pistol with criminal intent. Can you tell her I have no idea what she is talking about? And if you are backing away because you also think I am the mad gunman of Edfu, let me give you the same assurance. Whoever shot Purbright, it was not I. Is that clear?'

'If you had tried to shoot me . . . I wouldn't necessarily blame you.'

'How sweet of you. That's my dear, if somewhat pathetic, Ethelred speaking there. You'd forgive me for attempted murder, as long as you were the intended victim? I suppose that's nice to know. I'm glad you and I are no longer an item, Ethelred. You really are completely useless. I could forgive you for being a failure as a crime writer if it were not for your pathetic ambitions to write a great literary novel.'

'I understand why you are angry,' I said. 'And I'm sorry about the sale of Muntham Court.'

'Oh, you don't need to be too sorry,' she said.

'It's good of you to be so understanding,' I said.

'Yes, I am, aren't I? And hopefully you'll be equally understanding when I tell you that your buyer has dropped out.'

'Has he?'

'Sadly, yes. It was the deathwatch beetle holes in the cellar that convinced him that Muntham Court was not a good purchase.'

'There's no deathwatch beetle.'

'But there *are* holes that do look very much like deathwatch beetle – at least on casual inspection. Of course, they might equally have been made by a Black and Decker eighteen-volt cordless drill – I couldn't honestly say.'

'But,' I said, 'the survey will show up that there is no trace of live beetle, so you've wasted your time with the drill.'

'There will be no survey. Unlike you, I did actually meet your buyer – remember? He told me, over a very friendly coffee, that he had pulled out of a previous purchase because of the merest suggestion of dry rot. People who aren't used to old buildings do panic over very little. So I was reasonably sure that when he saw the holes on his second visit a few days ago, he would decide to fly home without further ado. The estate agent, regrettably, has no other prospects at present. Of course, who knows what will put off other potential buyers – stories of ghosts, for example, or the threat of legal action from the current occupant? I do wish I could rule out either of those possibilities. People can be so picky.'

'Do you think you can stop me selling for ever?'

'Maybe not for ever. But perhaps for quite a long time. We'll see, won't we?'

'Yes,' I said. 'We'll see.'

'I hope,' said Annabelle, 'that the shopkeeper hasn't understood our little conversation. But if he has, I think the purchase of that lovely reproduction of the Sphinx over there will probably buy his silence. It's been good chatting, Ethelred. I'll see you back at the boat, shall I?'

CHAPTER TWENTY-NINE

Elsie

'What's that?' I asked Ethelred, when I managed to find him again.

He looked vaguely at the newspaper-wrapped object in his hand. 'It's Thoth,' he said. 'He's the god of scribes – and by extension crime writers.'

I compared the only available crime writer with the ibis head sticking out of the paper. They had a certain beaky similarity.

'How much did you pay for him? Don't worry – whatever it was, you were robbed. People just see you coming, whether it's sellers of statuettes or scarlet women. Talking of which, I saw Annabelle a little while ago. I let her know we're onto her.'

'Yes, I saw her too,' he said.

'And what did she have to say for herself?'

'She says she's never been a pole dancer,' he said.

'Absolutely. Far too old.'

'She also said she's going to wreck any attempt I make to sell Muntham Court.'

'Can she?'

'She's having a good try. And if she challenges the will, then I guess buyers will not be too keen to pay out good money on something they may never get their hands on.'

'So you can't sell it?'

'I think I might give it away,' he said. 'It's scarcely the sort of place I'd like to live in myself. And, frankly, I'm not comfortable having the sort of money I'd get if I sold it – I've done nothing to deserve it, after all. I'll find a suitable charity and offer it to them. Maybe it could become a hospice? Their lawyers may have to fight Annabelle's claim, if she really decides to make one – but I don't think she will. And the courts are less likely to rule against a charity.'

'You wouldn't like to give it to me, I suppose?'

'No,' he said. 'You wouldn't want it either. Anyway, she clearly didn't need to kill me. That was never her plan. She always had another perfectly good way of getting what she wanted. As far as I'm concerned, we are back to having no female killer matching Tom's theory.'

It still seemed to me that Annabelle might have had Plans B and C as well as a Plan A, but there didn't seem much point in explaining this to Ethelred. Short of some sudden last-minute revelation, we would just have to accept the official version of events.

'Well,' I said, 'this literary novel of yours had better be good if you're going to make your fortune from writing.'

Ethelred fingered the newspaper wrapping, as if consulting his personal deity. 'I've gone off the idea of a literary novel,' he said. 'I think I'll carry on writing crime. I may not sell that many, but as long as anyone wants to read them and I can get somebody to publish them, that's what I'll do. Crime – and maybe the odd spy story.'

'What will the next one be then?' I asked. 'Crime or spies?'

'Maybe both,' he said. 'I think I could probably write something that overlapped the two genres.'

'It has to be one or the other,' I said. 'Anything that mixes up spies and crime will just be a mess.'

'I'll work on the plot while we travel back to Luxor,' he said. 'Good luck,' I said.

He looked at me uncertainly. He knew deep down that I was right.

'You're meeting Masterman there, aren't you?' I asked.

'Yes, just before we fly back. He said he wanted to tie up a few loose ends.'

'Good luck with that too,' I said.

THE END

'I think that pretty much ties things up,' said Masterman.

We were on the sun deck of the *Khedive* again, now securely moored at Luxor. From the direction of the engine room came the constant sound of activity as the repairs to the engines were finally completed.

'I'm still not sure I understand it all,' I said.

I had toyed with the idea of explaining to him that Annabelle had possibly shot Purbright in mistake for me, but Masterman was in 'transmit' rather than 'receive' mode. He therefore proceeded to tell me what had happened.

'The two terrorists, Mahmoud and Majid, were both British citizens, as you'd possibly worked out,' he said. 'Hence our involvement. We'd been onto them for some time and had followed them out here. We knew too that they'd made contact with a group based in Egypt. Their initial plan was to blow up the *Khedive*. It was an attempt to resume the attacks on tourist targets in Egypt. Unfortunately the boat's progress was slow and they were going to miss their rendezvous with their local friends, who had the explosive. So they got Captain Bashir to go faster – hence the engines blowing when they did. They had also decided they would have to get rid of our man, Purbright, before the rendezvous, to improve the odds. One of them – Mahmoud we think – arranged to meet Purbright alone on some pretext and shot him. Then, or perhaps a bit later, he dumped the pistol in the cabin by the dining room, which Miss Watson had carelessly left unlocked, according to the captain, after her inspection of it. Afterwards he joined Majid and the boat's captain on the bridge.'

'But Captain Bashir said they were *both* on the bridge when the shot was heard.'

'Yes, we've thought about that. I had a word with your Mr Proctor – a very astute man. He'd come up with what seems to me to be the solution to that problem. His theory is that Purbright was killed a bit earlier, using a gun with a silencer. The "shot" people heard shortly after was just part of a very old engine giving up the ghost. When Mahmoud and Majid discovered what people *thought* they knew, the two of them threw the silencer over the side of the boat, deliberately allowing people to find a gun that apparently *had* to be audible. Very clever. So there was confusion about the timing of the shot.'

'Jane Watson was convinced,' I said. 'She said she knew what a gunshot sounded like.'

'Typical woman,' said Masterman. 'Absolutely sure of herself but totally wrong. She'd have scarcely misled you all deliberately, of course, but if she was right about when the shot was fired, none of the rest of it makes sense. On the other hand, take out that one small piece of incorrect information and it all fits together, doesn't it?'

'Mahmoud and Majid were adamant that it was somebody else,' I said. 'They said they had abandoned their initial plan to blow up the boat because Purbright's death convinced them that one of the other passengers must be from another group with similar aims. They didn't want to kill somebody from their own side and needed time to confirm whether they had sympathisers on the boat. They were pretty sure it was a woman, by the way. Apparently when the Egyptian agent was shot he was talking on his mobile and said something about a woman he was going to have to watch out for.' But I was aware that I was losing my audience.

Masterman shook his head and gave me another of his sad smiles. The quality of my thinking was clearly only just above that of Jane Watson. 'The Egyptian security people said nothing to us about a woman terrorist.'

'Or maybe one of their own agents?'

'You have to remember,' said Masterman, 'that Mahmoud and Majid were just stringing you along. Obviously they had to make up something vaguely plausible. There was a great deal of play-acting for your benefit – that bit of Majid's phone call, for example, about wanting to come in from the cold – thrown in simply for you to overhear and assume to be a Le Carre reference. Ridiculous. Anyway, to continue the story, when the boat ran aground, they realised that they simply wouldn't have time to plant the bomb before our people arrived. So they decided to switch to a Plan B that they'd had in reserve for some time – kidnapping a prominent member of the party.'

'Me,' I said, 'but they decided I wasn't important enough.'

'Of course you weren't,' said Masterman. He smiled at me understandingly. 'At one point they were considering taking Lady Muntham, but it would seem that your agent – Elsie, isn't it? – persuaded them you were the one to go for. Anyway, though we knew, as I say, about the original plan, we didn't know about the change in tactics until after you had been taken.'

'For a while, I genuinely thought Majid was on our side.'

'As I say – poor-quality play-acting. The pretence that Majid was a double agent was purely for your benefit, to persuade you to carry the bomb back on board the boat. Having discovered you were no earthly use to them, it was the best plan they had left. The whole story they told you was laughable when you think about it. Why did they have to take you back to the boat, when they could easily have dumped you at some remote spot to find your own way back? And why should anyone have resorted to such a clumsy way of communicating with us as passing on a briefcase full of papers? An encrypted CD ROM, maybe, or a data stick . . . They must have thought you were completely unacquainted with modern technology in any form.'

'Possibly,' I said.

'What beats me is that they were stupid enough to think that anyone would fall for something so crude and unsubtle.'

'I did fall for it,' I said.

'Yes, but how likely was it that somebody like you

would fetch up just when they needed them?' Masterman chuckled and shook his head, inviting me to share the joke.

'Pretty unlikely,' I said.

'But to continue the story,' said Masterman, 'Purbright was supposed to be accompanied on this mission by a thoroughly reliable member of the Egyptian security service – the Egyptian was to pose as the tour guide, so that he could watch the crew while Purbright watched the passengers. It had all been arranged with the owners of the boat; but none of the crew, even Captain Bashir, knew. Unfortunately, as you say, the local man was killed before he even got to the boat – hence Purbright boarding alone and hence your not having a guide.'

'I'd wondered if Purbright's colleague was the missing passenger.'

'Yes, we wondered about this missing passenger too. We checked up on him. It turned out to be somebody called Raffles – no one of any importance or significance as far as this is concerned.'

'What happened to Raffles exactly?'

'He was stopped at the airport.'

'The Egyptians thought he was too unsavoury a character to allow him in?'

'No. They thought he had swine flu. He's still in quarantine at a hospital in Cairo. Hopefully he'll be able to join the *Khedive* for its trip next week. Apparently he knows Mr Proctor. He's been trying to get through to his mobile all week, but it doesn't seem to be working.'

'No, it isn't,' I said.

'That would explain it,' said Masterman.

'So,' I said, 'in the absence of anyone better, Purbright recruited me to help.'

'Yes, that was a silly mistake,' said Masterman. 'He'd confused you with some other writer.'

'Paul Fielder,' I said.

'That's the one. He's really good. Have you read him at all?'

'No,' I said.

'You should. Exciting, accurate stuff. He's always in the bestseller lists . . . I suppose you also sell a few books though?'

'Now and then. I'm apparently going to be quite big in Latvia.'

'Yes,' said Masterman. 'So your agent tells me. Well done, you. Anyway, our conclusion, and that of the Egyptian police, is that Purbright was shot by Mahmoud. The gun, by the way, had been stolen from a shooting club in Cairo. And the two of them could have been responsible for that incident with the rock at Edfu. It's just possible. Even though they claimed to have been back at the boat, it would have been easy for one or both of them to get to the temple by one of the horse-drawn carriages and back again before the rest of you. Purbright had been standing with you shortly before the rock fell. Whichever of them went up onto the roof wouldn't have realised Purbright had moved on and that Proctor had taken his place. But my own view is that the rock was simply displaced accidentally by somebody who went up there ignoring the safety signs. That's what my Egyptian colleagues think too, and that's likely to be the official version.'

It all made sense. Everything that Masterman had

described – the rock at Edfu being an accident, the silencer causing the confusion about the timing of the shot – could have applied if the killer was Tom's female suspect. But in the end, Masterman had made a convincing case for it being the two terrorists, who had the motive that was missing from Tom's version of events.

'Since Purbright, Mahmoud and Majid are all dead,' said Masterman, 'we'll never know for sure exactly what happened – but that's it more or less. Trust me.'

'So all the loose ends are in place then?'

'Pretty much. One rather sad task remains – to tell Purbright's wife.'

'Doesn't she know yet?'

'It was difficult to track her down. They'd been separated for a very long time, but apparently she's still technically his next of kin. We've finally got a mobile number for her. Jones is going to contact her once we have put you all on the coach back to the airport.'

We hadn't seen much of Jones – very much the junior partner in the operation, and now clearly given the least desirable of tasks. I didn't envy him that one.

'Good morning, Mr Masterman.'

'Good morning, Miss Watson,' said Masterman, switching his attention to the new arrival. 'All of your little bits and pieces packed?'

'I travel light,' said Miss Watson. She was again wearing the dust-coloured dress I had seen her in on the first day. She had also resumed the floppy hat. She had acquired a suntan and some more silver bangles, but otherwise she looked pretty much as she had done when she arrived. It was clear that Masterman regarded her as being of little importance, and he was about to leave when something occurred to him.

'A mutual acquaintance sends his good wishes,' said Masterman to Miss Watson. 'Colonel Ahmed Mohammed in Cairo.'

'Ah, yes, dear Ahmed. I saw him when I was passing through a week ago. He is an old, old friend. You know him well?'

'We've been working with him on the case. He was concerned that you had come on this boat in spite of his advice – he knew Purbright was planning to join the boat, of course, but wouldn't have been able to tell you that. He wanted me to check that you were safe. I'll tell him you are.'

'You may add that the trip was very satisfactory,' she said.

'Satisfactory? A strange way of describing it, if you don't mind me saying so,' said Masterman.

'Is it? I have had a most pleasant and informative trip. I have visited a number of very interesting places and met some very special people. It would be ungrateful to suggest that my visit to his lovely country had been less than satisfactory. You may tell him that I hope to return very soon. I'm looking forward to seeing him.'

Masterman grunted dismissively. Duty had been done, and he was now anxious to be on his way. He made a brief pretence of looking at his watch then said: 'Excellent. If you'll both excuse me, I'll go and find out whether your coach has arrived.'

* * *

The coach ride to Luxor airport was short and the check-in surprisingly quick and efficient. We were through immigration, and our X-rayed baggage was probably already heading happily across the tarmac towards the plane, when the inevitable announcement was made that we would be delayed for an hour. Our group dispersed around the departure lounge, in search of last-minute souvenirs or, in the case of one literary agent, the possibility of exotic chocolate. Just as we had coalesced over the first hours and days of the trip, the group was now rapidly decaying. The glue that had held us together for a week was drying and cracking, unperceived but relentlessly, in the arid heat of the departure lounge. One by one we broke away and became a handful of passengers who just happened to be heading in a similar direction.

I had already weighed up all of the known advantages of purchasing a fluffy toy camel or some bright piece of pharaoh-related jewellery; nor was there anything in the small selection of books that appealed to me, though I noticed two of Paul Fielder's spy stories. Both had, I observed with pleasure, been much thumbed and then returned unbought to their shelves. I also noted smugly that a markedly inferior statuette of the ibis-headed god Thoth was ten times the price that I had paid for mine in Aswan. Thoth, currently nestling amongst the socks in my suitcase, would look well in my sitting room, once I had cleared a space for him on the mantelpiece.

Halfway through my second circuit of the terminal floor, I opted out and located the only spare table in the cafe, where I sat drinking a farewell *karkade*. Jane Watson must have had much the same idea and appeared shortly afterwards, clutching a small cup of sweet Egyptian coffee but no other purchases, looking round for a vacant seat. Though we had spent so much time together on the *Khedive*, the change in location seemed to demand a formal enquiry from her as to whether she could join me. I could think of no reason why not. After a few minutes her mobile rang.

'Hello?' she said. 'Mrs Purbright? Yes, speaking – though I haven't used that name for many years. My husband? Dead? Dear me, what a shame for him. But you say he died in the line of duty? That will be a great comfort to somebody, I'm sure. It has of course been many years since we were together. And his earthly remains . . . eaten by crocodiles, you think? I hadn't realised you still got them below the Aswan dams, but if you say so. At least nobody will have the annoyance of transporting him back home for burial. Thank you so much for telling me. I've always tried, over the years, to keep up with what he was doing, so it's good to have one last update . . . yes, you too, Mr Jones. And I really do appreciate your condolences so much. Have a nice day now.' She snapped the phone shut and put it away. Around us the buzz of conversation continued. Only I had overheard the call.

Then I suddenly realised what Tom had noticed over dinner. Jane Watson had concurred that the murder weapon had an automatic firing-pin safety – which was odd if she'd never seen it or handled it before.

I looked at her and she smiled back at me unconcerned. The case was, after all, now officially closed. Colonel Ahmed might know the whole story, but it was unlikely he would be telling it to anyone. There was nothing I could do, and she knew it.

'Just out of interest,' I asked, 'what was your event in the Olympics?'

'Pistol,' she replied. 'I was pretty good. I almost won a medal once.'

POSTSCRIPT

Q: What's the worst possible way to end a detective novel?

A: Too many explanations. Stuff about what the characters all did afterwards or how minor characters fitted in. A crime novel should end with the revelation of the murderer. You don't need to explain every last detail. Let people go back and reread bits if they can't work it out. You don't want the book to tail off.

Q: Our readers are always interested to hear how authors work. Describe the room you are writing in at the moment.

A: I am back in my flat in Sussex after a research visit to Egypt. Outside, the village square is covered in snow. It's early morning. Nothing is stirring in the winter darkness. From a window I can see, a little way down Horsham Road, the lights of a Christmas tree shining on the pristine white blanket. In front of me is my computer and a pot of coffee. I've just started writing a new book. It's surprising how little you need to be happy.

Q: *A recent press release from your agent says that your ambition is to marry a pole dancer. Is that right?*
A: I think that may have been irony. I'll check *Fowler's Modern English Usage*.

Q: *What's the most exciting thing to have happened to you recently?*
A: When I went to Egypt I was kidnapped by terrorists. I don't think it made any of the newspapers here, in spite of our having a journalist with us.

Q: *Recently published interviews with you have apparently resulted in death threats from the Mayors of Sunderland and Dunstable and from the Margery Allingham Society. We understand Dan Brown's next book is to feature a pathetic failed writer named Ethelbert Trossider, who is brutally murdered in the first chapter. Are you planning to be more cautious about what you say in future?*
A: Yes. And that's the truth.

ACKNOWLEDGEMENTS

This book took shape during a trip on the Nile (where else?) and I would like to thank the captain, crew and passengers of the *Misr* for making my research so enjoyable. Nobody, I'm pleased to say, was murdered on that voyage, nor were we ever marooned even for a moment on a sandbank, but I have borrowed one or two minor features of the journey.

My debt to Agatha Christie is perhaps too obvious to mention. Those familiar with her work may enjoy spotting the parallels with and references (sometimes deliberately obscure) to *Death on the Nile*.

Two characters in the book bear the names of real people. One was a fellow passenger on the *Misr* with whom we shared many pleasant meals and temple visits. The other very generously bid in a charity auction to 'name a character' in what was then no more than half of a first draft of a novel. Neither of the fictional characters purports to be a totally accurate portrait of the genuine owners of those names.

I must thank my agent David Headley and everyone

at Allison & Busby for their help with this new edition, especially my editor Lydia Riddle, who patiently went through this and the other books in the series ensuring that they were fit for the digital age. I am also grateful to Susie Dunlop, Kathryn Colwell, Christina Griffiths and Sophie Robinson for their help and to David Wardle for his brilliant cover designs.

I must also thank my original editor at Pan Macmillan, Will Atkins. The book is dedicated to him and to the other writers who are, or were originally, published under the Macmillan New Writing imprint – in gratitude for support in good times and bad.

Finally, I would like to repeat my thanks to my family, both two-legged (Ann, Tom and Catrin) and four-legged (Thistle), for putting up with having a writer amongst them.